Half Way There, Haole

By Howard Boylan

Published in the USA by
Conquering Books
210 E. Arrowhead Drive, Suite #1
Charlotte, NC 28213
(704) 509-2226

FIRST EDITION - FIRST PRINTING

Copyright © 2005 by Howard D. Boylan. All rights reserved: No part of this book may be reproduced, stored in a retrieval system, or transmitted by any means, electronic, mechanical, photocopying, recording, or otherwise, without written permission from the author.

ISBN# 1-56411-378-7
YBBG# 0374

Library of Congress Control Number: 2005933729

Contents

Chapter 1	5
Chapter 2	15
Chapter 3	27
Chapter 4	39
Chapter 5	45
Chapter 6	55
Chapter 7	73
Chapter 8	85
Chapter 9	91
Chapter 10	97
Chapter 11	101
Chapter 12	107
Chapter 13	111
Chapter 14	117
Chapter 15	127
Chapter 16	137
Chapter 17	147
Chapter 18	151
Chapter 19	167
Chapter 20	175
Chapter 21	193
Chapter 22	205
Chapter 23	213
Chapter 24	223
Chapter 25	229
Chapter 26	239
Chapter 27	247
Chapter 28	259
Chapter 29	263
Chapter 30	273

JAMES A. MICHENER
TINICUM, BUCKS COUNTY
PENNSYLVANIA

June 17, 1960.

Dear Mr. Boylan:

I appreciated very much your letter of February 8 in which you tell about the people you have known in Hawaii, and find that you have a real gift for summarizing experience and for characterizing people in very brief and sharp form.

Your letter reached my home while I was working in Mexico on other projects and I hope you will forgive the long delay in acknowledging it, but I have only today had an opportunity to read it.

I hope that whatever work you are doing will be successful and that you will find as much fun in your occupation as I do in mine.

Most sincerely,

James A. Michener

Chapter 1

The axle on the two-ton Ford truck groaned wearily as the driver aimed the front wheels from the narrow street, across the shallow gutter and up onto the covered truck scales. The brakes on the truck grabbed, causing the load of damp cow manure to shift forward. Inside the scale house, the scale beam clattered as Dean Burns whirled from his stool and shouted, "That nigger never will learn how to drive that thing. If he breaks these truck scales again, I'm sending the bill directly to King Edward Tobacco Company. I don't care if they are the best customer on the Burns & Johnson books." He charged out the door to challenge the driver.

"But Mister Burns, I done tol' the foreman three times 'bout them brakes grabbin'. I'll tell him agin," replied the driver in his most respectful tone.

Inside the scale room, Allendale Burns carefully released the scale hand lock, moved the beam to an even balance, relocked the scale and reached for a punch ticket in the nearby cigar box. As he searched thru the dusty scale room window for the truck number, Allendale noted the rapidly forming puddle beneath the sagging Ford frame. Somebody was getting screwed on this load. Allendale located the tare weight for King Edward truck #17 scribbled on the scale house wall and quickly wrote it down on the punch ticket, calculated the net weight of the load, and wrote up the transaction in the thick double-carbon scale book. By this time he knew the driver was inside the scale house from the strong manure odor that penetrated his nostrils. The driver handed Allendale a matchbook cover that had scribbled on it –"Thomas Fletcher 15-acre shade." Allendale recorded the destination on the scale ticket, tore out the white copy and gave it to the driver who jammed it into his cigarette pocket without thinking.

"Mister Red had me water it down good to keep the dust down," said the driver with a hint of a gleam in his eye. Allendale knew that water was cheaper than manure and that an extra dollar would go a long way toward another pint of Old Heaven Hill for his bossman.

"Well, move it on out," cried Allendale, "You're pissin all over the truck scales and there's two loads of peanut hulls waiting to be weighed."

"You tell Mister Red to have those brakes fixed, or that's the last load across my scales," Dean Burns added.

"Yes suh," replied the driver as he crammed the manure laden boots into the cab of the battered Ford. As the truck eased off the scales, the condensation formed a cloud of steam off the warm manure on this cold February morning. Only then did Allendale notice the second man slouched in the passenger side of the cab. Thomas Fletcher just got screwed by another 150 pounds. Forget it, mused Allendale, Thomas Fletcher probably screwed King Edward a dozen times already. So it went in Gadsden County.

Pocket brought in another load of slabwood for the pot bellied stove, dropped it with a clatter on the cement floor and waited for his Saturday morning instructions from Mr. Burns. Allendale weighed the two loads of peanut hulls, deposited the two fifty-cent pieces in the small black leather purse, and also awaited instructions from his father. At 7:30 on a Saturday morning, Allendale was surprisingly alert and ready to work even though his legs were sore from all the running last night. As a reserve forward on the Quincy High basketball team, he had started last night and played most of the game. It had been a good game, as Quincy had beaten Apalachicola on their own court by four points. At 5'11" Allendale was convinced he had to make up in quickness what he lacked in height. Starting assignments were rare, even though it was his senior year. It had not occurred to him that his basketball skills were just average.

This was Allendale's favorite time of year working at the Burns & Johnson warehouse. Another crop of shade tobacco was germinating in the seed beds and with only Saturday work, it did not compare with the hot North Florida summers when he was expected to put in ten-hour days on a six-day week, along with all the warehouse help. He hated the dusty peanut-buying season most of all. But now he and Pocket were getting their instructions from Mr. Burns and both listened with careful respect.

Dean Burns spoke, "For the first time in four years we got the King Edward contract for shade tobacco fertilizer. We're making our first delivery to the La Camellia farm this morning and I don't want anything to go wrong. There's hardly any money in it for us and one torn bag can make the difference between any profit or not, on the whole load."

Pocket listened carefully for he remembered that his seventy-five dollar bonus for 1946 had been possible because Burns and Johnson had had a good profit year. He shoved his huge black hands into his torn jacket for warmth while he listened for further instructions from Mister Burns.

"Both of you know the La Camellia superintendent and how he would like to stick one on Burns & Johnson. I was up there yesterday with the King Edward purchasing agent and we agreed to use Tobacco Barn #2 for all fertilizer storage. The end doors are cut higher on #2 and you should be able to back the truck all the way to the center of the barn. The way I calculate, you can get eight stacks between each support post. I want 'em stacked five high with the tags out where they can be easily read."

Dean Burns drawled, "Do you both understand? Allendale? Pocket?"

"Yes Sir," both replied, Allendale knew his father demanded the same respect from his son that he did from his

Half Way There, Haole

Negro employees. He did wish, however, that his father would agree to call him AB, like everyone did at Quincy High, including most of the teachers, the principal, and occasionally, his mother.

Dean Burns continued, "Pocket, take the new Dodge truck and load up six tons of shade special marked with the red King Edward tags. Get Albert and Raymond to help you."

Pocket ambled off to back the new Dodge truck to the warehouse platform. He already knew about the special order with the red tags for King Edward. After all, he had handled rail cars of the stuff, getting it from the rail siding to the warehouse. The new 100 pound burlap bags marked Burns & Johnson with huge green letters had handled very well and caused Pocket to heave a sigh of relief when the 796 bags had been stacked neatly on the warehouse platform. The four torn bags had been dutifully turned over to the Seaboard Railroad agent as a claim -- where Dean Burns had just completed paperwork declaring the value at retail delivered price.

Allendale followed his father back into the scale room, where they both warmed their hands over the roaring little stove. Allendale looked out the side window at the new deSoto parked next to a single Cities Service gasoline pump. Someday, he would be president and general manager of Burns & Johnson. He wouldn't fool with a deSoto, but go directly to a Cadillac – maybe even a convertible. But then Allendale did not always understand how things worked in Gadsden County. The Chrysler dealer had a part-interest in two huge tobacco farms and bought his supplies from Burns & Johnson. The General Motors franchise was held by a member of the 'other group' in town who did their banking at Gadsden State Bank and who purchased farm supplies from Bates Supply Company – a long-standing competitor of Burns & Johnson. It had never occurred to Allendale that

Burns & Johnson did not own any General Motors trucks or cars.

"Son," said Dean Burns, "I want you to supervise the delivery of the shade special to all the King Edward farms this year. We need to have this contract go well so we can repeat next year. Pocket has been with us for six years and he's a reliable Negro, but I want you to go with him on every load to each of the farms. We'll make arrangements to work around your basketball practices. You'll want extra money to start college this fall and I'll make it right with you. By the way, you only have about six weeks to decide on your college. Better go check up on the boys loading the La Camellia delivery."

"Yes Sir," replied Allendale, "We'll take care of King Edward."

Allendale left the warmth of the scale house, headed across the truck parking lot, and wondered if he would ever feel close to his father. Their discussions were somehow only about business – even the selection of a college was somehow turning into a business-like evaluation of schools. His father had not even asked about the basketball game last night. Dean Burns had seen the last half of the first game of the season, and Allendale had not even played in that one. Suddenly, he was jolted from his thoughts as his nostrils were filled with the pungent odor of cottonseed meal. Freshly ground cottonseed meal was a major ingredient of shade special, and the fragrance permeated the entire warehouse. Allendale had learned to appreciate the smell of freshly ground cottonseed. Soybean meal, sometimes used in shade special, did not compare in fragrance. As he approached the neatly loaded truck, Allendale instinctively began counting the evenly stacked rows – six bags high, three rows deep, with the top two bags 'splitting the crack' to tie the tier together. Pocket was starting the last row on the back of the truck bed by putting the two bags on either side

Half Way There, Haole

and tying the load in with the middle bag – exactly as Mister Burns had taught him several years ago. Raymond and Albert tossed on the last two bags, with Pocket making certain that the bags were properly arranged to tie the back tier into the center of the load. No chance of losing a bag on the road that way. Allendale noted that all the tags were placed toward the center of the load to prevent any loss of product identification.

Pocket climbed into the driver's seat, lit a Camel with a one-handed thumbnail flick of a kitchen match and eased the truck across the parking lot while Allendale prepared the delivery ticket. Dean Burns looked over his son's shoulder at the scale house desk while Allendale very carefully wrote – King Edward Tobacco Company, La Camellia Farm --- 120/100 lb sx 5-3-8 King Edward Shade Special. Dean Burns smiled to himself; his son was following instructions in exact detail. Without saying anything, Allendale slipped the delivery book into his jacket pocket, strode from the office and climbed into the passenger side of the truck cab.

Pocket moved the truck past the scale house office and into early morning traffic of West Jefferson Street, not noticing the deSoto follow him to the Burns & Johnson retail store just west of the Square. He turned north on Attapulgus Highway and headed toward the Georgia state line.

"Maybe we can get Goldie to help us unload," Pocket drawled as he took the last possible pull on the Camel.

"Who's Goldie?" finally responded Allendale.

"Mister AB, you know Goldie – Goldwire Cohens. His daddy, Moses, sells tater drawers to Burns & Johnson every spring. He's the labor foreman at La Camellia and has a special 'rangement to grow sweet potato plants on the low land near the pond. Goldie plays basketball for Carter Parramore High."

Allendale didn't have any knowledge of the sports program at segregated Carter Parramore. The weekly

Gadsden County Times reported all Negro community activities on the back page, and he seldom read beyond the sports page. The rest of the paper seemed to be filled with endless reporting of Coca Cola bridge parties, weddings in complete detail, and activities from the County Agent's office.

"We're supposed to deliver and unload, but if we can get some help, it is OK by me," replied Allendale.

With a full load, the new Dodge truck rode smoothly over the North Florida hills. As Pocket turned from the blacktop and crossed the cattle gap into La Camellia, Allendale was struck by the early morning scene that unfolded through the windshield. The narrow gravel road ahead was lined on both sides with eighteen or maybe twenty four-room cottages, wood smoke trailing into the cool February morning from chimneys on each end of each cottage – indicating that two families were housed in each dwelling. This was "The Quarter'" familiar to every shade tobacco farm in Gadsden County. Unlike the unpainted wooden shacks with tin roofs on many farms, the King Edward quarter could be readily identified by the dark red paint and fresh coat of black roofing tar applied to each tin roof. Moses Cohens had seen that all windows were intact and had insisted that each family sweep the bare ground surrounding each house. Two small girls were sweeping one yard as the fertilizer truck slowed to stop in front of a larger house at the end of the row. Pocket leaned on the horn several times.

"Tell Goldwire to come here," yelled Pocket to a young boy in a heavy stocking cap. The youngster rolled his eyes from side to side to get a better view of the loaded truck, then headed to the house. Shortly, the solid wooden door opened onto the sloping porch and Goldwire approached the truck, immediately recognizing Pocket and sensing the reason for the call. He jumped onto the running board, directing Pocket to the #2 Barn.

Allendale stepped from the truck cab as Goldwire gave signals to Pocket from the rear of the heavily loaded truck. Pocket backed the vehicle into the tobacco barn with considerable skill since the clearance was such that the side mirrors had to be folded up, preventing a rear view to the driver. Just as he approached the center of the darkened barn, Pocket heard an agonizing rip of burlap. He immediately spiked the brakes causing the load to shift to the rear. Goldwire scrambled to the top of the load to see where an overhead beam had cut an open gash in three of the bags. Allendale moaned to himself—just what his father had said to be wary of! Allendale feared the worst from the La Camellia farm manager.

Pocket emerged from the truck with a cigar box he had taken from beneath the driver's seat. He climbed to the top of the load, allowing time for his eyes to get accustomed to the darkened interior of the barn. Pocket took a large curved needle from the cigar box and proceeded to thread the needle with coarse sewing thread. Allendale observed from atop the load without saying anything.

"Here, let me do that," said Goldwire. He scraped the loose fertilizer back into each bag, and with a skill that amazed Allendale, proceeded to sew each bag back to its original condition, even bringing the Burns & Johnson green letters back into perfect alignment.

Allendale smiled at Goldwire, "You do good work."

"Aw, it ain't anything. I been helpin' sew shade cloth since I was twelve"

Pocket and Goldwire jumped to the dusty dirt floor while Allendale remained to slide the bags from high atop the loaded truck. They all inhaled the fresh odor of cottonseed meal as Allendale slid the top bags to the broad shoulders of the two black laborers. He reminded Pocket of their instructions from Dean Burns to stack eight rows, five high between each support post. All tags to the center of the barn.

"Gimme two of 'em, "said Goldwire, "one on each shoulder." Allendale obliged and was amazed at the grace and strength with which Goldwire moved to unload two-hundred pounds at each trip to the rapidly growing pile between the posts. The truck was quickly being unloaded, as Goldwire was now easily carrying a one-hundred pound bag under each arm. Pocket stayed with one bag per trip. He knew there were many more trips to be made before fertilizer season would be finished in May.

Pocket moved the empty truck slowly from Barn #2 while Allendale made a recheck of the bag count. Forty bags in each tier, times three rows was one hundred and twenty bags or six tons. He looked up to see Red Thompson approaching the barn.

"OK, let's count'em," yelled Red. "Burns & Johnson ain't going to screw me on this load." Red and Allendale proceeded inside the barn to inspect the delivery. Red surveyed the stacks, looking for torn bags or missing tags. He counted to 120. As he signed the delivery ticket, Allendale caught a brief hint of whiskey. He felt relieved that all had gone well.

The empty truck came to a halt in front of one of the houses in the Quarter that had a Coca Cola cooler on the sloping front porch. Everyone knew that the Coca Cola cooler was signal for the location of the on-site bootlegger. Gadsden County was officially dry, but unofficially wet – especially when Sheriff Woodbury was in charge of local law enforcement. Allendale dug into his pocket and produced three nickels to buy a round of Coca Colas to clear the dust and cottonseed meal from dry throats. Even on a cool February morning, a cold Coca Cola tasted great. Pocket lit his last Camel.

Half Way There, Haole

"Pocket says you play basketball for Carter Parramore," said Allendale as he drained the bottle and returned it to the wooden crate next to the cooler.

"Yes sir, I tries, Mr. AB. Made seventeen points in the last game, but we lost anyway to Stevens High in Tallahassee," replied Goldwire.

"How tall are you?" asked Allendale.

" 'Bout 6-1 or 6-2, I'm not sure," said Goldwire. "I started this year at forward, but the coach asked me about playing center my senior year."

Nothing was said about Allendale playing for Quincy High, for Goldwire never saw anything but the back page of the *Gadsden County Times*. Except for daily job contact between black and white in Gadsden County, there wasn't much reason for either race to follow the activities of the other. Each group knew their position in the community.

Pocket cranked the Dodge and adjusted the rear view mirror, while Allendale checked his pocket one more time for the delivery book. The truck clattered across the cattle gap, turned left and disappeared down the road to Quincy.

Chapter 2

Goldwire broke into a jog as he headed down the narrow `quarter road' to his house. Unloading the truck had just begun to loosen his muscles from the stiffness experienced from the game on Friday night. He knew he didn't have to help with the Burns and Johnson truck, but Pocket was a friend, and besides he had considerable respect for Mr. Burns and his arrangement to buy sweet potato plants from his father.

The dilapidated Chevy labor bus with February-frosted windows was parked next to the Cohens house. The faded "Gadsden County Schools" sign on the side of the bus had been haphazardly painted over, but was still legible. The 1938 Chevy had served the school system well during the war years, but was now urgently in need of repairs. King Edward Tobacco Company had purchased it from the School Board as a labor bus to haul extra farm labor from Quincy during "the season," and to haul La Camellia labor to Quincy each Saturday morning for shopping. A rolling store appeared twice a week at La Camellia, but prices were too high and the owner had a reputation for cheating his customers.

Moses Cohens emerged from behind the solid pine plank door just as Goldwire jogged up to the porch steps.

"Son, let's see if the bus will start. We got to make a run to Quincy at ten-thirty to take the hands to town. Most of 'em don't have no money 'cause it was too cold to work the shades this week, but we gotta go anyway," said Moses.

Goldwire was planning to make the trip this morning too, and he knew his father was depending on him to help with getting the bus started. After all, he had already spent many hours under the hood of the old Chevy bus to keep it running. He had helped his father with pumps and irrigation equipment at La Camellia since he was ten years old, and had developed an interest in things mechanical. It was the ability to handle many of the odd chores around La Camellia that had earned Moses the privilege to grow two acres of potato plants on the land near the pond. Red Thompson recognized good Negro farm hands, and it had helped him earn a tidy crop bonus from King Edward for several years. King Edward was aware of the 'rangement with Moses for growing potato plants and even allowed a few bags of shade fertilizer to be directed to the sweet potato crop.

"I'll go get the John Deere and cables."

Within minutes Goldwire was back, sitting atop the big green John Deere, belching huge white puffs of exhaust into the crisp morning air. He hooked the battery cables from the tractor to the bus, while Moses sat inside with his foot to the floorboard starter. The motor of the old bus grudgingly started, heaving masses of blue smoke from beneath the drivers seat.

"We gotta work on that muffler one of these days," yelled Moses. "Them fumes will git to ya."

Goldwire's four younger brothers and sisters were the first to board the bus and take the window seats near the front. They all began scraping frost from inside the windows to have a peephole to view the trip to Quincy. Moses drove the creaking bus past the sideyard Chinaberry tree and into the narrow road through the quarter. The bus filled quickly with families, dressed in layers of ragged clothing to keep the morning chill away. Some had home-made stocking caps fashioned from ladies rayon hosiery – hand-me-downs from the ladies of Quincy to their maids. Goldwire was to look after the younger brothers and sisters while his mother stayed behind to boil clothes in the backyard. The wire fence behind the Cohens household already held a scattered array of heavy work clothes from the first wash.

Moses stopped the bus at the cattle gap to scrape more frost from the windshield. Goldwire worked on the windows of the folding door to allow more side vision for the driver. As he cleaned the windows, Goldwire hesitated to get a good view of Shade #3, the 18-acre shade near the blacktop road. He noticed all the shade posts were in perfect alignment, the rotten ones having been recently replaced with newly-treated posts. The shade wires had all been tightened and carefully positioned to support the cheesecloth. In thirty days the tender tobacco plants would be ready to transplant from the seed bed. The cheesecloth would have to be sewn to the wires and the soil prepared in the next three or four weeks. There would be plenty of work for the adults as soon as this cold weather moved through the area. By May, all the children would have steady work and the bus would be jammed with happy families going to Quincy to spend their new-found wealth.

Goldwire remembered well those days when he was a youngster and had twenty cents to spend on a day's outing in Quincy. At age six he had started to work in the shades at thirty-five cents a day. His job was to work as a 'toter' with the 'primer' during the harvest days of late May, June, and July. The heat and humidity under the cheesecloth were unbearable, but he soon learned to carry the large and tender tobacco leaves to the end of the row with great care. The primer, an adult who could reach all heights of the fast-growing tobacco plant, would snap or prime the leaf from the heavy stalk and hand it to a runner who positioned the stack of leaves carefully between his hands and carried the stack to the end of the row. There, a mule-drawn sled, meticulously

Half Way There, Haole

lined with burlap, was waiting to haul the tender cargo to the tobacco barn for the intricate curing process. His weekly earnings were turned over to Moses for family expenses, but during `the season' there was always twenty cents left over for a Roy Rogers or Tom Mix movie, popcorn, and Coca Cola in the upper balcony of the Leaf Theater near the square in downtown Quincy.

At age ten, Goldwire was promoted to work in the tobacco barn where it was cooler, but always subject to more direct supervision of the white barn foreman. He worked hard at transferring the tender leaves from the mule-drawn sled to the smooth sewing tables. He was kept busy picking up falling leaves which somehow slipped from the sticks as they were handed high up into the interior of the cavernous barn. Goldwire returned the leaves to one of the sewing tables, always conscious of preventing cracking or breaking of the leaf. The barn foreman was paid an incentive for prime quality cigar wrapper tobacco and he constantly watched the activity of the female sewers and the helpers. Careless effort would be rewarded with an angry confrontation with the foreman and possible return to the heat and humidity of work in the shades.

At age twelve, large for his age and available when older men were being drafted into the war, Goldwire was earning $1.75 a day as mule driver for the sled. He also was tall enough to help with sewing the shade cloth to overhead wires. New babies were arriving at the Cohens household almost every summer and the earning power of the family was reduced while his mother was unable to work regularly in the shades or the barns. But now, his younger sisters were old enough to work as toters during the priming season. Moses maintained tight control over this family and saw that each member became an earner at an early age.

Within the following two or three years, Goldwire had had an opportunity to learn every job in the shade tobacco farming business, from priming tobacco, to tractor driving, to irrigation pump repair, and his newest job this coming season of supervising a field crew. He would have the 18-acre shade from soil preparation, fertilizer spreading, transplanting, to tying up, pesticide dusting, and priming. He would need full cooperation of the field crew of twelve – maybe sixteen, during the heavy priming time. All black schools in Gadsden County were in session from August to early April to make available a full work force for the major crop of the County. White schools were on the more traditional September/May schedule – among other things, to assure that the hot month of August in North Florida was available for families to escape to the cool North Carolina mountains, after successfully delivering another crop to the packing houses.

Goldwire was jolted back to reality as Moses brought the cold and balky Chevy bus through a change of gears on the blacktop highway. The three-dollars-day promised him for the new responsibilities of the upcoming season left a trace of a smile on his face. Maybe he would skip the last two weeks of school to get an early start on the crop. He hadn't discussed what portion of the salary would be his, with his father, but Goldwire knew it would be enough to buy the small red radio he had seen in the window at Bates Supply Company on the square.

"Goldwire, I want you to go to Burns & Johnson this morning with me," said Moses over the roar of the engine and the pungent odor of burnt exhaust oil. "I need to make 'rangements with Mr. Burns for another crop of tater drawers."

"Yes sir," replied Goldwire.

Half Way There, Haole

"You can trust Mister Burns more than the preacher," said Moses. "He's always been fair with me. I don't want to have nuthin' to do with them bankers. They'll get you every time.."

Moses guided the bus southward toward Quincy, a bright early February sun to his left was finally beginning to burn off the effects of the heavy frost. By afternoon the temperature would be in the sixties and the briskness of the early morning would be easily forgotten. The bus came to a quick stop at the red light in front of the Methodist Church. Moses crossed the intersection and joined the heavy flow of Saturday traffic around the courthouse square. He parked the bus on West Jefferson Street and behind the J. Q. Casey grocery store—the parking lot provided by the City merchants for labor buses. The sidewalks along West Jefferson street were rapidly filling with Negroes from other area farms—but nothing like it would be on an early Saturday in May when everyone had money to spend.

"We leaves at four-thirty. Be here," yelled Moses to the noisy group awaiting the opening of the school bus door. "Watch the clock at the courthouse building."

The Cohens children were left in the charge of an older sister, while Goldwire and Moses made their way down the crowded sidewalk to the Burns & Johnson store. Goldwire wondered if he would see Mister AB for the second time this Saturday. As the sidewalk crowd thinned, Goldwire could see the large red and white Purina checkerboard identification containing the Burns & Johnson sign. On a small brown grassy plot between the sidewalk and the street sat a shiny bright green John Deere tractor. A neon sign flashed in the window announcing the location of the local Westinghouse appliance dealership.

The Burns & Johnson agricultural supply business was housed in what had been the Quincy livery stable of many years ago. Dean Burns had formed the company during the Depression, twelve years ago on $4000 in borrowed funds. After a meager start, the business had prospered during the war years. All farm supplies and tractors had been in limited supply during those years and profit margins had been comfortable. The post-war years held more promise of profitability as tobacco farmers strained to meet the demand of the expanding cigar-smoking public. Yet the darkened interiors of the general store reflected a hodge-podge of shelves and displays reminiscent of the 1920's. An exception was an attractive arrangement of gleaming white Westinghouse appliances located near the front display windows.

Moses and Goldwire entered the front door, passing by the appliances and extensive display of seed bins containing local favorite varieties of butter beans, blackeye peas, field peas, okra, sweet corn, string beans, English peas, rape seed and collards. Goldwire had fond memories of visiting Burns & Johnson every Good Friday to buy garden seed with his mother. The family garden plot was her project, but she was allowed to charge the seed purchases against the "Moses Cohens Sweet Potato Account." All of Gadsden County knew the 'moon was right' to plant a garden on Good Friday weekend, to guarantee a bountiful garden crop.

Further within the depths of the store, the two visitors passed piles of mule collars, plow lines, and other supplies used to outfit the hundreds of mules used on the many acres of Gadsden County under shade cloth. The entire store had a curious mixture of odors, dominated by the aroma of freshly-ground Purina hog chow and chicken feed, but with a hint of chemical pesticides, leather, and rope supplies. Goldwire had visited the store many times and recalled the aroma as a distinct part of the experience. He liked the smell; he inhaled deeply to catch the full bodied flavor as he followed his father through the building to the office.

To their surprise, a line of seven farmers had formed, some with wives, to see Dean Burns about 'making arrangements' for another crop season. Many of the smaller farmers in Gadsden and nearby Liberty County, and from south Georgia—those not engaged in shade tobacco farming—looked to Dean Burns to finance their spring fertilizer and seed purchases until the crop 'was made' in the fall. Burns & Johnson had become their bank as well as the principal source of farm supplies. A distinct feeling of total trust had developed over the years by many of these people in the line – including Moses Cohens.

Moses approached the sliding glass window of the office area, where he was greeted by a middle aged lady wearing thick rimless glasses and a smile.

"Moses, how are you today! Are you ready for another year?"

"Sure am, Miss Alice," responded Moses with a broad grin. "If I can just do as good as last year, I'll be happy."

"Mr. Burns will see you in a few minutes; you follow Josh Hall and his wife."

Alice Morgan instinctively moved to the vertical ledger file on her glass-topped desk and thumbed through the "C" index for the Cohens account. She reviewed the activity in the account for the previous year, noting that all purchases had been covered by the delivery of potato plants and that the account had been cleared with delivery of a $220.00 check in July of last year to Moses Cohens. Alice placed the ledger sheet on the lower left corner of Dean Burns' desk, underneath the ledger sheets of other waiting customers.

Goldwire found a comfortable seat atop an unopened cardboard carton marked 'mule collars', with a label of a hardware supply company from Dothan, Alabama. He had a complete view through the sliding glass window in the clerk's office and directly into the inner office of Dean Burns. The room was extremely cramped, with space enough for a desk, chair, and two unmatched wooden customer chairs. The walls were lined with wooden shelves haphazardly heaped with books, cigar boxes, mementos, advertising brochures, and small paper bags containing fertilizer samples. Directly behind the two customer chairs was a huge black safe, open to reveal small shelves stacked with ledger sheets, more wooden cigar boxes, and a black metal box holding a cash drawer. Behind Dean Burns was a cloudy four-pane window partially covered with dusty venetian blinds.

Although Goldwire could not hear the conversation, he could see that Dean Burns was engaged in deep and serious conversation with a white farmer and his wife. He could see the cold stare of deep-set brown eyes through small rimless glasses. His furrowed brow of the reddish-brown complexion reflected a multitude of long hours of hard work and was topped with a heart-shaped receding hair line. Dean Burns was quite aware of his thinning hair and made a futile effort to part his hair in the center, and sweep back the remaining dark brown strands well over each ear. His nose was a parrot-beak shape with a high bridge, but was somewhat small and out of proportion for the firm mouth and heavy chin. He wore a brown checked flannel shirt with a corduroy jacket and leather elbow patches. He listened intently as the farmer discussed at length his inability to complete payment of last year's crop note. The farmer's wife sat rigidly and with a look of concern and anticipation on her face.

Finally, Dean Burns leaned back in his overstuffed chair and stared intently at the ceiling, his hands cupped and holding a long yellow pencil. He suddenly leaned forward toward the farmer across the desk, obviously making a profound statement as the result of his decision-making posture. The farmer's wife relaxed in the chair as a faint smile crossed her weathered face. Dean Burns had decided to finance the farmer for another year and to carry forward the old crop note. He then reached for a large black ledger book and proceeded to write down the fertilizer and seed order, and calculate the total by adding $2.00 per ton to the posted fertilizer price for the risk of carrying a customer with questionable credit. The farmer nervously signed the new crop note with a huge rough red hand. As his wife signed, Dean Burns extended his hand to the farmer without emotion and the couple left the office.

Other customers repeated the process. It readily became evident to Goldwire from the reaction of Dean Burns which customers had successfully paid their previous year's account, and those who had not. Josh Hall emerged from the office, and Alice Morgan motioned for Moses and Goldwire to enter.

Dean Burns stood and greeted Moses Cohens with a smile. Goldwire returned the broad smile, flashing even white teeth in contrast to his light brown skin, as he was introduced to Dean Burns by his father.

"Goldwire is goin' to supervise a field crew this year at La Camellia, and he's goin' to help with the tater crop in his spare time. He's seventeen and will finish Carter Parramore next year," said Moses with obvious pride.

"Good boy," responded Dean Burns. "If he has your ambition and head for business, he'll do all right." Moses accepted the compliment, and sat forward in his chair ready to discuss the results of last year's ledger sheet held in Dean Burns left hand.

"Looks like you did all right last year, Moses. That $220.00 check helped pay some of your bills?" questioned Dean Burns.

"Yes sir, what are you paying this year for first class tater drawers?'

Dean Burns was somewhat surprised, "Same as last year."

"I need five cents a bundle more this year," responded Moses with a stern appearance on his dark face.

Dean Burns leaned back in his arm chair, folded his cupped hands with the long yellow pencil protruding. He stared at the upper corner of his office ceiling with a concerned look on his face. He needed fifteen percent markup to cover general overhead expenses. Potato plants sold well last year at sixty percent markup. His only competition was at Greensboro, twelve miles away. He could improve his markup....

After what seemed an eternity to Goldwire, Dean Burns lowered his head, his piercing brown eyes staring directly at Moses, "I can make it two cents a bundle."

"Three cents," shot back Moses.

"Three cents it is," said Dean Burns without hesitating. He admired anyone who drove a hard bargain, but Moses Cohens was the only Negro he knew in Gadsden County with instincts for 'doing business.'

Goldwire had never seen his father speak up to a white man in such a determined voice. Moses certainly never had been so forward with any of his white bosses at King

Edward. Somehow, for the first time in his seventeen years, Goldwire had a different feeling about the white people of Gadsden County. He had met someone who, at least on a business basis, recognized a Negro as an individual.

"Miss Alice, step in here a minute," called the Burns & Johnson manager. "Open up a new account for Moses Cohens. The price for sweet potatoes drawers is up three cents a bundle over last year; and tell LuEthyl Potter not to leave....I need to see her."

All three men rose from their chairs simultaneously, shaking hands on the completed deal. As Goldwire turned to leave, Dean Burns noticed the broad shoulders and heavy legs of the younger Cohens. He made a mental note to keep him in mind next time he was hiring temporary warehouse help for peanut buying season........even more important, perhaps was the Moses Cohens strategy of inviting his son to join him in the Dean Burns visit. Maybe it would payoff sometime!

Chapter 3

Allendale circled the courthouse square in his mother's Plymouth looking for a convenient parking spot. It was a beautiful sunny March afternoon – the kind that only North Florida could produce this time of year. That feeling of an early spring was in the air, so why was he saddled with the horrible thought of registering for the military draft. He would get a deferment to attend college, and maybe after that the government would forget the whole idea about needing warm bodies for the military. After all, the big war was over. He remembered how only last summer the draft law had been suspended by the Congress, and then, within months, reversed itself and reinstated the conscription of 18-year olds. The senior Current Events class at Quincy High had carefully monitored the heated debate in Washington on the subject. As Allendale turned to circle the area once again, he spotted a pickup truck backing from a parking space at the end of the block. He eased the Plymouth into the curb and glanced up at the courthouse clock—ten to five; just time enough to visit the Selective Service office.

The basement room door read – ROOM 104 GADSDEN COUNTY SELECTIVE SERVICE. Allendale opened the wide wooden door only to be nearly blinded by the late afternoon sun streaming in the high basement window. Out of the confusion, a high pitched female voice asked if she could help him. Allendale stood to one side, away from the sun light when his eyes finally narrowed and focused to reveal an extremely overweight young lady with long straight and unkempt black hair. She wore no makeup. Her heavy upper arms strained the short sleeves of a yellow print dress. He had seen the same yellow flower print on the

Purina chicken feed sacks in the Burns & Johnson feed warehouse.

"Is this where you register for the draft?" said Allendale, finally collecting his thoughts from the shock of his sunlit entrance, and the unattractive female.

"Yes," she said, "Fill out this form, and if you want to apply for a college educational deferment, complete the green form too." The clerk recognized Allendale, as she did almost all young male Quincy residents. As the unmarried daughter of Sheriff Woodbury, she made it her business to keep up with most of the males in Gadsden County. Her appointment as Selective Service clerk aided in her avocation. She knew which local families would be sending young men to college.

Allendale picked up the forms and retreated to the side of the room protected from the strong western sunlight. Four chairs with writing arms were pushed back against the wall. He selected a seat and utilized the writing surface of the chair next to him in order to accommodate his left hand. He had become accustomed to making arrangements for his left-handedness in public places. Few of the classrooms at Quincy High were equipped to meet the needs of left-handed students.

The clerk placed the completed forms in a soiled manila folder and reminded Allendale that he would receive notification within sixty days to report for a physical examination. She explained this was necessary to establish his physical profile for classification purposes but he would probably be granted a deferment to complete his college education. The local Selective Service Board, composed of the County Superintendent of Schools, a retired Quincy dentist, a tobacco farmer, and two merchants from Greensboro and Havana, routinely passed on all deferment requests for continuing education. Since the Negro community accounted for about seventy-five percent of the county population, and few Negroes requested college deferment, there was a sizeable reserve of men to meet the small quota allotted to Gadsden County each month.

Allendale left the office without further conversation, but somewhat taken aback by the immediate need to report for a physical examination. He hadn't counted on that. As a graduating senior, his life was becoming much more complicated – pushing him to adulthood before he was quite prepared. His eighteenth birthday last week had propelled him into decision-making situations that he had been delaying. The planned discussion with his parents at dinner this evening about college selection was something he would just as soon delay.

The dark green Plymouth stopped abruptly at the King Street traffic light, as Allendale was suddenly jolted back into reality. He waited for the two truckloads of baled cheese cloth to pass before turning left. He passed the Presbyterian Church on the corner and several huge southern colonial homes graced with curving driveways, magnolia trees draped heavily with Spanish moss, and masses of red, white, and pink blooming camellias carefully spaced in side yards and next to formal entrances. He approached the Quincy High School and was hailed by several basketball friends.

"Hey, AB, pull over," yelled Clay Bates.

The group piled into the parked car. Two friends had just received word of acceptance at University of Florida in Gainesville. Another was going to Florida State in Tallahassee – recently name changed from Florida State College for Women – to accommodate the huge influx of male veterans. The two seniors attending school in

Gainesville were from prominent Quincy families. Allendale considered them more acquaintances than friends since there was this feeling that the Burns family, having moved from Greensboro several years ago, was really not a part of the inner Quincy society that had grown up in the shade tobacco business since the early 1900's. AB did not want to discuss his visit of ten minutes ago to the Selective Service office, even though everyone had already or would have to sign for the draft. The boys jumped from the car as quickly as they had piled into the Plymouth, and AB was on his way down King Street, turning at the large live oak tree into his driveway. The neat white home with screened front porch reflected the Burns image of modesty, carefully masking and understating the Dean Burns financial condition. AB parked in the Plymouth-assigned spot, allowing extra room for the oversized deSoto.

Lucinda Burns returned the phone receiver to the hook. "Daddy won't be home until after seven-thirty. He's in a meeting with the fertilizer people from Cottondale," sighed Lucinda, as AB entered the kitchen.

"That's OK," replied AB, "I'll do some work on the term paper."

Lucinda needed the extra time to prepare dinner. The bridge club had run late at Sara Beth's house. She regretted somewhat that most of the other ladies had full-time maids to prepare meals. However, with fresh oysters from Appalachicola Bay, dinner wouldn't take long to prepare.

Appalachicola oysters were a Burns family favorite. Masonic friends from Panama City supplied fresh oysters at Christmas time each year, and were usually favored with a Burns & Johnson Purina-fed turkey. But, this mid-March, a surprise fresh oyster treat had been arranged by Dean Burns. Pocket was scheduled for a corn and peanut fertilizer delivery to Wakulla County and had been instructed to return via Panacea to pick up the freshly-shucked oysters. Lucinda retrieved the shiny half-gallon bucket from the refrigerator and prepared the corn meal for deep frying.

    AB sat at the end of the extended dining room table, cluttered with reference books and notes he had taken in preparation for his senior English project. He had struggled with the thesis, supporting statements, and outlines and was finally to the point of actually writing the text of the project. The dining room table had been enlarged so he would have sufficient room to work without the distractions of the trappings of his room. He would eventually type the theme from a hand-written draft copy. His mother entered with plates and silverware to prepare the other end of the table for the evening meal.

    "Mom," said AB, "Clay and Tom have been accepted in Gainesville, They just heard today. If they can get in, I'll probably be accepted too; but I don't really want UF. I know Dad wants me to go there, but that's not the place for me."

    "AB, your father has his mind set on his only child graduating from Florida," stated Lucinda Burns in a soft but firm tone. "He never had the opportunity to attend college and he wants the best for you." She quickly returned to the kitchen since she did not want to continue the conversation. Lucinda already felt the pressure between her husband and her son. AB understood. He knew she would have little to say about the final decision. As he sat there with his pencil poised in his left hand, he could see his mother busily preparing dinner, the small Zenith kitchen radio tuned to Lowell Thomas Evening News. The radio broadcast intentionally prevented a conversation between the two rooms.

Half Way There, Haole

AB sat there frustrated, but admiring his mother. She was tall with dark brown hair that was beginning to evidence some gray from her forty years. Her thin lips, smooth complexion and beautiful even teeth somehow drew attention away from the too-close set eyes. Her ready broad smile prefaced almost every word she spoke – slowly, distinctly, and with the trace of a South Georgia drawl. The smile effectively masked the frustration of living with the strong will and high motivational level of Dean Burns. The same smile also masked the disappointment of not being able to have the large family they had planned. In the long and difficult years of establishing Burns & Johnson as a successful Gadsden County business, Lucinda Burns had not been asked once to participate in any decision making. She felt ignored but never did it occur to her to express an opinion on how Burns & Johnson should conduct business. Instead, she directed her hidden talent for managing to church, school, and community activities. She had been named President of numerous local groups and now was active in state PTA and church groups. She also felt the need to establish her position among the Quincy tobacco and banking matrons.

AB had recognized her frustration of living with his father and identified with it. The two of them never discussed their mutual frustrations; that would have betrayed Lucinda's love for Dean. AB turned his thoughts as to how he would explain his own decision to attend a Liberal Arts college in Pennsylvania.

Both mother and son recognized the motor sounds of the approaching DeSoto to the Burns household. AB would have to wing the college conversation. Lucinda hurried to finish the fried oysters – a Dean Burns favorite. The oyster stew was simmering on the back burner of the Westinghouse range. Cornbread sticks were warming in the oven.

"Sorry I'm late," said Dean, "but those fertilizer people from Cottondale wouldn't agree to a trucking allowance increase over last year. I got what we needed, though." Dean stopped suddenly. He had already said more than he intended. He seldom brought home any small talk from the day's activity.

"The oysters smell great," said Dean as he passed through the kitchen to the dining room. "How you coming along on the term paper, son? I saw Professor Hanson at the Rotary meeting today and he was bragging on the talent and leadership in the class of '47. He says for the first time since Pearl Harbor, the senior class isn't dominated by talk about being drafted or joining up in some branch of the military. Instead the boys are talking about competing with Veterans for dormitory space at Florida and FSU."

"Yes," replied Allendale, getting up from the books and papers on his end of the dining room table. "They say that all kinds of temporary buildings are being thrown together on both campuses to house the Vets. Even some temporary apartments for the married students." Allendale kept the conversation going to warm up to the discussion on his own personal college decision.

Lucinda Burns carried a tray of three bowls of oyster stew from the kitchen, carefully placing the steaming delicacy in front of each diner. She seated herself and Dean Burns quickly repeated a prayer, before reaching for the pepper shaker.

Allendale decided to open the conversation.

"I went to the courthouse today to sign up for the draft. The lady said I would receive a deferment as long as I was enrolled in college. I do have to take a physical exam in Jacksonville in the next few months."

Dean Burns' brown eyes flashed, "Why do you have to take a physical if you're not going to be drafted?"

"They have to know what physical classification to put you in, even if you're being deferred for college. That's the law."

"OK, I can understand," said his father, "but maybe they'll change that ridiculous draft law by 1951 when you graduate. This country….the whole world…has had enough war for this century." He tipped the bowl to one side to get the last spoonful of oyster stew. Lucinda smiled as she arose to remove the empty bowls and returned with heaping platters of fried oysters and corn bread.

"Son, I think you know your mother and I want the very best for you. The Burns & Johnson business is now established in Quincy and we both look forward to you becoming an involved partner. Things weren't always this way. It's been difficult to move from Greensboro and be accepted in the Quincy business community. I'll have to admit if it hadn't been for the shortages in supplies during the war, Burns & Johnson probably wouldn't have been successful. But farmers and tobacco corporations would buy from anyone who could deliver. We need to continue to earn our reputation and the right to serve the public here. There are some bankers here who said Dean Burns would never make it in Quincy. I've worked hard to prove them wrong. But in order for Burns & Johnson to prosper, we need to grow and serve the community. I want you to feel a part of this company, but you have to finish your college degree first. The University of Florida offers an excellent business course…."

"Dad, I don't want to go to Gainesville," interrupted Allendale. "I want to be a part of Burns & Johnson someday, but Gainesville isn't for me."

Dean Burns' piercing brown eyes narrowed through his glasses to focus on his son. Allendale had not challenged his father since an incident in eighth grade, but he had prepared himself for the glaring response and proceeded to hold his composure. Finally, Dean Burns finished chewing the cornbread, swallowed, and spoke softly.

"You don't seem to understand, son. The Woodbury's, the Monroes, the Gates, the Edwards, the Allens.....all the prominent families of Quincy send their youngsters to Gainesville. You can join a fraternity......"

"I don't want to go to Gainesville," interrupted Allendale for the second time. "And I don't want to go to FSU in Tallahassee either."

Dean Burns was caught speechless. Lucinda had never seen her husband when he was not fully in command of the moment. She stopped eating and placed her fork on the edge of her plate with the composure of a British queen. She glanced to her left at the long mirror over the buffet to get a full view of her husband as he stared, without blinking his eyes, with astonishment at Allendale. Dean Burns' ruddy complexion reflected a mellow glow as waves of anger alternated with ripples of confused frustration. He leaned forward over his plate with both elbows on the table, his hands dangling but holding a fork and half-eaten cornbread stick. The silence of the moment was broken only by the ticking of the mantle clock in the adjoining living room, and the occasional sound of a passing car on King Street. Allendale had recently learned the effectiveness of the technique of total silence during a confrontation. He realized his father often used this technique in negotiating with visiting salesmen, as well as certain customers when price negotiations were stalled. Allendale was determined not to break the silence between the two of them. Lucinda fetched the coffeepot from the kitchen. She returned to find the situation unchanged. Allendale continued to eat with deliberate movements, occasionally glancing at his father. The coffee cups filled, Lucinda returned to her chair.

An unexpected feeling of compassion for his son suddenly crept through Dean Burns. He relaxed, leaned back and placed his elbows on the arms of the captain chair. His narrow-set eyes contained a hint of a smile. The reaction of his father disarmed Allendale. He suddenly felt he was losing control of the silent standoff with his father. Lucinda nervously reached for her coffee cup. Dean Burns simultaneously reached for his cup and finally broke the impasse.

"Well, son, just where would you like to go to college?" said Dean Burns, with the tone of a soft south Georgia drawl usually reserved for Church, Rotary, and Masonic gatherings.

Still shaken by his father's unexpected reaction, Allendale was determined not to let his voice show any evidence of concession.

"Daddy, I've been accepted at Allegheny College, and I'd like to go there. Allegheny is a small Liberal Arts school in Pennsylvania. It's associated with the Methodist Church. Doctor James down at the church told me about it. His brother graduated from Allegheny before the war."

Dean Burns, who prided himself on being in control of every situation, conceded meekly. "Allegheny it will be. Do you have an Allegheny catalog? I'd like to see it."

"I'll bring it home from school tomorrow," said Allendale, excusing himself to answer the telephone.

"That was Billy Joe. I'm going over to his house for a few minutes."

The timing of the phone call was perfection – for all members of the family.

Chapter 4

AB wearily lowered his frame into the newly re-upholstered chair in the den. He had washed up for supper, but the dirt and dust from the peanut warehouse remained in the folds and creases of his work clothes. There were four more truck loads of peanuts to unload at the warehouse and only time for a brief supper break before returning to work. The den had been added to the Burns household when AB was in his third year at Allegheny, and had been the result of much detailed sketching and planning on the part of Dean Burns. Lucinda Burns had given an allowance of four-hundred dollars to furnish and decorate the new room. The re-upholstered chair had been a compromise—funds had been exhausted before she could purchase a much-inspected new lounge chair at Shelfer Furniture on the Square.

With a quick glance at the wall clock, AB dialed the radio to a Tallahassee station to listen to the Lowell Thomas Evening News. While off at college he had not made much effort to keep pace of current news events, but since graduation he carefully followed the progress of the war news coming out of Korea.

"Good evening, ladies and gentlemen—this is Lowell Thomas with the evening news. On this Labor Day in 1951, the reports out of Korea are mixed. The First Marine Division has driven the North Koreans from key hillside positions in the Punchbowl area north of the 38th Parallel. Indications are the Marines are well poised to drive the enemy to the Suyong River. Meanwhile, the US 2nd Army Division has run into stiff North Korean resistance in the attack on Heartbreak Ridge and on Bloody Ridge. US casualties are reported as moderate to heavy……."

AB listened intently, unaware that his mother observed his reaction to the radio program from the kitchen while she prepared dinner. She had seen her son mature gradually as he returned from college each summer. The freshly scrubbed face revealed, beneath a deep tan, the best features of his parents. From his father came the dark brown eyes, but not nearly so deep-set, and the light brown straight hair – parted in the middle and swept back from his forehead. Fortunately, his father's parrot nose had been replaced with a non-descript model from elsewhere within the family tree. From his mother came the quick smile, near perfect set of gleaming white teeth, and the calm calculating manner. Missing from his personality was the personal drive, sense of urgency, and self assurance of his father – but maybe some aspects of that would develop under the careful tutelage of his father now that AB was in a training program to become a partner in Burns & Johnson.

The news report of a hurricane entering the Gulf of Mexico caused AB to sit up and listen carefully. He knew that a successful peanut harvest in North Florida and South Georgia called for weeks of dry weather in August and September. A hurricane with accompanying heavy rains would be a real problem to peanut farmers. He began to make plans to keep the peanut buying warehouse open for extended hours to accommodate weather-conscious farmer-customers.

Lowell Thomas closed the news with late reports from Korean battlefronts. AB wished he could hear from the Bureau of Naval Personnel in Washington. In May, before graduation, and unbeknownst to his parents, AB and two fraternity friends had driven to Pittsburgh to take examinations for Naval commissions. Allegheny did not offer an ROTC program and the termination of the draft deferment occupied much of the conversation at the SAE fraternity among the non-veterans. One friend had failed the eye examination, and the other had been drafted into the Army in August. AB had been told by BUNAVPERS that he had passed all physical and education requirements, but that direct commission programs were full and he would be notified of the next opening. The draft situation in Gadsden County was most uncertain. The quotas varied each month and the large backlog of Negroes eligible made educational deferments an unknown element in the selection process. AB had privately scanned the list of draftees each month in the *Gadsden County Times*. None of his school friends with deferments had been listed, although some had been accepted as volunteers by various branches of the military. He also read with keen interest the multi-columns of news stories from activities of Gadsden Countians in the military services. New army arrivals were being sent to various parts of the country with no apparent consistency, for basic training and technical schools: Fort Jackson, South Carolina; Fort Dix, New Jersey; Camp Campbell, Kentucky; Schofield Barracks, Hawaii; Fort Devens, Massachusetts; Fort Ord, California; Camp Blanding, Florida; Camp Gordon, Georgia; Fort Meade, Maryland......

"We'll not wait for Dad for dinner tonight," said Lucinda, "I know you want to get back to the warehouse and finish early."

Lucinda brought her son a large dinner plate piled high with chicken and yellow rice, fried okra, squash, and the usual cornbread sticks. She followed this with a bowl of banana pudding and a giant glass of sweetened ice tea. AB polished it all off in fifteen minutes and was on his way back to the warehouse in his new dark green Ford pickup truck.

The new Ford pickup was waiting at the warehouse on the first day he reported to work after graduation. Although owned by the Burns & Johnson partnership, it had been assigned exclusively to AB (his father now called him AB), as assistant manager of the company. AB had always had access to a vehicle; usually his mother's, but it was a way Dean Burns had chosen to give his son an immediate active position within the organization. The second manner in which his father had chosen to provide physical evidence of his acceptance at Burns & Johnson, was to build an office for AB in the retail store on West Jefferson Street. AB was less impressed with this token of acceptance. The Westinghouse ranges, refrigerators and freezers had been rearranged to allow floor space for construction of the office. Although adequately furnished, it was located adjacent to the general office where Miss Alice and the two clerks maintained records and prepared payrolls for the thirty-two employees. Somehow AB felt isolated from the decision making that transpired in his father's office, and the glassed-in office gave him the feeling of being on display. The store employees, many of whom had been with the company since 1937, had expected AB to be part of the business and had welcomed him graciously to the group. They had watched AB grow from a child and worked with him on various summer jobs during his high school and college years.

AB was particularly pleased now that everyone was calling him AB rather than Allendale – even his father. Ever since the dinner confrontation with his father concerning college selection, there had begun to be a different feeling between father and son. At Allegheny, in his freshman year the one or two letters he had received from his father carried a "Dear AB" salutation. AB had suspected his mother's intercession on the subject.

The dark green Ford pickup sped down King Street, turned at the football field, and arrived at the warehouse within the allotted four-minute driving time from the Burns household. Both windows had been lowered to cool the truck cab on this Monday evening. The humidity seemed unbearable, perhaps signaling the hurricane that lay several hundreds of miles south in the Gulf. AB parked the pickup next to the truck scale house and stepped inside the office. Pocket and Goldwire sat on an old truck seat that had been removed from a junked Dodge, dusty sweat caked to their shining upper black bodies. They had each just finished a pan of rice, beans, and chicken, brought from home for the occasion. This time of year, both knew that peanut-buying season either meant a late supper or two meals brought from home.

Goldwire had been hired two years ago as truck driver and store porter for the retail store on Jefferson Street, but from August through early October he assisted at the warehouse as handyman in unloading customer peanut trucks, driving semi-trailer loads of peanuts to Graceville; and generally serving as mechanic in keeping the peanut elevator and belt conveyers in good working order. Dean Burns had observed Goldwire carefully and was impressed with his natural mechanical ability. At next opportunity, he planned to transfer Goldwire to the John Deere tractor repair shop – another department of the Burns & Johnson complex.

"Mr. AB," said Goldwire, "Reckon we can be out of here by eight-thirty tonight? I sure would like to stop by the Blue Star before catching a ride to La Camellia."

AB offered a broad smile, "Keep the elevator working and we'll close up by eight o'clock. I heard on the radio we may be having a hurricane in the Gulf next few days. You know those trucks will roll in here ahead of that storm. I'm going to talk to the Federal Inspector in the morning about keeping the peanut grading table open extra hours at night."

Pocket ground the remains of a Camel on the cement floor of the scale room office and headed for the warehouse to unload the last four trucks. Goldwire stretched his huge frame and joined Raymond and Albert shading their eyes against the strong rays of the setting sun as they approached the warehouse. AB pulled the high stool over to the grading table to attack the mound of paper, grading sheets, and truck weight slips. He was determined to show Miss Alice he could turn in a day's receipts without error. Sweat trickled off his brow and onto the government inspection forms.

Chapter 5

AB wasn't terribly surprised when it arrived – an official-looking brown window envelop. "GREETINGS, you have been selected . . . . . " The real surprise came in the attached list of fellow draftees. Immediately below his name on the list was someone he had come to know very well – Goldwire M. Cohens. AB's mind began to work overtime on that hot September evening. How would he feel traveling and living with a Gadsden County Negro – one whom he knew and respected as a laboring warehouse employee? Could he enlist? What about the Navy commission application? What would he say to Goldwire? The only other name in the fourteen-member group he thought he recognized was Clayton duPont from Chattahoochie, a tobacco-chewing basketball player he had played against four years ago. He heard that Clayton was now driving a logging truck for International Paper and running 'shine to Tallahassee on weekends. Most of the other names on the typewritten list sounded Negro –Ezekial, Roosevelt, Jonah . . . . .

With sweating palms, AB again read the letter. He had thirty days before reporting to the Quincy Greyhound Bus Station at 14 South Munroe Street, at 7:15AM. The group leader had been designated as the first man on the list – Roosevelt Abernathy. AB carefully folded the letter and placed it back into the brown envelop. Neither parent was aware of the notice since his mother was on a two-day bridge playing trip to Panama City with a group of Quincy matrons. His father was attending a Chamber of Commerce dinner at the Sawano Club.

Half Way There, Haole

AB turned his thoughts toward his probable early morning discussions with Goldwire. He knew that the Goldwire would have received his mailed notice that evening also, when returning from a long day at the dusty peanut warehouse. What would the two have to say to each other? What had been a white boss/Negro worker relationship would suddenly change. What would it change to? AB recalled his first encounter with Goldwire four years ago on that cold February morning, unloading shade tobacco fertilizer. How Goldwire had eagerly pitched in to help unload the truck; how he had carefully sewn the torn burlap bags; how they talked vaguely about basketball; and how AB had respectfully maintained his distance in a feeling of genuine friendliness, but with the expected reserved white superior attitude.

AB's mind continued to play games as his thoughts raced from one image to another. He sat alone at the kitchen table staring at a tepid plate of pilau he had warmed in the oven for himself. He had picked out the best of the chicken but the cool rice had lost its appeal, even though he was starved from another long day at the peanut warehouse. The sweetened ice tea was gone – a Falstaff beer would have tasted better, but it had turned into too much of a hassle with his parents to keep beer in the refrigerator. Falstaff had replaced the Iron City brand he had learned to appreciate at the frat house at Allegheny. Maybe he needed to get away from Quincy....His long hours at the warehouse kept him from further developing any real relationship with Carol Ann at FSU. Tallahassee was just too far away after 12 or 14 hours in a grimy warehouse. Besides, Carol Ann was in her senior year and was preparing to practice teach in Sopchoppy. The war news out of Korea wasn't very encouraging these days. The Chinese were all over

Heartbreak Ridge. The 2nd Army Division continued to report heavy losses . . . with a college degree and being drafted, could he qualify for specialized service? Something other than the dogface infantry? Everyone being drafted these days didn't end up in Korea; Maybe he would be lucky and get a stateside assignment. Maybe he could still get a Navy commission – he had passed all the exams. What would his father say, losing a son and two employees from the Burns & Johnson organization in one draft call? If he had gone to Gainesville to school, as his father had insisted, he could have been in ROTC and avoided some of this draft bullshit . . . . and what about Goldie?

The silence of the moment was broken by the slam of a car door in the Burns' carport. AB stared at the kitchen clock. It read ten-thirty. Where had the time gone? AB quickly retreated to his room. He would get up early and clean the kitchen of the dirty dinner dishes when he fixed breakfast. He couldn't face his father tonight!

Goldwire failed to show for work the next day -- a Wednesday. It wasn't unusual for Raymond or Albert not to show up for work, but that was always on Monday. AB had learned the procedure well on how to get employees released from the Gadsden County Jail after a weekend of jookin'. . . . . But Goldwire failed to appear on a Wednesday! Everyone at the warehouse assumed his was sick. Only AB knew.

The phone in the truck scale house rang several times. AB sent Raymond from the warehouse to answer it. AB wearily climbed down from the stake body truck piled high with huge burlap bags filled with peanuts from Wakulla County. It was 11 o'clock and already he was hungry for a big noontime lunch at home. Lucinda had returned from Panama City Beach earlier that morning.

Half Way There, Haole

Lucinda Burns nervously held the phone in her left hand, "AB, there's a letter here from the Navy in Washington. It says it is from the Bureau of Personnel. It's a thick letter in a window envelop."

AB's heart leaped into his throat. He could barely find the breath to respond.

"Well, open it up and read it to me," he finally gasped.

Lucinda Burns followed instructions, "Allendale Burns is appointed a commission as Ensign in the Navy Supply Corps." She read on quietly to herself-- then suddenly realized that AB was anxiously awaiting the rest of the letter.

"You are to report to either Bayonne, New Jersey or Quonset Point, Rhode Island on October 17, 1951. The letter goes on to tell you how to complete the enclosed forms."

AB could hardly breathe the hot, humid September air. He told his mother not to notify his father, but he would be home for an early lunch and discuss it with both of them.

Sitting at the kitchen table, he read the Navy letter intently, while his mother prepared hot lunch of fried ham and potato salad. Lucinda was troubled by the letter, but refrained from expressing concern. AB went to his room and returned with the brown envelop from the Draft Board in his back pocket.

Dean Burns entered the room, threw his sweaty straw hat on a chair and went immediately to the kitchen to down a huge glass of sweetened ice tea. The humid September weather was bothering him even though he had spent his entire lifetime in Gadsden County, and......he had just installed a window air conditioning unit in the small office at the Jefferson Street store. He joined Lucinda and AB already seated at the kitchen table, refilling the iced tea glass from a pink Depression Glass pitcher.

"How was the beach? It must be cooler than Quincy."

Lucinda responded half-heartedly, "Fine, it got pretty hot in the early afternoon, but the evenings were cool. The new Woodbury cottage is beautiful. Wish we could have stayed a whole week."

Dean Burns turned more to the business at hand.

"AB, how long would it take to get the lime spreader trucks in working order? I'm working on a deal with American Sumatra Tobacco Company to lime all their pastures. That would keep us busy until Thanksgiving, but we'd have to close out the peanut buying business first."

AB answered the question by placing the two envelopes on the dish-crowded kitchen table. Dean Burns stared in disbelief, immediately noticing the return address of each envelop. Lucinda could read the Draft Board return address upside down. A feeling of terror struck her, but she did not demonstrate any emotional reaction, keeping it all well within her. She recalled their last discussion concerning their son's future – the one about attending school away from Florida. The news from Korea was somewhat improved but with every newscast there came reports of more Chinese crossing the border into North Korea.

A lengthy discussion developed after Dean Burns had read both letters with great care. AB wanted to accept the Navy commission, but would the local Draft Board permit it? A quick phone call to the Draft Board Clerk indicated that it was not possible to delay or reject induction after a name appeared on the monthly draft list. The final word, however on such matters was in the hands of the Draft Board Chairman and Board members. Arrangements were made for AB to take the afternoon off to visit Talmadge Norton's office—County School Superintendent and Chairman of the Gadsden County Draft Board. Dean Burns felt a swelling fear of frustration. He had ways of demonstrating influence within the County, but he felt somehow this was beyond his control. He was also frustrated in losing two key employees from the Burns & Johnson organization. He had planned for Goldwire to move to the John Deere tractor shop at the close of the peanut harvest……

"Son, the law is very clear on something like this," said Talmadge Norton. "Once you are sent a formal notice for reporting on a specific date, you must appear for induction on that date. The Gadsden County Board has been ordered to deliver fourteen men on October 15th, and each man must be given 30 days notice. There would be not time to get a replacement for you and obey the law."

AB had feared the worst.

"Now I know, and you know that this country would be better served if your talents could best be used by serving as an officer in the US Navy. Perhaps you could apply for an Army commission after being drafted. You have the privilege of asking each Board Member for a review of your case, but I feel you are wasting your time. You can also appeal to State Draft Headquarters in Tallahassee by writing them a letter and explaining the situation."

AB left the Superintendent's office with a list of the Board Members: Dr Harrison, a retired Quincy dentist; Clay Johnson tobacco farmer from Gretna; Paul Fletcher of Fletcher Hardware in Havana; and Adrian Sunday, a merchant in Greensboro. He studied the list intently as he sat in his pickup truck. To hell with running around the County talking with these people; he'd write a letter to Tallahassee and if that didn't work, he'd go and make the best of it.

~

Red Thompson guided the new GMC pickup through the La Camellia quarter, cursing the high growth of ragweed that nearly bridged the roadway. By the dog days of August and early September in Gadsden County, dry weeds and dust, encouraged by the heavy humidity made him wish for the opportunity to escape to the North Carolina Mountains like most Quincy townspeople. But King Edward farm superintendents were employed year round and were required to be on the scene while their managers and families escaped the heat, ragweed, and humidity. Red reached the Cohens family house at the end of the road and wheeled into the front yard in a cloud of dust, blowing the horn endlessly to scatter stray dominecker chickens. He stopped just short of the big chinaberry tree and waited for two of the Cohens children to appear from under the front porch. He was distributing mail in the quarter and there was seldom anything to deliver.

"Here's a letter for Goldwire," said Red, pulling a brown window envelop from the glove compartment reeking of Old Heaven Hill. "It's from the Selective Service Board in Quincy."

The ten year old boy took the letter, knowing it was something important, and disappeared within the darkness of the house. Red nipped at the bottle, placed it back in the glove compartment, and reached for the reverse gear of the truck. He roared out of the yard and back to the narrow gravel road in a repeat cloud of dust. The first cloud had barely settled on the ragweed from his instantaneous arrival.

Goldwire sat on the top step of the front porch trying to read the letter in the little daylight remaining.

"GREETINGS, you have been selected….." The attached list included the names of the other thirteen draftees. He turned to the attached list. . . . Roosevelt Abernathy, Allendale Burns…..ALLENDALE BURNS….Goldwire was stunned. Would Mister AB really be going into the Army with him? Maybe he would get a deferment or a release. Mr. Burns knows people in the County. And what about the money that went from his pay envelop each week to help support the Cohens family?

Goldwire was now getting $30.00 in his pay envelop every Saturday afternoon. Of that, $18.00 went to his father. At age twenty-one he was ready to be on his own, but somehow strong family ties had kept him from marrying. He didn't lack for female companionship, especially from the Hava-Tampa quarter that joined the La Camellia farm on the Attapulgus Highway toward Quincy. And what about his job at Burns & Johnson when he returned from two years in the Army? He had clearly decided he didn't want to return to King Edward as a farm hand, or even as a foreman. He wanted to live in Quincy and work at Burns & Johnson.

And where would the Army send him? He had been to Tallahassee, and one time the basketball team had gone to Panama City on a school bus, for a tournament. That seemed further than Tallahassee, but he wasn't sure. He had heard about the big cities of Jacksonville, Atlanta, Detroit. Yes, a cousin from La Camellia had gone to Detroit to work in the car factories at the end of the War. He was making good money. Maybe the Army would send him to Alabama. There was a camp near Dothan; maybe that wasn't too far away.

Goldwire had taken an Army physical exam in Tallahassee over two years ago. He didn't remember hearing any more about it, but had assumed he had failed, or maybe they didn't need him. There was a war going on in Korea. He heard some war stories from Army men in neat

Howard Boylan

tailored uniforms at the Blue Star Grill in Gretna. A younger sister brought him a pan of rice and beans with a small piece of chicken on top. It had been a long day . . . . .maybe he wouldn't make it to work tomorrow. . . . .

Chapter 6

The Greyhound bus driver adjusted the sun visor and glanced at his watch. He was crossing the Little River, and at 7:30 he was about on schedule. The bright early morning October sun was belting him directly in the eyes as he sped toward Tallahassee. This was the express bus; the local made a stop in Havana every other day. They had been delayed in Quincy as the fat lady from Selective Service Board read names and gave last minute instructions to the group leader. Then, the Salvation Army lady had arrived from Tallahassee, just as the fourteen were boarding. The three white draftees had occupied front row seats while the eleven Negroes found seats toward the rear. The group leader, feeling the sense of responsibility to keep the group together, had attempted to seat all of them toward the center of the bus, but both groups resisted. The leader had considered taking a seat near the front, but one glance from the bus driver had quickly changed his mind. The experienced driver was used to handling such situations since a group of draftees left each month from several of his North Florida stops. It was easier when the group leader was white.

AB and Goldwire had talked briefly before boarding the bus. Dean Burns was there to bid both of them farewell, but had spent much time in small talk with AB and Lucinda. Both parents held back a tear during the farewells, but later found a private moment to express concern over the future of their only child. Things were not going well for UN forces in Korea. AB promised to write.

Half Way There, Haole

    The sign over the driver's seat read "Seats – 54, Standees – 14." AB estimated there were only about twenty-five people on the bus. He sat in the seat – alone, and contemplating the activities of the last fifteen minutes. He stared out the dusty window, not comprehending the view. He vaguely remembered the bus lumbering awkwardly through the narrow Quincy side streets and returning to the town square, where he had taken a quick glance at the yellow brick courthouse amid the shedding magnolia trees. Two small boys were squirting water from the drinking fountain marked "COLORED."
    Route 90 east was dotted with pastures, and in a distance AB observed the remains of several tobacco shades bordered by rows of huge wooden tobacco barns. The tobacco crop had long since been harvested and the cheese cloth removed from the overhead wires. Some shade land was already showing early growth of a fall crop of oats or rye. Other shades were still being prepared for fall planting by mule-drawn plows. Burns & Johnson had supplied much of the oats and rye seed for the fall cover crop. AB had supervised loading and paperwork for Pocket to deliver truck loads of seed to farms. Goldwire had helped also, as warehouse operations had slowed from the peanut-buying season. The bright green cover crop would later be disked into the soil under the shades to provide more plant nutrients for the next season's tobacco crop. A few scattered farm hands were standing on benches repairing overhead wires. The work pace was slow and leisurely this early bright October morning.
    The bus tires made a slapping sound on the tarred crevices of the old cement highway. It was easy to tell the speed of the bus as the slapping sound increased or decreased over the gentle slopes of the North Florida

countryside. As the bus crossed Little River into Leon County the scene outside the dusty bus windows changed quickly to wooded areas of pine trees -- some growing in neat rows as planted by International Paper Company for pulp wood. Other pine tree areas were natural growth coming from a confusing undergrowth of palmettos and other swamp plants. While AB had made the Quincy-Tallahassee trip what seemed like hundreds of times, this trip had a feeling of finality about it—even though this was his first ride on a Greyhound bus. It would be another four or five hours from Tallahassee to Jacksonville. Having traveled to Pennsylvania and other states in the East, AB did fear the unknown of military life, and continued to notice each small home, farm, tree, shrub, and cross-road along the route. His mind was attempting to grasp onto something—anything --- familiar, even though his many previous trips on Route 90 east to Tallahassee he had taken no notice of the mundane roadside scenery.

Seven windows behind AB on the Greyhound sat Goldwire Cohens, also by himself and in deep thought. He, too, was glancing out the window at the passing sights. He wouldn't miss the many hours of following a mule in a freshly-turned furrow of the tobacco shade, the many hours of backbreaking work digging holes for shade posts, tying overhead wires in place, hauling fertilizer and forking cow manure into wagons and on to shade land. The move to Burns & Johnson had served him well to escape the long hours of laboring at La Camellia, but on many days that was replaced by working in dusty bins of peanuts or unloading rail cars of bagged fertilizer. The rumored move to the John Deere tractor shop as a mechanic trainee would be the final escape. On the other hand, Goldwire was anxious to be fitted into a well-tailored Army uniform—like the ones worn by the brothers at the Blue Star Grill in Gretna. And he heard the Army pay wasn't that bad, especially after you made corporal or sergeant. The seventy-five dollars a month would be better than his Burns & Johnson pay envelop, since he wouldn't have to continue to help support the family on La Camellia. He hadn't really discussed this with Moses. The thought of exploring the world beyond Gadsden County didn't carry any fears. Maybe he would go to South Carolina, Alabama, or even Kentucky!

The bus slowed for the Tallahassee city limits and students rushing to early morning classes on the FSU campus. Two students got off the bus at the campus entrance. Heavy truck traffic prevented the easy left turn into the Greyhound parking lot. The driver finally succeeded and aimed the huge vehicle into an angular parking slot. AB observed every move from his vantage position, and was somewhat surprised to see a Salvation Army lady handing kits to a group of anxious-looking young men. Another group from Leon County would be joining them for the trip to the Jacksonville Army Depot. He surveyed the five white men for a familiar face – no luck.

The white group leader, in bib overalls and dirty corduroy jacket, feeling very much in charge with his newly-discovered authority, shepherded the fourteen aboard the bus, with the Negroes joining others from Gadsden County in the rear of the bus. The group leader, continuing to attempt to demonstrate strong leadership capability, made a final count as all settled into their seats. As the bus sped east on Route 90, he finally sat in the seat beside AB, immediately opening his Salvation Army kit and devouring the two Hershey bars while carefully removing the almonds and throwing same beneath the seat.

As his seat mate removed the dirty jacket, AB detected a familiar smell – turpentine, from the piney woods stumps. AB introduced himself.

I'm Potter Allison from Woodvul," said the new passenger with a deep rural accent. AB knew of Woodville, a small community in south Leon County. He guessed it was a wood pulp logging area. Potter seemed surprised when AB explained that he too was headed for Jacksonville and Army induction.

"Whadda ya think of them niggers in the back? Ya gotta tell 'em everythin' to do. None of 'em ain't ever been on a Greyhound bus before. They gonna' find a home in this here Army," said Potter.

"I don't know, I guess they'll do all right," responded AB in a non-committal tone. "One of them is our group leader from Gadsden County." AB knew well that the first man in the alphabetical listing was automatically made the group leader. Potter would have been deflated to know this, but AB didn't want to make the point—at least right now. Potter ignored AB's comment.

"I worked a bunch of niggers on the loggin' trucks," said Potter. "They all alike – drinkin', cuttin', and chasin' after pussy. Come to think of it chasin' pussy ain't so bad."

AB decided not to comment further. He knew what Potter was referring to, but he also knew there was one Negro aboard this bus that didn't fit the mold. His mind wandered, as to how Goldwire would survive the stereotyped image. He certainly could hold his own among his own people—if for no other reason than his size and physical conditioning. Yet there could be problems with the whites and maybe the Northern Negroes from large cities. Maybe AB could help some way if they were stationed together. On the other hand, Goldie would have to look after himself, too.

Chances are they aren't going to be too many college-educated Army trainees. AB decided to play down his educational background since he didn't want to be tagged with a 'college boy' label. It should be interesting spending two years with buddies like Potter. Maybe they all wouldn't be directly from Woodvul'.

With the remains of the Hershey chocolate on his stubbled chin, Potter drifted of into a deep sleep, in spite of his newly-found leadership ability. Before doing so, Potter finished a detailed conversation with a friend across the aisle of the last evening he had spent with the $3.50 Tallahassee whore. The sexual conversation immediately led AB's thoughts to Allegheny and his brief fling with the Italian girl from Beaver Falls last April. It wasn't until one of the graduation parties in June that AB discovered the dark-haired sophomore had spent numerous weekends with fraternity brothers at Conneaut Lake cottages. She had seemed so naïve in helping them both discover the capabilities of their bodies on that rainy April night at the lake.....

The bus had made numerous stops – Monticello, Madison, Lake City – taking on and discharging passengers at every stop. The towns looked amazingly alike, a yellow two-story brick courthouse in the center of the town square with stores located around the perimeter. The bus was now nearly full, and as it crossed the Suwanee River a heavy flash rainstorm appeared from nowhere – the kind the Florida coastal plains are noted for this time of year. The sun would be shining five minutes later. The roadside landscape was now taking on a less familiar appearance to AB, and once again he became apprehensive about what the Army might have to offer him. His thoughts suddenly took a brighter turn as he realized that numerous acquaintances had made it through basic training, many with much less education and capability than he. He could do it, but possible assignment to Korea as an infantryman would have to wait his chances. Some assignments to Europe and the Canal Zone were being made. A few even had stateside assignments as reported in the *Gadsden County Times* and the *Tallahassee Democrat*.

The noise level in the rear of the bus reached a peak at times as the Negroes became acquainted and began to relate Army stories about others they had heard who had gone through basic training. Most stories poked fun at ignorant mistakes made by Negroes. AB recognized Goldie's voice as he relayed a story about a trainee who had spent a weekend cleaning his gun after failing to pass a Saturday morning inspection. The trainee had used Colgate toothpaste to clean the bore of the gun and the inspecting sergeant had recognized the peculiar antiseptic odor when holding the weapon to his eye for bore inspection. Goldie had become so engrossed in his trash-talking friends' stories that he failed to notice that the bus was entering the more populated areas of Jacksonville.

Potter awoke and began scrambling overhead for the brown envelop containing Selective Service records and directions for his group from Leon County. He withdrew a stub pencil from the center chest pocket of his bib overalls, put on his "in charge" appearance and proceeded to the back of the bus to call the list of names one more time. After all, someone may have slipped out during the numerous stops. Abernathy felt compelled to do the same for the Gadsden County group.

As the Greyhound bus slowed to enter the large Jacksonville bus terminal, AB noticed evidence of considerable military presence. There were several school busses painted in brown military shade with the US ARMY clearly marked on the side. Five or six uniformed men stood grouped in front of the first bus, smoking and talking. One of the group, a sergeant, moved from the group and followed the progress of the Tallahassee bus to the assigned parking slot. As the driver opened the door, the sergeant jumped aboard and announced that all military personnel should remain seated on the bus. He picked up the brown envelopes from the two group leaders while the civilians gathered their belongings and emerged from the bus.

"My name is Sergeant Martin," he announced. "I will be in charge of your processing while at the Jacksonville Replacement Depot. You will only be here about three hours. Please answer as I call your name. Abernathy, Burns, ...

AB carefully scrutinized his first Army contact. Sergeant Martin was probably about 24 years old, but something about the appearance around the eyes indicated he may have seen experiences beyond his apparent age. He wore his khaki uniform well with a heavy upper chest displaying two rows of various colored ribbons. The dark flat-top haircut was topped with a military cap neatly trimmed in light blue piping and carefully placed two fingers above the right eyebrow. The smooth complexion was outlined with evidence of what would have been a heavy dark beard, if allowed to grow. His dark deep-set eyes seemed to glisten, and almost snap as he spoke with total and complete authority. He wore a large yellow and black patch on his upper right arm. AB believed he recognized this as being the emblem of the 1st Cavalry Division – a unit that had seen heavy fighting in Korea. His boots were stained a dark brown and shined, and were topped with a two-buckle strap, thus avoiding the appearance of having the pants merely stuck into the tops of the boots. AB would have to work on learning how that was accomplished, since he had seen some new Army recruits in movie Newsreels who had a sloppy appearance in an effort to blouse boots.

The draftees filed from the bus, forming two lines as directed by Sergeant Martin. In contrast to the sergeant, the group gave a varied and disheveled appearance – all heights, manner of dress, some carrying unnecessary heavy suitcases…..

"Hey Martin," shouted one of his buddies, "looks like you robbed the corn crib again."

"Naw," shouted another, we shook the pine trees for this bunch."

The group silently filed across the paved terminal area to the first of the Army busses. AB felt embarrassed to be associated with such a country-looking group. Goldwire followed AB in line, unaffected by the remarks.

AB selected a seat near the center of the small bus. Without thinking, he slid to the window seat and motioned for Goldwire to join him. With little hesitation, Goldwire sat down, but after being seated a moment a very awkward, uneasy feeling came over him. Other Negroes in the group filed to the rear and filled the seats toward the front, finally filling in front of AB and Goldwire.

For the first time, it occurred to Goldwire that relations with whites MIGHT be different in the Army, particularly his relationship with Mister AB – his former 'bossman.' Suddenly his mind panicked on how to act … what to say. . . He had always followed orders from anyone at Burns & Johnson in strict obedience, and with an attitude that he owed total allegiance to the Burns family, almost as an unquestioning servant. Now here he was sitting next to Mister AB and he didn't even know what to call him….

Half Way There, Haole

"All right, listen up," said Sergeant Martin standing in the front of the bus beside the civilian driver, "the Jacksonville Replacement Depot welcomes you to the U. S. Army. We don't have much time here. Some of you will be taken to a 5:15 train headed north; others will be catching buses for training camps in the southeast. I will accompany those who leave by train. While at the Center you will fill out a number of forms and will be sworn into the Army. The Marine Corps has a quota of twenty-four men to come from the two hundred seventy-five men who are processing here today. If you are interested in volunteering for the Marines, you will be given an opportunity to do so after we get to the Center. Are there any questions?"

Goldwire and AB exchanged blank looks. The Marines – no way!

"The Marines are getting chewed up in Korea," said AB. "I didn't know you could get DRAFTED into the Marines! They really must be getting hard up for recruits."

"I might think about it," replied Goldwire. "That blue dress uniform would look good on South Munroe Street in Quincy."

"Aw, come on," snapped back AB. "Maybe we'll get assigned to the same camp for basic training. I wonder where that train Sergeant Martin is talking about is going."

AB found himself wanting to stay with Goldwire. It helped relieve some of the uncertainty of what lay ahead. Goldwire didn't necessarily share the same feeling. He was excited about just seeing the tall buildings in Jacksonville, the wide streets, and all the traffic.

The Army bus joined numerous other busses in discharging at a long metal warehouse-looking building in the industrial section of the city. The groups were kept together and seated in a crowded room filled with school-type chairs—all with right hand writing tables. AB looked around for a left-handed chair, but to no avail. Besides he wanted to sit next to Goldwire who might need some help with the forms. He compromised, as usual, by preparing to write sideways on the right handed desk/chair. He'd done it many times before. Sergeant Martin stood aside while a corporal proceeded to give instructions for the form completion.

AB looked at the clock. It was 2:45 and there was no indication they were going to be fed. He was hungry. As he reached for the Hershey bars in the survival kit, he realized that those people at the Salvation Army knew what they were doing when they provided the snacks. Maybe the soap, washcloth and small towel would find a similar emergency use. He'd have to write home and tell his parents to contribute to the Salvation Army, at their next opportunity.

Finally the group assembled in a large open area of the warehouse where they were sworn into the Army after repeating an oath and taking one step forward. It all happened so quickly there wasn't much opportunity to grasp the gravity of the moment. They must have filled the Marine quota!

A Captain stood on a raised platform with a group of Army personnel. He spoke over a crackling loud speaker system. He introduced Sergeant Martin.

"The following named personnel will assemble with Sergeant Martin over near the large open door. This group is assigned to Fort Meade, Maryland for further processing as Pineapples. This group must leave immediately for the train station, so listen up carefully."

AB and Goldwire stared at each other.

"What the hell is a Pineapple," said Goldwire.

"Damned if I know, but I don't think I want to be one," replied AB.

The Captain began the name calling and the group began to assemble slowly near the assigned spot with Sergeant Martin.
"Abramson....Adams....Aiken.....Andrews....Ashley...Baldwin....Belk....Bonamo......Burns.....Carpenter....Cohens....Cooper...

AB and Goldwire exchanged grins as they made their way through the crowded assembly of men and baggage to the assigned area. The list of names rattled on until a large group assembled near the Sergeant. Two other sergeants joined the group with stacks of brown envelopes and official looking lists.

"Move out to the bus area," Sergeant Martin called. "When we get out there we'll recheck the names. We have to be at the train station in forty-five minutes."

As Goldwire and AB again settled into seats on the small Army bus, they guessed there was about fifty in the group. AB saw Potter and the bib overalls getting on one of the other busses marked with a hand-made sign, CAMP GORDON, GEORGIA. He wouldn't miss Potter.

As Goldwire and AB sat aboard the sleek train awaiting departure from Jacksonville, a similar train pulled beside their car. As the shiny train slowly moved along, ATLANTIC COAST LINE SILVER METEOR, Goldwire read printed above the windows. The southbound train had every seat filled with Northerners escaping to the Florida sunshine for the winter months. AB had heard of the winter exodus to Florida but had never experienced the phenomenon. Suddenly, their train bolted to a start and they were getting further instructions from Sergeant Martin who stood in the middle of the long car. He shouted over the noise of the rapidly moving train.

"Gentlemen, we are guests of the U. S. Government and the Atlantic Coast Line Railroad. This car has been checked and there is no damage to any of the seats or equipment. If you damage or destroy anything, this group will pay for it when we get to Fort Meade. Act like gentlemen. We are the last car of this train and will soon go to the diner for a meal. We will eat early – ahead of the civilian passengers. When we pass through the other cars, act like gentlemen toward the other passengers. We will be divided into two groups; the first group leaving immediately. We will return to this car as a group. No one leaves early! Sergeants Keys and Cirrone will accompany the first group. I will accompany the second group."

The two sergeants proceeded to count off thirty-five men toward the front of the railcar. AB and Goldwire would be in the second group. They guessed they could wait, but they sure were hungry. Goldwire headed for the men's room and soon returned perplexed. He told AB there was no restroom for colored – only men and women. AB went to the end of the car to verify the arrangement. He told Goldwire to use the room marked `men.'

Sergeant Martin gathered the remaining men toward the center of the car.

"We arrive in Baltimore at 8:20 in the morning. The seats in this car recline some – make the best of it to get some sleep. This group will be responsible for policing the trash from the car at 7:30 tomorrow morning. That includes both latrines –you can use both mens and womens rooms. We will clean and polish the latrines with a detail of six men finishing by 8AM," he said in a very certain and precise manner. "Now about what happens to you."

Everyone strained to hear every word.

"Each of you has been selected a Pineapple because you have a Class A medical profile. You will process in Fort Meade for about two days and then ship out to Camp Stoneman, California where you will board a troop ship for Hawaii and eighteen weeks of infantry training at Schofield Barracks."

The men listened in stunned silence. No one said anything. Facial expressions were without emotion. The car swayed as the noise of the wheels on the tracks continued to pick up speed. Finally someone spoke.

"Do we get overseas pay?"

The group doubled up in laughter, almost in unison. This broke the tension. Even Sergeant Martin broke into a half smile.

"Yes, as a matter of fact, you are eligible for overseas pay the minute you leave the coastal waters of California" he said.

AB and Goldwire returned to their seats when it became obvious that Sergeant Martin told them all he intended to.

"Now you know what a damn Pineapple is," said Goldwire. What do you think of it?"

Well, that is a little more than I bargained for," responded AB after some thought.

"Mr. AB, just where is Hawaii," said Goldwire. "I know its an island somewheres with volcanoes; I remember something about it and December 7th in history class at Carter Parramore, but the teacher didn't seem very sure of where it was."

"First place, you got to stop calling me MISTER AB. Just AB is ok."

It suddenly occurred to AB that he and Goldwire were the only integrated seatmates in the car. The Negroes and whites had no problem in locating their respective areas of the Greyhound bus, but which was the front and rear of the rail car? Most had settled anywhere in the car as long as the seat mate was of the same shade. Many had already learned it didn't pay to become too friendly with someone because you were soon separated again – as in Jacksonville. Some had turned seats around to face each other. Others had noticed AB and Goldwire's relationship and both races had simply avoided any contact. Neither AB nor Goldwire, however, had sensed the feeling.

Finally the first group returned from the dining car. They had been informed of their destination while eating. One even attempted a poor imitation of a hula dance.

The dining car steward seated the second group, seeing that all tables of four were filled before going on to the next table for seating. The steward was perplexed and hesitant when AB and Goldwire sat together. The steward finally compromised by seating Sergeant Martin and a Negro trainee across from the mixed pair.

Goldwire was amazed and confused by the array of china and heavy silverware, the weighted coffee pot, cream pitcher and sugar bowl. The experience of eating with white folks in such elegance caused him to withdraw from the conversation. The other Negro seemed equally uncomfortable and said nothing. Negro waiters brought a plate served with a thick cut of ham, mashed potatoes with ham gravy and yellow string beans. Both Negroes were hesitant, but their hunger soon convinced them to reach for a fork.

"This is probably the best meal you will ever have while you are in the Army, so dig in," said Sergeant Martin. "They ain't all going to be this way."

AB decided to seize the opportunity to seek additional information from his leader, but he too was so hungry that the ham and mashed potatoes occupied his immediate attention.

As AB paused to prepare his coffee with cream he asked, "Sergeant Martin, isn't that the First Cavalry insignia on your arm?"

"Yes, I was in Korea for nine months. Got a leg wound and was sent back to Tripler General Hospital in Honolulu. Been assigned to this duty about a month. Best duty I've had since joining two years ago."

AB paused to continue, "What's this about Class A profile and Hawaii?'

"Well, said the Sergeant with a wry smile, "Seems like the Army is looking for only trainee candidates with no physical problems to send to Hawaii for eighteen weeks of infantry basic. If you go there, you get mountain training experience sort of like Korea. Then when you finish training, you're half way across the Pacific and ready to ship out to Korea. They need replacements bad over there right now."

The three trainees at the dinner table froze.

Now AB understood about the Class A profile pitch. He and Goldwire returned to their assigned seat in the rear car in total silence, leaving the cherry cobbler dessert untouched. Finally, Goldwire spoke up.

"I wonder if you get any leave time back in Florida, Mr. AB."

"Who knows, it sure doesn't sound very good to me."

AB pushed the lever to recline his seat. The sun rattled through the pine trees as the train sped north through Georgia and into South Carolina. How could he explain to his parents about the assignment and the high probability of going direct to Korea as an infantryman? Why hadn't that damn Navy commission come through three days earlier? Maybe he wouldn't get back to Quincy before going to the Far East.

In his own way, Goldwire had the same thoughts. Maybe he wouldn't get to wear that uniform on South Munroe Street on Saturday night, or go to the Blue Star Grill in Gretna. What is this place Schofield Barracks, anyway?

The train was slowing as they approached a large city. Who cared where they were? Pineapples, ugh!!!

Chapter 7

"Goddam you, shut up in the back row," shouted the Corporal in a high squeeky voice. "You can make your stay at Fort Meade just what you want it to be. We've got a lot of processing to do here and not much time to do it in. You are in MY command for the next few days...."

His voice was buried in the laughter and catcalls from the huge passing group of men, in uniform, but sloppily dressed. Caps were at numerous angles, some boots were bloused – some not, shirt tails hung out below wool Eisenhower jackets. AB guessed this group was all of two days ahead of their newly-arrived group, which was still dressed in a crumpled array of civilian clothing. The group remained quiet and impressed by the "veterans" of two days.

The Corporal with the high squeeky voice waited patiently for the last remnants of the rag-tag army to move on.

"If I catch anybody in this group doing that, I'll bust your ass. The first thirty six men I call off will be assigned to the second floor of Barracks 18E."

A tall dark-haired kid with the Brooklyn accent—the one who was talking in the back row—grabbed the first bunk in the row, in a show of bravado.

The Corporal reassembled the group after a pairing off for headcount, and marched them double file off to the mess hall. Enroute, Barracks 18E was the subject of catcalls from various other "veteran" groups. It didn't take long to figure out that the second man in each formation was in a vulnerable position. As Barracks 18E approached a main thoroughfare within the camp, the high-pitched Corporal shouted, "Road Guards Out," whereupon the second man on each side of the formation ran ahead to halt vehicle traffic for the passing formation of men. As the group passed, the road guards were instructed to fall into the rear of the marching group. When the formation finally arrived at the mess hall, the road guards found themselves at the rear of the chow line. *AB and Goldwire were to learn the 'art of positioning' in the Army, as one of the major forces for survival in the next two years.*

    Barracks 18E finally arrived at the Mess Hall after several repeats of the "Roadguards Out" routine. Two lines wound around the low flat building, nearly obscuring the structure. AB and Goldwire were in line near the kitchen entrance where lines of garbage cans dominated the scenery. The kitchen was in chaos. White-uniformed cooks were ordering KP's to duties. Other KP's were washing metal trays in a dishwasher room with a loud and continuous clatter of trays being slammed into wooden racks. Still others were engaged in scrubbing rows of garbage cans with hand brushes and hoses. The scene was frightening to a new recruit.

    The chow line moved more rapidly than AB had anticipated. When he finally approached the serving line he found out why. A huge Negro cook in white uniform standing on two milk crates screamed endlessly at those being served, to keep the line moving. Goldwire and AB reached for metal trays that were so hot that one had to alternate hands to keep from being burned. They also were given a fork and a handle-less cup. The cup was also screamingly hot from the dishwasher. KPs served lumpy mashed potatoes with a slap at the tray. A second KP attempted to ladle cut hot dogs in thin gravy on to the potatoes. A third KP placed red jello onto another tray compartment. Milk was ladled into the cup as the two recruits were hustled from the end of the serving line and directed to a table toward the rear of the mess hall. Goldwire and AB stared at the tray. The jello had already melted to a soup from the heat of the tray. The milk was lukewarm from the warmth of the cup. The hot dogs and potatoes were scattered in remnants across the three of the remaining sections. Nothing was said by anyone at the table, until the kid with the Brooklyn accent sat down.

"You can't eat this shit," he said. "Look at this." The jello, mashed potatoes and hot dogs had all been piled into one overflowing compartment of the tray. His cup was less than half full of warm milk.

AB looked at Goldwire with a grin, "It doesn't pay to open your mouth when going through the chow line."

"Nah sir," said Goldwire, as he tasted the potatoes and hot dogs. All gave up with the soupy jello -- a fork just wouldn't do.

The corporal strode down the aisle of the dining room yelling for Barracks 18E to finish up and meet outside immediately. AB gulped down the remainder of the meal, even though it wasn't at all appealing when he first sat down.

The rest of the long day was spent in endless lines at the Quartermaster warehouses being outfitted with a barracks bag full of clothing. AB and Goldwire had become separated in the many lines for boots, jackets, hats, and trousers – summer cotton khakis, winter wools, and olive drab work clothing—all jammed haphazardly into a nearly non-liftable barracks bag. AB dragged the bag up the stairs of Barracks 18E and to his assigned bunk, only to find Goldwire already trying on his fatigue uniform--both had learned quickly that the olive drab work clothing was referred to as fatigues.

Half Way There, Haole

The barracks was now filling with exhausted men outfitting themselves in newly-acquired boots and clothing. The corporal entered the room and shouted for quiet.

"I need two men for latrine orderlies – you and you," as he pointed to the vocal kid from Brooklyn and the body in the second bunk.

"What's your name?" said the corporal as he reached for a note pad and pencil in his upper left pocket..

"Why me," replied the vocal one.

"Shut up, fuckhead, what's your name?"

"Barrigan – B-A-R-R-I-G-A-N," he spelled out.

"Forsythe," said the other victim, in a deep Southern accent.

"Fall out in fatigues in twenty minutes for supper. We have to be up at four-thirty tomorrow for testing. Barrigan, you and Forsythe see me when we get back from chow," said the corporal, turning to go down the steps.

"*See what I mean about positioning*," said AB to Goldwire.

"Yes sir, Mister AB, but what do we do to get out of KP? I didn't like what I saw down there today," smiled Goldwire broadly, and showing his mouthful of even white teeth.

"I can't handle everything," replied AB. "And quit calling me Mister AB."

Goldwire smiled again, "Yes, sir."

Barracks 18E returned from their second army meal – diced hot dogs, noodles and bread, vanilla pudding garnished with endless screaming and clattering of trays. As they rounded the corner, Barracks 18F was being occupied with new arrivals. The veterans from 18E let out a barrage of catcalls and comments about how rough it was in this man's army – much to the dismay of the wide-eyed civilian-clad recruits.

The October sun was settling behind the water tower and cold air was beginning to move between the barracks. Barracks 18E had been dismissed with instructions to be ready for reveille at 4:30AM. AB and Goldwire moved inside the barracks to catch their first free moment of the day. Both realized how tired they were from the long sleepless train ride and a day of standing in long lines. Much to their surprise, someone had placed two folded clean sheets and a pillow case on each bunk. A corporal, whom they had not seen before, called the recruits from the second floor to one end of the room to demonstrate the art of making an army bunk using the "hospital corner" technique on the sheets and blankets. He showed how a quarter would bounce off the covering blanket to demonstrate the required taughtness. Each recruit retired to his bunk to duplicate the accomplishment, as the corporal disappeared down the stairs for a repeat demonstration to the men on the first floor.

Goldwire tried in vain to duplicate the bed-making procedure. AB wasn't having any better success – the quarter refused to bounce. Barrigan proudly finished his bed-making effort only to have it torn apart by the squeaky-voiced corporal, who appeared to usher him -- and Forsythe to the latrine to explain their cleanup responsibilities. Barrigan started a comeback remark to the corporal, but for the first time in his army career decided against it. AB glanced at Goldwire to exchange a broad grin. A group of the white recruits gathered near the water fountain to exchange bad information and experiences. AB joined the group but noticed Goldwire remained near his bunk to inspect and repack newly issued clothing.

Half Way There, Haole

"Wait until I call home and tell the old lady I'm going to Hawaii," said a short, hairy Italian-looking kid with a Boston accent.

"Ya, that's half way to Korea," replied his buddy.

"I wonder how much the airfare is from Honolulu. I got to see my girl before I go over there. I'm horny already."

"What do we do tomorrow?"

"I hear we take tests for four hours in the morning, and then get issued more clothing in the afternoon."

"Then we get a flying twenty."

"What's that?"

"That's when you line up and tell somebody your serial number and they give you a twenty dollar bill. It's an advance on your monthly pay."

"Have we earned twenty yet?'

"Who knows, but I'll take it anyway. We get overseas pay in Hawaii."

"Maybe everybody doesn't go to Korea. Some may get Germany, Alaska, or the Canal Zone."

"No luck here. They need warm bodies for Korea that's why we are going to Hawaii."

"I only got 727 days to go."

"Where can ya get a beer around here?" drawled a tall lanky kid, who earlier had said he was from North Carolina and proud of it.

"Recruits don't get no beer."

"Then what do we do with the flying twenty?"

"I got the dice," said Barrigan as he rejoined the group after his latrine-cleaning instructions.

"I'm going to bust that fag corporal right in the mouth before we leave this place. Just you wait and see," said Barrigan.

Suddenly the lights flickered in the barracks and conversation ceased. A voice from downstairs announced that lights would go out in fifteen minutes.

The group quickly broke up as there was a rush to get bunks made for the night. AB returned to his bunk next to Goldwire, and looked up to see a young kid with eyeglasses, in striped pajamas and fuzzy slippers headed for the latrine with toothbrush and water glass in hand.

"Hey, check this out," hollered Barrigan from the far end of the barracks. The entire group broke out in laughter and cat calls.

"This is going to be an interesting two years", said AB to Goldwire.

"Ya, and only 727 days to go," replied Goldwire as both prepared for their first night of sleeping with thirty-six others. The bunks were quite comfortable – maybe it was because this was their first full night of rest in a horizontal position since leaving Quincy. It seemed like weeks ago they were standing in front of the Greyhound Station saying goodbye.....

AB's mind began to sort through the experiences of the last few days. The thought of 727 days of this madness rolled through his mind. The food was awful, only eight of the fourteen shower heads worked, his dress uniform fit but one set of fatigues was sizes too big, cigarette butts littered the floor, the latrine smelled. There was no place to escape for privacy. His fellow `pineapples' in 18E were all basic rednecks – whether from North Carolina, Brooklyn, New England, or Pennsylvania. He again decided to downplay his educational background. In spite of four years of schooling in Pennsylvania where he had learned to appreciate Yankee attitudes, interests, and humor, AB was much more comfortable in the presence of Southerners, regardless of

Half Way There, Haole

color and educational level. Thank God for Goldwire! His mind still couldn't surround the concept of 'pineapple.' Hawaii . . . . . maybe there would be time to call home tomorrow, but what would he say . . . .

Goldwire was experiencing his first night ever between clean white sheets and in a bunk of his own. Sleeping in a room with many others was no new experience for him. Back in the quarter at La Camellia there was always a roomful of family – all ages—sleeping in unison. At the foot of his bunk he had strapped a duffel bag full of clothing, two sets of fatigues with side pockets, a matching combat jacket, two sets of khaki pants and shirts. Which would he wear when he returned to Quincy and south Munroe Street on Saturday night, or the Blue Moon in Gretna? The food wasn't half bad, but he hated the long lines and the waiting. He feared the KP duty – not the hard work, but the intimidation. The people in the barracks are OK. But he decided to stay clear of the big city northern Negroes…., the brothers intimidated him with the fast jive talk and actions. Mr. AB would help him with the situations he didn't understand.

The overhead lights came on with an instant glare. A corporal with a "CQ" arm band was yelling at the top of his voice and kicking the sides of the barracks walls with a thunderous clatter.

"Get up, you mothers! I ain't had no sleep and you've had enough," as he reached into a breast pocket to retrieve a police whistle and blow it with stunning effect.

It was dark outside as AB squinted at his watch. It was 4AM. The residents of second floor 18E were in various states of shock. The corporal stomped downstairs and repeated his performance for the first floor recruits.

"What the shit is wrong with that guy?" hollered Barrigan to no one in particular. "What does CQ mean?"

"Damn, the floor is cold," said someone in the far end of the room.

Others silently scrambled for socks and boots to protect their feet from the cold wooden floor. Still others merely rolled over. Goldwire headed for the latrine in his newly issued khaki underwear and bare feet. Cold floors were nothing new to him!

Forsythe sat on the edge of his bunk in contemplation of nothing in particular. He reached for a cigarette. "I'm going to have my first ever cigarette before breakfast. Anybody want to join me?" Even he scowled at the bitter taste of his newly-lit Lucky Strike.

The squeaky-voiced corporal climbed the stairs to remind Barrigan and Forsythe of their latrine cleaning duties and to scream at those who were still bed ridden. Barracks 18E was finally assembled in the street ready to march to breakfast. AB and Goldwire carefully positioned themselves in the center of the formation to avoid road guard duty. After a long wait in the dark with breath steaming, breakfast was an amazing combination of left-over hot dogs in some kind of thick gravy, poured over cold hard toast. Coffee was too hot to drink in the time allowed.

All AB could think of was 726 more days.

Upon return to 18E, most recruits eagerly descended on the latrine, only to find the door blocked by Barrigan and others. It was closed for cleaning, and just when everyone needed to use the place! A major confrontation, and near riot, occurred, but the cleaning crew prevailed. AB decided he had lost the 'the war of positioning' – at least for this morning.

Half Way There, Haole

    In total darkness, 18E was called into the street for a roll call. The squeaky-voiced corporal called names from the light of a small flashlight while reading from a typed page on a clipboard. After a ten-minute delay to locate Barrigan, who was still in the barracks struggling with boots and long shoe laces, the 18E recruits were marched off in the night to have their mental ability tested for future Army careers. At 6:20AM, AB was assigned to Chair #43 in a large Army warehouse. He made the usual compensation for the left-handed writing on a right-handed chair/desk, and tried as best he could to collect himself to listen to instructions on the battery of tests to be completed. The steaming cup of coffee he dumped into the garbage can forty-five minutes ago sure would help now...He had lost Goldwire in the mass of humanity, all smelling strong from the newly-issued uniforms. He was reminded of the same odor that hung heavily from the 2nd floor work clothing department of the Tallahassee J C Penney store.

    The testing program was to last for five hours with a break at 8:30 for personal needs. AB wasn't sure he could hold out until the appointed hour, but soon was deeply engrossed in a simple math test, followed by a history and current events multiple choice series. By the time the sun was up, the testing group, including AB and Goldwire, were completely engrossed in a test interpreting a train schedule, reading up and down the page to determine elapsed times for the best train arrivals. Goldwire had never seen a train schedule and became totally confused. AB determined the nature of the schedule, but failed to complete the test segment on time. Barrigan, and others from the big city areas whipped through the train schedule test with ease. The mechanical aptitude test featuring squares, triangles and rectangles was readily comprehended by Goldwire. AB was probably one of the few with a college background, but at this early hour and with little sleep and a full bladder, he had found the whole matter extremely frustrating. How could this affect his Army career if he was already destined for pineapple infantry training in Hawaii?

Upon return from another non-descript meal to 18E, the group was surprised by a small cluster of officers assembled around a raised platform. A captain moved to the microphone while the men stood at attention. His wool Ike jacket was neatly tailored and colored with an array of ribbons. AB tried to identify the small red and yellow patch on his right arm.

"At ease, men. My name is Captain Lewis. I am responsible for your processing here at Fort Meade. With the exception of your medical inoculations, you have all completed each processing step here, and are ready for your next assignment. You will each be given a copy of your orders. All men in 18E barracks are assigned to the 210th Replacement Depot in Camp Stoneman, California. You leave by troop train at 10:45 tomorrow morning. After further processing in Camp Stoneman, you will be assigned to the Hawaiian Infantry Training Center at Schofield Barracks near Honolulu. Your medical profile will be verified by the medical teams at Camp Stoneman. After completing your shots this afternoon you are on your own time. I suggest you contact your families by letter or phone and advise them of your assignment. The Army does not recommend you have mail sent to the Replacement Depot address in Camp Stoneman since you will be there only a very short time. Good luck."

Each man was then handed a four-page mimeographed sheet giving details of the Camp Stoneman address and a very long list of names in carefully prepared alphabetical

Half Way There, Haole

order. AB and Goldwire located their names on the list as they climbed the stairs of 18E. The rest of the afternoon was spent in long naked lines, as the medics punctured arms and buttocks with an endless series of shots. Each recruit was supplied with a sheet entitled MEDICAL RECORD. As each shot was administered, the details were duly recorded by the medics. The squeaky-voiced corporal advised each man to protect his shot record with his life, otherwise each subsequent army medical exam would call for a whole new series of shots. AB folded the record into a deep recess of his wallet. He didn't have any intention of submitting to another afternoon of square needles in the butt. He tried to concentrate on how he would break the news to his parents about his overseas assignment in a phone call that evening. As he lay on his bunk he shifted his weight to the left side to ease the pain in his right butt. Others lay in similar fashion, smoking and throwing cigarette butts on the floor.

Chapter 8

The olive-colored school busses lined up beside the parade field in double lines; too many to count. The Pineapples from Barracks 18E had been joined by about six hundred others, all struggling in wool uniforms, ill-fitting Ike jackets--and new, but unpolished boots. They tried as best they could to stay in line with a heavy barracks bag balanced on one shoulder and carry-all bag in the other hand. A handful of corporals and sergeants also tried in vain to form a company and battalion parade grouping. With no knowledge of what was desired, the new recruits cussed endlessly while the cadre moved and shifted men around, trying to form a battalion front for presentation to a group of officers on a covered review stand. Finally all was in order, groups of about one hundred men standing at attention with full barracks bags wedged between knees to remain upright.

From nowhere, an army band struck up a military march at the end of the parade field, and hidden behind the school busses. The band stepped smartly on the field and marched past the massed recruits. The huge drum carried an identification of the 413th Army Band, Fort Meade, Maryland. AB felt a twinge of pride and patriotism pass through his body, even though he was extremely uncomfortable and the hour was early. The band returned from the end of the field, passed the recruit formation a second time and with a smartly executed maneuver came to rest to the rear of the reviewing stand. Goldwire caught the beat of the band. He was excited about just being there. Barrigan could be heard to mumble something about "Fag musicians blowing their brains through tin horns."

Half Way There, Haole

Upon completion of several brief speeches by Fort Meade officers, the band again trooped the parade field and the recruits were ordered to board the busses. Struggling with the heavy barracks bags in the narrow aisles and cramped seats of the bus, AB and Goldwire finally settled in for a short ride through the Maryland countryside to a remote rail siding, where they were greeted by a steam engine hitched to a long line of ancient Pullman cars. The school busses pulled along side the Pullman cars – two busses to a rail car. The alphabet again came into play as all the "A's" and "B's" and "C's" were assigned to the first Pullman behind the coal car and steam engine. AB, Goldwire and forty-six others settled into what was to be their home for the next five days.

Soon, a sergeant and lieutenant visited the car and requested attention of the troops. The sergeant introduced the officer as the Train Commander. The lieutenant appeared younger than AB, and was probably fresh out of an ROTC unit. The gold bars had a newly-issued appearance. He had no medals, ribbons or patches. AB was sure the officer was ROTC material. He felt a twinge of remorse and would have liked to approach the officer for a friendly conversation, but determined that was not the thing to do.

The lieutenant spoke in his most convincing manner, "Men," he said, "You are in MY command while aboard this train. No one, that means NO ONE will leave the train for any reason. Our destination is Pittsburg, California and we will be enroute for about five days. You will not leave this Pullman car to visit a buddy in another car for any reason. A car commander will be assigned to each Pullman and he will be responsible for your well-being and whereabouts. There are two mess cars on this train. You will be assigned mess hours. Food will be adequate, but without much variety.

(Where had AB heard that before?) For that reason the car commander will be permitted to leave the train at certain train stations to purchase food, candy, or cigarettes for you. Sergeant, who is the car commander here?"

The sergeant referred to his clip board, "Where is Private Aaron?"

A tall gawky fellow with a deep West Virginia accent stood as his name was called. AB noted the alphabet was working again. Private Aaron had been someone most of the men in 18E had avoided. His bad teeth were matched only by his bad breath and body odor. Five days aboard a troop train with Aaron in charge would be a challenge to anyone. The lack of showers aboard the train wouldn't help. AB and Goldwire awaited Barrigan's comment as soon as the train commander moved to the next car.

The ancient Pullman cars couldn't compare with the facilities of the Atlantic Coast Line "Silver Meteor." For one thing, the passenger car behind the steam engine was constantly dusted with smoke and soot from the struggling steam engine. Upper and lower single compartment bunks were made up each night by the recruits, utilizing army-issue wool blankets, without sheets. The five-day journey was to be a dull blur of repeated events: standing in line weaving from car to car to get to the chow car for another meal of non-recognizable food; endless hours of looking out of windows at the back yards of low income homes; breaking the boredom with an occasional game of cards or exchanging lies about sexual exploits. Private Aaron, body odor intact, proved to be an acceptable and willing courier of Camel cigarettes, Baby Ruth candy bars, and an occasional newspaper. AB, Goldie, and others came to envy Aaron for the opportunity just to get out of the Pullman car and walk platforms of small railroad stations.

Half Way There, Haole

Most of the time there was little in the scenery or cities to identify where the train was actually located. Finally, in the middle of an endless harvested wheat field, the train came to a screeching stop. Outside the car, and in the wheat stubble stood the young ROTC lieutenant waving his arms for all six hundred Pineapples to join him.

At the direction of the car captain, the Pullman quickly emptied of the human cargo. The men were instructed to run around the front of the railroad engine – indeed around the entire train. This took only a few minutes while the group returned to the position in front of the Train Commander. There was time for a cigarette break before returning to the Pullman seats--all men had already learned the art of 'field stripping' cigarette butts. AB noted that the geography of the land had been perfectly selected – miles and miles of wheat stubble on level land, leaving nowhere to escape to – nowhere to hide. Everyone HAD to go back on that train!

After many uncounted hours of travel through New Mexico and Arizona, the train finally arrived in Pittsburg – California, that is. AT 3:30AM, few aboard the train were ready to dress, make up their bunks, and depart the train for a long hike through the vacant and lonely streets of Pittsburg. The dimly-lit sign at the end of the wide street read CAMP STONEMAN REPLACEMENT DEPOT.

The exhausted troops were greeted in the pre-dawn cool of the San Francisco Bay area by several tough-talking sergeants. The deep Oriental facial features of the cadre were lost in the darkness of the early morning hour.

"Listen up, men, my name is Lieutenant Soong. Welcome to Camp Stoneman. We know the hour is early and you are all tired from your cross country trip. You will be assigned to barracks where hot showers are available.

Your breakfast meal is now ready in the mess hall. Sergeant Watanabe will assign you to barracks."

Sergeant Watanabe used the same roster that was used by the troop train commander, and proceeded to assign barracks in the same grouping as used for rail car assignments. AB and Goldie were again bunkmates in the same barracks. Everyone dug towels from barracks bags and lined up for the long-awaited showers. Aaron didn't seem to be in any hurry.

Camp Stoneman was to be much more than just another stop along the way to Schofield Barracks. The barracks and other buildings at Stoneman were an exact repeat of those in Fort Meade; the comparison stopped there, for the huge bare California mountains surrounding the area seemed to consume everything.

The barracks assigned to the Pineapples were some distance from the chow hall. To get to a meal, Pineapples were "marched" past other military units that were obviously well trained, and, as it developed, were awaiting transport direct to Korea. These men had completed basic training in the States, wore their uniforms well, and were obviously in good physical condition. The Pineapples, always the last to eat, were again the subject of catcalls and foul remarks as they struggled to march in some semblance of a formation.

Once in the mess hall, however, Pineapples were treated to a meal the same as that offered to the Korea-bound replacements. And what an unexpected surprise—steak cooked-to-order with all the extras, and seconds on apple pie with ice cream – all on a china plate—no metal trays here. No one ordering the Pineapples to speed up the chow line; and all served by civilian employees with no unhappy KP's in sight. It seems the Army decided to do something right for a change – particularly when it's finest trainees were being sent from home to a war zone.

Chapter 9

The events of the next morning at Camp Stoneman came as a complete shock to all. The oversized movie theatre was filled with troops – Pineapples and Korea-bound replacements. On the large stage was a reconstruction of a rural home from a Korean village. The huge screen in the background contained an outline of a Korean mountain scene focused from a slide projector. An Army Captain with a chest full of ribbons stood at a podium, backed by several sergeants and corporals with numerous battlefield ribbons and sleeves with multi-year diagonal service stripes. One sergeant was on crutches with a missing lower leg.

The Captain spoke in clear and precise deep tones: "Gentlemen, what you see and learn here today is for your eyes and ears only. When you leave this room today you will discuss this information with no one: I mean NO ONE. Our session today is to discuss HOW TO ESCAPE FROM BEHIND ENEMY LINES!"

The entire audience froze—absolutely rigid – in their seats. AB looked at Goldie seated to his right. Their eyes met in near absolute terror. How had they gotten to the point of prisoner escape instructions so early in their military career?

The sergeant on crutches approached the makeshift podium near the door of the Korean hut, "Gentlemen, you need to know that your best opportunity to escape from the North Koreans is within hours or even minutes after you have been taken captive. We have learned that there is often confusion when the front line North Korean troops transfer prisoners to rear echelon authority. You will be stripped of all weapons and most personal property by front line troops

Half Way There, Haole

and sent to the rear in groups of about twenty-five, normally under guard of two or possibly three front line soldiers. Your opportunity to escape is when you are placed in a single line headed to the rear. First thing you do is to lag behind the man in front of you. SPREAD OUT THE LENGTH OF THE LINE. Then when you approach a curve in the path ahead, and when you cannot be observed easily by your captors, take a dive for the underbrush and let others pass you by. Stay there until after dark and proceed on your own, back toward the front line area that you just left."

The sergeant continued, "Another opportunity could occur when you are on a Korean train headed further to the rear area of the countryside. The Korean coaches are normally crowded with prisoners with a guard at each end of the coach. Make your way to the vestibule area between each car where the guard stands on duty. Indicate you want fresh air, or maybe even offer him a cigarette. Select a time to leap from the train when the train is making a curve TO YOUR LEFT, then jump off the RIGHT SIDE of the train as it moves forward. The guard will attempt to shoot at you, but chances are he is right-handed and shooting at a target from a moving left-handed position will cause him to miss. Even though the train may make an emergency stop, your chances of escape are excellent if you remain in the underbrush until after dark. Then proceed to the South."

The Captain returned to the podium, "Gentlemen, the sergeant know what he is talking about. He successfully escaped not once, but twice from North Korean trains using this technique. Now, please refer to the large background picture of the Korean mountainside. We know that the North Koreans normally occupy the top of the mountains with observation posts and sometimes anti-aircraft units. The army also often controls the areas from halfway down the mountainside to the valley below. This leaves an area about two-thirds up the side of the mountain that is open territory. This is your area of travel to the South. Often it is rough travel, but your chances of being surprised by enemy troops is almost negative."

The Captain moved to the large backdrop picture with a long pointer to indicate the area he was speaking of. At that point a Korean corporal in US uniform approached the podium. He spoke in excellent English, "Gentlemen, we have here a reconstruction of a typical Korean farm house. The purpose of this is to familiarize you with the possibility of local family support for food and water. Most lower mountain areas are terraced for rice production. As you move at night time through the upper areas of the mountainside you may want to spot an isolated house similar to this. Do not approach a village. Look for a single farm house. The main family meal, usually of rice and vegetables, is prepared in late afternoon – before dark. See if you can approach a single Korean man working in the rice paddy in the late afternoon. He may indeed provide assistance as long as none of his neighbors are aware. Do not approach females; they cannot make such decisions for you. Take what they offer you, but do not stay long. Return to your protected area, preferably wooded, for the night. Do not approach children for assistance. If assistance is not offered, make a second appeal, but do not force yourself upon the farmer."

The other non-coms approached the podium and told their story of escape from behind enemy lines by using some of the techniques just described.

Barrigan whispered to his Italian friend from Boston, "How do you like this shit? They haven't even taught us to

Half Way There, Haole

shoot a gun yet, and now we hear how to escape from behind the Gook lines."

AB made an interesting observation to himself. All but one of the escapees on the stage was wearing the same unit patch on their right upper arm sleeve – that of the 24th Infantry Division. AB recognized the 24th Division "Taro Leaf" patch from NEWSREEL movie stories shown at the Leaf Theater in Quincy. He clearly recalled how the storyline went – the 24th Division had been stationed in Japan in post World War II. From there, certain units of the 24th had been sent to South Korea as UN occupation troops. It was these units that later had been devastated by the North Koreans, and the remnants finally forced into the Pusan Perimeter in the first few weeks of the invasion from the North. AB had not realized that Sergeant Watanbe and other Oriental cadre at Camp Stoneman also wore the 24th Division patch. The left arm patch was a bright blue circle with a red arrow and stars.

As the Captain indicated the formal program was over, Corporal Kam and Sergeant Watanbe appeared before the Pineapples from Barracks 22 and ordered them to remain seated until the theater was emptied. Then Sergeant Watanbe counted off thirty men as they remained seated.

Sergeant Watanbe spoke firmly, "Gentlemen, the thirty men we have counted off are to go with Corporal Kam to police up the area around the Officers Club and PX parking lot. The Commanding Officer of Stoneman observed cigarette butts and candy wrappers in the area early this morning. OK, follow Corporal Kam. The others of you remain seated and then fallout for formation to return to Barracks 22.

Goldie glanced at AB, "Well, we missed that one!"

The remaining Pineapples of Barracks 22 marched back to their area. AB thought about home. If they have the rest of the afternoon off, he would write a letter. There had been a postcard and letter written on the train, but that was all he had any interest in doing. As the Pineapples were dismissed, Goldie went directly to the latrine to check the showers for hot water. There was plenty. AB smiled to himself, Goldie was finally developing his own *'theory of positioning'* – getting in the hot showers while half the barracks was off policing up cigarette butts.

Goldie stripped and wrapped himself in a white towel as he headed for the latrine in flip flops. AB was still considering the letter-writing task as he rummaged through his duffle bag for his writing pad. He finally decided to delay the letter writing until they were advised of their ocean travel plans to Pearl Harbor. He, too, wrapped himself in a towel, found flip flops, and headed for the shower.

Goldie had been joined by several others, including Barrigan and his Italian sidekick from Boston. AB never could remember this kid's name.

Goldie was rinsing off and finishing his shower, but he wanted to talk, "AB, what do you think 'bout all the stuff 'bout escapin' from behind enemy lines? Do you really think we will go to Korea after training in Hawaii? . . . . It sure gives you a lot to think about."

AB followed with a brief conversation to convince his friend that somehow it would turn out all right. Goldie left the shower room to dry off in the latrine area.

AB proceeded to shampoo his GI haircut with the only thing available—a new bar of Lifeboy soap, while Barrigan and his Italian friend carried on a conversation about southern accents and the fact that they had never heard anyone from Florida with an accent like AB and Goldie.

Barrigan commented, "I don't think they are really from Florida; it sounds more like Georgia or Alabama to me."

"What the hell difference is it to you anyway, Barrigan," said AB, with a shut-your-face attitude.

Barrigan bristled, "By the way, what is it with you and the nigger. Every place we go, you and the nigger are buddy-buddy next to each other – all the time talking about something back home. Don't tell me you grew up together – not in the South, you didn't. What goes with you guys anyway – are you sweet on each other? What do you think Vinnie?"

Vinnie made a couple of crude hand signals; both doubled up in laughter.

AB was furious, firing the bar of Lifebuoy soap with his left hand, hitting Barrigan in the lower jaw. AB charged with doubled fists and proceeded to whale away. Vinnie stepped between them, separating the two amid the spraying hot water and steam.

"You stupid Brooklyn piece of shit. You and your friggin' asshole buddy Vinnie hang together all the time and nobody says a word. You got a fuckin' warped mind. If you ever say anything again about Goldie and me being fags, I'll bust your ass in a New York minute. One more thing, I dare you to call Goldwire Cohens a nigger to his face. He'll wipe the floor with your ass, and you know it."

Chapter 10

Lieutenant Soong spoke to the formation of Pineapples from Barracks 21, 22, and 23. "Gentlemen, welcome to the 55th Company of the 50th Battalion of the Hawaiian Infantry Training center stationed at Schofield Barracks, Oahu, Hawaii. The 50th Battalion will be housed in Quad K and is made up of four other training companies – 51st through 54th. I can tell you right now that the 55th Company will be the best in the Battalion, by far. I'm saying that because I am the Company Commander of the 55th. Now, look around you. These are the men who will be training with you in the 55th. But, don't get carried away – only HALF of the Pineapples are here this morning. The other HALF of the 55th is already at Quad K awaiting your arrival. These Pineapples are truly Pineapples – they are from the Hawaiian Islands and other Pacific island territories."

He continued, "You have already met Sergeant Watanbe and Corporal Kam. Now, let me introduce you to some of the newly-arrived cadre who have come to Stoneman to escort you back to Schofield. Will the following please step forward: Sergeant First Class Sidney Mapa, Sergeant First Class Raymond Los Banos, Sergeant First Class Wilfred Paaluhi, and Sergeant Daniel O'Conner."

The four sergeants joined Lieutenant Soong and offered a sharp salute in unison. AB's mind was in turmoil.

Lieutenant Soong continued," Gentlemen, there are at least ten other cadre members waiting for you at Schofield. These are the four platoon sergeants for the 55th Company. We will have about two hundred and fifty Pineapples in the 55th Company – about sixty men in each platoon. The 50th

Half Way There, Haole

Training Battalion will consist of approximately twelve hundred Pineapples. Welcome to the HITC."

"Now, about plans for travel to Pearl Harbor. We sail on Saturday on the USS ALTMAN, along with about five hundred other Pineapples. Your names are now published on an IBM printout posted outside of Barracks 24. Be sure you check the listing when you fallout from this formation. Between now and Saturday, the Medics will be checking your shot records and Quartermaster will have one more clothing check. Dismissed."

All Pineapples converged on Barracks 24 to check the manifest for the USS ALTMAN. Instead of the usual alphabetical listing, the IBM sheets organized the 55th Company by platoons and squads. Sergeant O'Conner was designated as Platoon Leader for the 1st Platoon. The first squad of the 1st Platoon read as follows: Aaron, Jacob B.; Allen, James R.; Barrigan, Francis J.; Burns, Allendale D.; Cohens, Goldwire; del Fucci, Vincent R.; Forsythe, Joshua D.; Knight, Matthew R.

Goldwire found AB in the crowd, "How 'bout it. We're still hanging together. If you can handle it – I can."

AB didn't react.

"What's the matter, Mister AB?"

"Look, for the last time, don't call me Mister AB," he said with a frown. "Didn't you see Barrigan and his sidekick Vinnie listed in the first squad, too? The damned alphabet won't let us get separated from these guys."

"Screw 'em," said Goldie, as he field stripped his last Camel cigarette.

The next morning Sergeant O'Conner called the first platoon of the 55th Company into their first formation. He was in a near state of shock when he observed the rag-tag collection of scrubs – poorly dressed and out-of-shape Pineapples.

"Corporal Kam, this bunch of recruits ain't for shit. They'll never make it. Just remember, for the next eighteen weeks your ass is mine. That's right, your ass is mine; so you better make the best of it."

Barrigan whispered to Vinnie, "Fuck Sergeant O'Conner and the horse he rode in on."

Vinnie responded with, "Up his ass with a crosscut saw –sideways."

Goldie rolled his eyes. AB winced.

Sergeant O'Conner shouted, "Knock it off with you guys in the back row. We're going to have friggin' discipline in the first platoon."

AB initiated his own evaluation of Sergeant O'Conner. He must be at least 35, or maybe 38 years old, shorter than most his peers, and that small Budweiser gut didn't help. There was that chicken-shit mini mustache under the pug nose. The sandy colored hair showed an occasional sprinkle of gray. What was really confusing was the buck sergeant stripes – no rockers to designate a master sergeant or even tech sergeant – yet he was clearly older than Sergeant Mapa and the other platoon sergeants. AB did note and respect the service hash marks on his lower sleeve and the 24th Division insignia on the right arm. He figured the bravado and the GI language were to make up for the lack of size and stature. Sergeant O'Conner, however, was someone to be respected and perhaps feared. Only time would tell.

Upon return to the barracks, AB dumped the latest issue of gear on the bunk.

"Now what in the hell are we going to do with a pile-lined overcoat in Hawaii," he said to the equally confused Pineapples from the first platoon. Sergeant O'Conner just shook his head – he didn't have an answer, except to say something about an Army order from the Pentagon that all troops leaving Camp Stoneman would be equipped with winter gear. Obviously, this was intended for Camp Stoneman Korea-bound trained replacements, but no exceptions could be made.

AB, Goldie, and others jammed the winter gear in the top of the repacked barracks bag with considerable effort – the thing was full and non-liftable.

Roll call was early the next morning. It seemed like it was still the middle of the night. The first squad of the first platoon lined up with eyes squinting toward the East as the powerful early morning sun peaked over the bare California mountains surrounding the San Francisco Bay area. This would be their last day in California – and their first day of overseas pay outside the States.

Chapter 11

Zachary Alexander Marley sat on the top step of the small front porch of a two-room cottage. It was early Sunday morning near Pago Pago, Samoa; but Zack had already stepped down to the beach for an early morning swim before the family awoke. The other four cottages in the quarter were silent with sleeping families. The small Missionary Church on the far side of the lagoon awaited the arrival of early church members.

Zack was puzzled and angry – all wrapped up into one emotion of frustration. His father, Caleb Marley, was a major landowner on Tutulia Island; yet Zack (the only son) and his family were relegated to the workers' quarters on the large dairy farm. Caleb, Zack's mother, and older sister lived in the "Big House" with manicured lawns, tennis courts, and a large free-form swimming pool.

The frustration with his father all started about eight or nine years ago when Caleb contracted with the U.S. Marine Corps to provide a tropical jungle orientation program for young Marine officers, identified as Raiders. Temporary tented living quarters for groups of twenty-four officers had been established near the "Big House" for a two-week jungle warfare orientation. Caleb had graduated in the mid 1930's from a military school in New Zealand where Zack's grandfather had sent him. In World War II, when Marine Raiders, like the British Commandos, were preparing to invade or harass the Japanese armies on Pacific islands, there was a significant need to orient new Marine officers in the art of jungle warfare and jungle survival. Caleb had seized upon the opportunity and had become somewhat wealthy as a result of his contracts with the U.S. government.

Half Way There, Haole

    Zack, at age fourteen, was subject to the Marine discipline and had somehow become a military ward of his father, rather than just a son. Zack was on a strict military schedule for school, homework, and farm work – with no free time to fish or just be a kid. While Marines were subject to daily lectures and jungle field trips learning the art of jungle cover and concealment, camouflage, bird and animal life habits, and the dangers of coral reefs and jellyfish – Zack was living a life of hell by just being there. At times, Zack would be called upon to identify the jungle dangers of poisonous snakes and threatening insects, and to demonstrate the art of cracking coconuts and identifying other edible jungle survival foods. By the time he was nearly sixteen, he hated everything about the Marines AND his father. His school work at the Missionary School was deteriorating and Zack was in a stage of family revolt.

    The war with Japan was in the closing stages when Caleb decided to send Zack to Queenstown, New Zealand to attend military school. Zack boarded a flight from Pago Pago with one simple instruction from his father: "Keep that thing in your pants."

    Military school in New Zealand for Zack was a welcome relief from the constant badgering of his father. He learned the finer points of British Army military routine – the open palm salute, the boot-stomping during close order drills, and the long arm swing in unison with other cadets. Now, at over six feet, Zack had learned to hold his own in a rugby scrum and on the tennis courts. Academic work was going very well.

    Zack had brought with him from Samoa, his lavalava – a sarong-like garment used in native dances on the island. He and several other native Samoans had formed a Samoan Knife Dance routine using huge machete-like knives, and accompanied by native drums. The group performed at special school functions and, unknown to school officials, on weekends sometimes performed at a local Queenstown Polynesian nightclub.

The nightclub owner was a motorcycle buff and at times would lend a German-made machine to Zack to take to the nearby mountains.

On one occasion, Zack took an afternoon trip to Shotover Canyon when he encountered a serious accident. The right motorcycle handlebar penetrated his lower abdomen leaving a noticeable scar from his hip bone into the groin area. Now, when Zack wore his lavalava he lowered it in such a manner as to show the nearly full length of the heavily stitched scar. He became the lead knife act of the group!

This incident somehow lead him to Melanie – his future wife-to-be. Melanie was a beautiful young Chinese-Maori girl from Queenstown. Her father, a porcelain artist and owner of a dragon kiln from Cheng du Chen, China, had emigrated to New Zealand to pursue his skills in the Queenstown artist colony. He had married a Maori native and Melanie was the beautiful result of their union.

Zack and Melanie had discovered an abandoned gold miner shack at Shotover Canyon on one of their many motorcycle adventures to the area. Melanie had become pregnant and they were married by the military chaplain at his school.

It had been nearly two years ago now that Zack and his family returned to Samoa – and Caleb still did not accept Zack, Melanie or the baby – even though little Moana was his only grandchild.

The Marine Raiders had long since left; yet Zack mentally reviewed all the past years as he sat on the porch of his small cottage. Upon return to Pago Pago, Zack learned that Caleb had contracted with a Hollywood movie studio to provide South Seas settings for a series of movies starring Jon Hall and Dorothy Lamour. Zack and his sister had played the parts of extras in the movie production. He even teamed up with other locals to perform Samoan knife dances – displaying his lower body scar with the carefully arranged lavalava.

Zack had, at the suggestion of a movie contact, gone to the States as part of a tour group performing knife dances at clubs from Manhattan to San Francisco. After several months of missing his family, he had signed on as an entertainer on the "Lurline" – a California-to-Hawaii cruise ship. He returned to Pago Pago occasionally for home visits.

Still, his father failed to provide any significant form of support for Zack and his family. At the military school library, he had read of a technical school in Trinidad, West Indies offering a two-year course in tropical agricultural management—sugar cane, pineapples, and other tropical fruits produced commercially for export. Zack had approached Caleb to send Zack and his family to Trinidad for schooling, so he could return and help manage the plantation – but to no avail.

Now he sat on the steps pondering a future for his family. Melanie knew Zack was thinking of another scheme to resolve their family problem.

"Melanie, this just isn't working out. I'm working in the dairy as an ordinary laborer and Caleb--he long ago gave up calling him father-- won't change his attitude. I approached him yesterday about school in Trinidad and he wouldn't even let me finish with my thoughts."

Zack continued, "The war in Korea has opened opportunities in the U.S. military for enlistment. When I was in Honolulu on the last Lurline trip, I visited Army and Navy recruiters. As a native of American Samoa, I can enlist. In Honolulu, the Navy will only enlist locals as house boys and valets for navy officers. No way will I do that! I can join the army and take basic training on Oahu. When I finish training, and with my military school background, I would be eligible for leadership school at Schofield Barracks and be qualified to train other recruits on the Islands. You and Moana could then join me there and we all could live in Hawaii."

Melanie reacted, "But Zack, Moana and I have New Zealand citizenship."

"I've already worked that out. I went by the Immigration Office in Honolulu, and you can both become US citizens once I finish infantry basic training and I can support you on a non-commissioned officer's salary."

Melanie offered her broadest smile, "Let's do it."

Next morning, Zack went to the harbor at Pago Pago to follow up on a notice he had seen posted at the Commissary. He signed on as a crew member of a forty-five foot yacht sailing for Honolulu. The owner was seeking a buyer in the wealthy Honolulu market.

Chapter 12

Goldie had never SEEN a ferry boat, much less BE ON one; yet there he was sitting crunched up with a duffel bag between his knees on a long bench of the lower deck. Beside him sat someone he wanted to talk to for some time—but somehow hadn't found the courage. His name was Forsythe and he was from North Carolina. He remembered Forsythe and Barrigan cleaning the latrine at Fort Meade, both of whom prevented him from using the spotless latrine facilities when he needed to in the worst way, that morning. Anyway, now was the time to talk.

Goldie said, "I heard you tell someone the other day that you grew up on a 'bacca farm. . . so did I."

"Ya, my father is a sharecropper on a 'bacca farm near Goldsboro," responded Forsythe, "We sharecrop eighteen acres   I'm from a big family….number four of 'leven kids. We worked 'bacca starting at six years old…..mostly picking off worms and puttin' 'em in mason jars."

Goldie picked up the conversation and discussed at length how they grew tobacco in Florida under cheesecloth, and how he started by carrying tobacco leaves to the end of the row when he, too, was age six. That lead to a lengthy discussion between the techniques of growing a crop of cigarette tobacco versus the complications of growing wrapper tobacco for the cigar trade. Goldie had found a friend…and his first name was Joshua, right out of the Bible. Goldie knew of his strong biblical feeling because he held a well-worn copy of the New Testament in his hands all the time they conversed.

Suddenly, Josh was quiet …reading the Book of Mark from pages scrambled with pencil notes in the margins.

Half Way There, Haole

Goldie ended the conversation and looked at AB who was sitting across from him about six seats closer to the edge of the ferry. All they could see were the dock pilings, rolling up and down from the wake of other craft passing by. AB glanced at Josh only to discover a sickly look on Josh's face…HE WAS SEASICK AND WE HAVEN'T EVEN LEFT THE DOCK. Forsythe proceeded to barf his breakfast into the crowded aisle among duffel bags and boots. Barrigan, seated opposite, and beside Vinnie took most of the unpleasantness. AB and Goldie exchanged eye contact with a hint of a smile. So much for this *theory of positioning* – even on a ferry boat.

There was a roar as the ferry engines reversed motion and moved away from the dock. Within a few minutes the boat was rolling side to side as it pushed across San Francisco Bay and past Alcatraz Island. Others were heard to become sick as the brief ride ended at another dock next to a huge gray troop ship with "USS Altman" painted on the bow.

As Sergeant O'Conner directed the movement of bodies from the ferry boat to the dock, the Pineapples were to endure yet another awkward moment. From the gangway of the Altman came hundreds of returning Korean veterans fresh from Inchon and ten days aboard ship. There was much shouting and hollering as the vets put their boots on US soil for the first time in many months. The unpressed fatigues of the Pineapples could not compare to woolen Ike jackets adorned with corporal and sergeant stripes and accompanied with rows of sleeve service hash marks and chest ribbons. The sullen Pineapples could only stand by as the gloriously happy troops paraded past, with well-chosen remarks about Korea—the Land of the Morning Calm. AB decided, with relief, that this had to be the last time they would be looked down upon by others as rookie dog faces.

Sergeant O'Conner proceeded to march the first platoon up the gangway, across the narrow deck, through an open passageway to the port side and into a Compartment marked C-4. After passing down awkward ladders and balancing duffel bags, the first platoon soon learned that the "4" meant the fourth deck down. There was no deck #5. The lower they went into the bowels of the ship, the worse the air became. Soon the atmosphere was one of foul air mixed with the smell of diesel fuel, and the odor of many human bodies. It would be a long five days to Honolulu.

AB climbed the ladders to return to the deck for a breath of fresh air. The Altman had pulled away from the dock and was proceeding through the Bay toward the Golden Gate Bridge. As the huge gray vessel passed beneath the bridge, Goldie joined him at the crowded railing.

"Who is Earl, " he said.

"What do you mean, 'Who is Earl?'" replied AB.

"Look up under the bridge."

AB strained to look straight up, to see in huge block letters:

"FUCK YOU EARL."

"I think he is the Governor of California," smiled AB.

Chapter 13

Tadao Sato sat on the top step at the local post office. Mail to the Sato family was infrequent, so a weekly visit to the post office at Waialau was more than adequate. It was no real surprise when he saw the envelop from the Selective Service marked "Official Business, if not delivered in 5 days return to Local Board No. 51, 441 Dole Street, Wahiawa, Oahu."

He opened the single-page letter and noted the letterhead: "Selective Service System" ORDER TO REPORT FOR INDUCTION. The letter was dated September 12, 1951 and read:

> "The President of the United States, to Tadao Sato, GREETING:
> Having submitted yourself to a Local Board composed of your neighbors for the purpose of determining your availability for service in the armed forces of the United States, you are hereby ordered to report to the Local Board No. 51, 441 Dole Street, Wahiawa, Oahu at 6:45AM on the 16th of October, 1951 for forwarding to an induction station."

Tadao read the small print about fine and imprisonment for failure to report as a violation of the Selective Service Act of 1948; about how the government would return you to your home if you failed the physical; and something about bringing sufficient clothing for three days. The letter was signed by Charles P. Hale, Member of the Local Board.

Tadao had expected to receive his notice in early summer. He had graduated from Waialau High School over a year ago and was working in the Dole packing plant as a warehouseman. His father, a twenty six-year employee of Dole had arranged for preferred employment in the warehouse – better than the field hand positions offered to most high school seniors.

Employment opportunities for young rural Japanese men on Oahu, even in 1951, were mostly limited to work related in some way to the pineapple or sugar industries. Tadao's parents had come from Beppu, Japan in the 1920's to seek employment opportunity in the rapidly growing sugar and pineapple industries of the Hawaiian Islands. Their plan was to earn $3,000 to return to Beppu and buy a small resort hotel on the beaches of the southern island of Kyushu. When the Satos signed for field labor in Hawaii they knew the rate of 90 cents per day would take many days to earn their $3,000 goal but it was better than no opportunity at all in Beppu.

The arrival of older brother, Isumi; then Tadao, and finally twin girls had pretty well put the master plan for return to Japan on hold. The attack on Pearl Harbor by the Japanese naval forces had clarified the Sato family situation, along with all other Japanese laborers – as being declared United States citizens ten years ago. Tadao, having been born in Hawaii, was a United States citizen and subject to the Selective Service Act of 1948.

It had been a different experience for older brother Isumi, who had joined the National Guard in the summer of 1941. On the day of the Japanese attack on Pearl Harbor, Isumi was on duty at Schofield Barracks as part of a 10-day period of active duty. Nine-year old Tadao had seen the swarms of clearly marked Japanese aircraft wing over the northern Oahu coastal village of Waialau. He, along with his parents, was stunned that their grateful fatherland would attack the islands of their home.

In the days following the December 7th attack, there were numerous rumors that all Japanese/Hawaiians would be forced to move to detention camp on the island of Molokai – much the same as Japanese in California were being moved inland to Utah, Colorado, and Nevada. The Sato family feared the worst. At Schofield Barracks, Isumi and other Japanese Guard members were forced to give up their weapons, stripped of any identification of authority and given full-time latrine or KP duty. Isumi later volunteered for duty to help with the physical work of cleaning up heavily damaged Hickam Field.

Japanese-Hawaiian loyalty to the U.S. war effort had been the subject of significant review and discussion by the federal government, by the mainland newspapers, and by local haole leadership. The easy response would be to follow the lead of California and evacuate all Japanese Nationals to camps – possibly on Molokai. Haole leadership readily recognized the need, however, to continue to depend on experienced Japanese labor to maintain and harvest the vital pineapple and sugar crops – yet it was well known that many first generation Japanese were quietly following the "glorious successes" of the invading Japanese forces into mainland China since the mid-1930's, and quietly supporting the effort with funds sent to the homeland through local Buddhist and Shinto religious leaders.

Most second generation Japanese, while still clearly demonstrating disdain for the local Chinese, expressed complete loyalty to the U.S. war effort as American citizens. In spite of major conflict with his parents, Isumi and others of his unit were seeking ways to serve their country. Relief came to the second generation Japanese in the form of the 222nd Combat Infantry Unit. A haole army officer recognized the support of the young Japanese from all the

Islands and convinced senior officers in Washington of the value of forming a fighting unit to combat the Germans on the European continent. In this way there was no question that Orientals should be subject to opposing their own in the Pacific war zone.

Isumi was one of the first to volunteer for the 222nd – one of the fifteen hundred Japanese men recruited only a few weeks after the Pearl Harbor incident! The Unit was sent to Mississippi for eighteen weeks of infantry training, where it was determined that the group would be integrated with haoles – man for man. In Mississippi, Isumi found himself involved in an incident in Yazoo City when he was told to use the colored toilet facilities at an Esso gas station. He had grown up accustomed to the haole superiority in the Islands, but as a U.S. citizen and Army volunteer, he clearly was confused with discrimination against Japanese on the mainland.

The 222nd Combat Infantry Unit went on to the invasion of Italy at Salerno and a place called Monte Cassino where heroism of the tough Japanese was established with considerable publicity in the mainland U.S., and of course, Hawaii. Isumi returned to Waialua three years later with a partially crippled left arm.

And now, five years after Isumi's return, Tadao was entering military service for another war – this time in Korea, where Orientals WOULD be fighting Orientals. The elder Satos in recent years had severed all family ties with Beppu, Japan. They had moved from the Dole company-owned quarters to their own small cottage in Waialua with a large backyard vegetable garden. Tadao was to report to Schofield Barracks where it was well known that Islanders would be "blended" with haoles for eighteen weeks of infantry training. The training cadre of these combined units was to be by former members of the 24th Infantry Division fresh from the Pusan Perimeter disaster in Korea – many of whom were Oriental/Hawaiians.

On October 16, Tadao reported to the bus carrying draftees to the Schofield compound. His parents had sent him off with the standard instructions to avoid all Chinese, the Eta Japanese, and most certainly Okinawans. After two years as running back for the Waialua High School football team and eighteen months of heavy duty warehouse work, Tadao knew he was in great physical condition for infantry training – just don't call him a "Jap" or a "Gook." As for the Chinese, Tadao reserved his personal feelings, having learned to appreciate certain Chinese high school team members who blocked for him on the Waialua football team. It was the Koreans he wasn't too sure of.

Chapter 14

The five days aboard the USS Altman became an endless blur of going through the motions of daily survival. The sleeping quarters in C-4 compartment were miserable. The five-high bunks made of pipe laced with canvas webbing gave absolutely no room for movement. The close quarters, foul air, and sea sickness had put everyone on edge.

The alternative to the compartment living was to find a spot on the steel deck of the Altman to sit and stare endlessly at the rolling waters of the Pacific. An occasional dolphin siting was the subject of innocuous conversation about how close to land they might be. Excitement for the morning came with the public address announcement:

"Attention All Hands…..clear the port side of the main deck for trash removal and washdown. All troops move immediately to the starboard side of the ship. Throw all trash over the fantail—that's OVER THE FANTAIL."

Whereupon about four hundred men moved immediately to the starboard side to join the other several hundred men and jamming together bodily with the other recruits. Laggards were subject to a faceful of high-pressure cold saltwater from an inexperienced crew of Army-assigned deckhands.

In twenty minutes a similar announcement would be made to clear the starboard side for washdown. Whereupon all would streak to seek favorite positions on the newly saltwater-dripping port side. This was the excitement for the morning. A similar exercise would occur in the afternoon.

Because of the unpleasant environment of compartment C-4 and the confusion on the main deck, AB and Goldie and others seldom spoke to each other, even at meal time in the mess.

Meals lacked variety. Chow lines snaked endlessly through interior passageways, and down ladders to the mess. Goldie was given an aluminum tray fresh from the steaming dishwasher that was so hot he could not hold it. Jello and other food turned to steaming mush even before he passed through the serving line – just like the meals at Fort Meade. Long stand-up tables were placed crossways of the ship. As the Altman rolled from side to side, Goldie attempted to hold his OWN food tray in front of him with one hand while trying to spoon his food with the other. The challenge was to finish a meal from your OWN tray. A particularly severe roll of the ship would send all trays flying against the messhall bulkhead. Numerous garbage cans were strategically bolted to the deck to serve the seasick needs of many barfing Pineapples.

On the fifth day the waters suddenly calmed as the USS Altman approached the entrance to Pearl Harbor. The railings were jammed with excited and exhausted Pineapples. There had been much confusion earlier that morning as the order had been issued for stowing the dirty fatigues in barracks bags, and the uniform of the day was declared to be Class A with neckties and dress woolen pants! All belongings were to be retrieved from below deck. For many, the island landscape continued to "tilt," as sea legs constantly braced for the non-existing pitch and roll of the Altman decks.

The USS Altman edged to the dock and revealed a stunning sight -- dozens of swaying hula girls, dancing to an Hawaiian band with loud speakers turned to highest possible volume. Confetti and bright paper streamers were everywhere. Again, the horizon continued to tilt for many of the Pineapples as they set foot on solid ground at Pearl Harbor. Around the neck of each excited GI was placed a paper lei by a real live hula girl as a true welcome to the Islands. The confusion, the music, the hula dancers were too much for the sea-dulled minds of the debarking troops. It would take a while to recover from the seemingly endless ceremony.

AB, Goldie, and other members of the first platoon of the 55th Company HITC were assembled in an alley beside a long metal warehouse. Near the end of the warehouse were parked open air semi-trailers with wooden steps from an open-end tailgate. The Pineapples were to become very familiar with the Buna Bus. The troops scrambled aboard the trailers and took seating on long benches. A soft rain began to fall against the canvas stretched across the body of the busses. The motorcade proceeded through numerous such showers as they passed the low mountain roads approaching Wahiawa and the entrance to Schofield Barracks.

The MP's in cool, crisp khaki uniforms gave each Buna Bus a sharp hand signal to pass through the main gate without delay. The main street was lined with tall coconut palms with whitewash base. Among the palms were huge white gardenia bushes and bright red hibiscus plants. The double lane boulevard was lined with three-story Spanish style stucco buildings neatly landscaped with more flowering plantings. They passed an open air theatre near tennis courts and a swimming pool. The pool was occupied by families — many of them Oriental in appearance.

"Where are the long, ugly wooden barracks," asked Goldie.

"I don't know, but wait till we get to where we are going to be at Quad K, "replied Forsythe. "You know this ain't the kind of place that WE are going to be staying."

The Buna Busses passed a golf course surrounded by small cottages with officers' names clearly printed on the mail boxes. AB noticed several groups of trainees in fatigues, mowing lawns and weeding flower beds. This was truly a paradise when compared to Fort Meade and Camp Stoneman. A vision of the nearby mountains came into view as the busses pulled into a compound with a huge "Quad K" sign in the center of the grass-covered quadrangle park surrounded by three-story permanent buildings, formed in the shape of a gigantic U.

Four of the slow-moving busses pulled near to one of the buildings in the complex with a small freshly-painted blue sign "55th Company, 50th Battalion." The place was swarming with men in new fatigues and helmet liners. Near what was obviously the kitchen area were four overweight Oriental cooks in white uniforms and tall white chef hats, and leaning on a pipe railing separating the loading dock from six gleaming garbage cans.

Although Schofield was located in the mountain foothills, the fresh Pearl Harbor sea breezes cooling the humid air were not to be found. Behind the Quad K barracks hung a low dark cloud – in the area of Kolekole Pass. The new recruits were to learn more about Kolekole Pass in the weeks to come.

Sergeant O'Conner rode in the cab of the first truck to enter the quadrangle. He jumped from the front seat as the vehicle came to a stop near the 55th Company sign. Sergeant Mapa was right behind him for the 2nd platoon. Both men quickly ordered the busses unloaded as the Pineapples lined up in a loose squad formation with Barrigan, del Fucci,

Forsythe, AB, Goldie and others struggled to find assigned positions. Each stood with his barracks bag in front of him. It was one o'clock, as the sun and humidity combined for the height of discomfort for the new arrivals in their wool uniforms.

"Damn," said Barrigan to Vinnie, "The sweat is running down the crack of my ass."

AB smiled to himself; he too felt a trickle of sweat on his butt and down the inside of his leg. With no showers for five days aboard ship, the first squad members were immune to the community aroma. The heavy woolen pants didn't help.

The Islanders, in their cool fatigues, stood in a similar formation opposite the sweating Pineapples -- a distance of about twenty paces. Their boots had been uniformly stained a dark brown, pants properly bloused just at the ankle. Goldie wondered how they made the bloused pants look so Army professional.

Barrigan peered across the twenty paces, reading the names clearly printed in white block letters on each helmet liner. "Goddam, everyone of 'em is a fuckin' Gook. Look at 'em – Japs, Chinks, Gooks and everything between yellow and brown."

"It's going to be fuckin' interestin' these next eighteen weeks," replied Vinnie.

Across the way, a stocky kid with "Loa" printed on his helmet liner, nudged a buddy to his left. "Screw all the haoles and the Buna Bus they rode in on."

Sergeant O'Conner bellowed, "First Platoon, attention! Now listen up. When I call your name, take one step forward with your bag. . . . platoon at ease." The sergeant then turned to a PFC with "Kong" printed on his helmet line. PFC Kong handed a clipboard to Sergeant O'Conner.

"Men," he shouted, "This is PFC Kong. You better get to know him – he's the company clerk and handles the mail for the 55th Company. It's hot out here, let's get started."

"Francis Barrigan," bellowed Sergeant O'Conner. Goldie snickered; he knew Barrigan hated the 'Francis' part. Barrigan took a step forward, dragging his barracks bag. Twenty paces away, as instructed, Alex Silva stepped forward and approached Barrigan. He offered a broad Portuguese grin, an 'Aloha,' and extended his right hand. The surprised Barrigan offered a weak handshake, while Silva hoisted the barracks bag to his shoulder and started toward the building behind the 55th Company sign.

"Allendale Burns," shouted Sergeant O'Conner.

Tadao Sato stepped forward, offered an 'Aloha,' and a handshake, then easily lifted the barracks bag to his broad shoulders. AB, also somewhat surprised, followed Sato to the wide sidewalk and through the double screen doors.

"They call me Tad."

" I'm AB."

Both men reached the second floor, crossed the screen porch – identified later as the lanai—and entered a large squadroom with endless rows of double-decker bunks carefully made with white collar sheets and pillow showing on each bunk. Tad turned left at the first row of bunks near the lanai windows. He stopped in front of a footlocker displaying a carefully centered helmet liner with the name 'Burns' spelled clearly in white block letters.

"You guys were really expecting us," smiled AB.

"We been busting our ass for more than two weeks now on this place," replied Tad.

AB looked around. The cement floors had been polished to a high sheen – the rotary polishing machine marks clearly showing up and down the aisle. The windows to the lanai were gleaming. M-1 rifles were cross-stacked nearby, shining from the pad locked rifle rack. Dozens and dozens of bunks were made with precision hospital corners.

Tad spoke hesitatingly, "AB you can have the bottom bunk."

"No, you take it," replied AB.

"No, its yours, I've already slept in the top bunk."

"OK, thanks."

The noise level of the room raised to a fever pitch as others moved in – Barrigan to the right of AB and Goldie to the left.

"Where's the latrine?" asked Barrigan.
Without comment, Silva pointed through the lanai windows and down the hall.

AB and Goldie sat on their footlockers trying on the new helmet liner head pieces, but still trying to shake their sea legs – the room would tilt occasionally for no particular reason. AB noted the private room in the corner near the main room entrance marked with a sign, 'Sergeant O'Conner.'

From the loudspeaker system came this: "Chow will be served in the messhall in ten minutes. The first squad of the first platoon will be first to be served. The cadre squad leader of each squad will take charge."

With this said, Corporal Kam appeared and made his way down the row of first squad bunks, introducing himself in an awkward manner. The huge Korean towered over most of the recruits. He then led the first squad to the lanai where he counted to fifteen squad members. Kam led the group down the steps to the main hall, passing a door marked 'Mail Room,' around the corner and a second door marked 'Lieutenant Soong Company Commander.' And, finally to the messhall where the Mess Sergeant stood blocking the entrance to the room.

"Kam, you're five minutes early,"

"That's OK, we'll wait."

The 55th Company messhall was a scene almost beyond description. AB blinked his eyes. Above the serving line was a large hand-lettered sign, 'WELCOME 55TH COMPANY'. Red hibiscus flowers adorned almost every flat surface in the room – a row of red flowers down the center of each table, the window sills, even between each aluminum pan in the cafeteria serving line. Numerous Islander KP's were standing by in the kitchen and messhall to assure that everything went as planned. KP's on the serving line had red flowered leis over white bib aprons.

Goldie, AB and others of the first squad proceeded to the serving line where trays were heaped with Maryland fried chicken, mashed potatoes and gravy, green beans and chocolate cake. Before being seated, they passed a special table in the center of the messhall containing piles of fresh pineapple halves filled with a scoop of cottage cheese covered with bits of red maraschino cherries. The Chinese cooks and Islander KP's had truly planned a successful Hawaiian luau for the arriving haoles.

"We been in the Army for almost three weeks now, and I ain't ever seen anything like this," said Forsythe to anyone at his table who would listen. "This here army ain't half bad."

Tad Sato had escaped KP duty, probably because he had been on Battalion guard duty the night before. He sat there with his tray nearly empty – playing with a fork in the white mound of mashed potatoes. He smiled at AB, "We like rice here."

Not knowing how to respond, AB inquired, "Tad, tell me about Schofield."

"Well, I'll tell you what I think I know. You saw the quadrangle buildings on the way in here. They're built sort of like a fort around a grass square. You enter through a tunnel called a salleyport, built in two sides of the main building. They're three floors high where the quarters open onto the lanai, like here at Quad K. These other Quads were built sometime during the 1920's."

"Quad K was built during World War II as a recovery hospital for men injured in the Pacific war. The 50th Battalion is the first group to use Quad K for infantry training. We worked hard on the cleanup of the third floor here in Quad K last week. I hear they're going to move the 3rd and 4th platoons to the third floor in a couple of weeks. That way they can take the top bunks and move them to the third floor. It's going to be crowded here for awhile with two hundred and fifty guys trying to live and sleep in one big squad room."

Goldie spoke up, "I'll help move the bunks to the third floor."

AB looked at his empty tray, but as he peered through the messhall windows at the nearby golf course, the horizon again began to tilt – his USS Altman sea legs were still with him. His inner ear told him he was still aboard an ever-shifting, sloping deck.

As the last of the 55th Company passed through the chow line, AB decided the wool uniform had to go. He was going to return to the second floor and hit the showers for his first hot bath in a week. Goldie and Forsythe had the same idea.

There was PFC Kong with several bags of mail. AB received five letters. There was one for Goldie with a carefully hand-lettered address.

Chapter 15

Today was to be the day that the 55th Company would really get organized. The four platoon sergeants separated their recruits in the Quadrangle by platoon formation, for instruction.

"Men, my name is Sergeant O'Conner. I am the platoon leader of the first platoon. I am in charge! Now, if you will glance up to your right you will see office windows on the second floor of the Battalion Headquarters. The Battalion Commander is Colonel Cottingham. He is responsible for the training of the 50th Battalion. From his office window he can readily identify members of this platoon – particularly those up front –in the first squad. He'll be observing this unit almost daily for signs of military training progress. You guys ARE going to be good."

First Sergeant Rubinal called the four platoon sergeants to the loading dock near the mess hall and the garbage cans. He gave instructions to have the platoons proceed to different parts of the nearby athletic field for purposes of instructions in close order drill and then to begin a program of physical training.

Sergeant O'Conner stood back from the platoon formation. The first thing to do was to line up each squad by individual height of the recruits. He would have to take special care with the first squad, since Colonel Cottingham had a closeup of this group. The tallest of each squad traditionally became the squad leader – the assistant squad leader would be the second in height.

"Corporal Kam," ordered Sergeant O'Conner, "come here and help me line up these guys by height." The good

Half Way There, Haole

Sergeant needed help since he was short in stature. Corporal Kam was over six feet tall.

Kam examined the helmet liner names and called Barrigan, Marley, Cohens, and Burns and had the four men remove their head gear. Sergeant O'Conner observed from atop a mound near the ditch and compared the relative heights of the men. He shuffled each into position.

"Barrigan, you're squad leader of the first squad. Then comes Cohens, Marley, and Burns. Now, return to the platoon formation in the order you are now standingl"

AB whispered to Goldie, "This isn't going to work. Barrigan is an ass."

The other squad leaders were selected and the balance of the platoon organized by height. At the rear of each squad formation stood one or two Guamanians – all about the same at 5 feet 3 inches—minimum Army height requirement.

With the newly-organized platoon in tact, Sergeant O'Conner ordered, " Attention, dress right dress. Men, listen up. This is the platoon arrangement you will always form – notice the guy to your right and left. It will be this way for the next eighteen weeks. You are ass-hole buddies now, so get acquainted. Now, Kam is going to march the platoon to the far end of the athletic field where we will start physical training – so get used to PT every morning. I'm going to follow along and observe the platoon formation."

Kam hollered in Pigin'English, "Toon tenshun, right face, fo'rd harch. Hup, two, tree, four – hup, two, tree, four – hup, hup, hup!"

The platoon struggled to keep in step, but individuals improved somewhat after fifteen minutes of getting accustomed to the stride of the man immediately in front of him.

Sergeant O'Conner ran ahead of the formation and motioned to Kam to halt the platoon.

"Barrigan, what the hell is wrong with you! You don't march, you don't even walk, you BOUNCE."

AB guessed what was wrong – it was of combination of 'Brooklyn swagger' and never having walked on anything but concrete. Barrigan had probably never walked on plain old solid ground before.

"And, Forsythe, what's wrong with you? You look like you're trying to follow a mule in a ditch, with one foot in front of the other. The rest of you guys need plenty of help. And you short guys at the end of each squad – learn to take a bigger stride and stay in step."

Kam marched the platoon to the end of the athletic field. Sergeant O'Conner spoke, "All right, men, now here's what I want you to do. Stand at double-arm's length from each other. Remove your fatigue jacket and your T-shirt, fold each, and place in front of you."

Kam relayed the order and watched while Sergeant O'Conner turned his back to the shirtless platoon and while still not facing the group gave the following instructions: "All right now, the first sonofabitch who laughs when I turn around will give me twenty-five pushups, …now."

With that said, the sergeant turned to face the troops. A curved tattoo over his left nipple read "SWEET"; over the right nipple was "SOUR".

"I was a drunk sonofabitch – enough said."

Barrigan grabbed his nose and snickered.

"Barrigan, hit the deck and give me twenty-five."

The daily PT program for the next eighteen weeks was to be commonly referred to by the recruits as "The Sweet and Sour Hour."

After an hour of strenuous PT, the Sergeant told the sweating recruits to get dressed and announced, "Barrigan, you've been squad leader for two hours. That's enough. Marley you are squad leader of the first squad. Cohens, you're Marley's assistant squad leader."

Goldie looked at AB in complete shock; how could this be?

AB grinned, "Just think of us as your crew in the 18-acre shade at La Camellia."

"You're full of bull crap, Mr. AB."

"And what did I tell you about this MISTER stuff," AB replied. After the La Camellia remark, Goldie's thoughts trailed off. . . . .

~

It was ten o'clock in the morning, and Goldie could smell the Old Heaven Hill whiskey on Mr. Red's breath. "Goldwire," said Mr. Red, "I been at the barn watching the wrapper coming from your shade—and it ain't for shit. You know that primings six through eleven are the best from the stalk. You are supposed to be pulling prime leaf number eight – and we are getting everything from sand leaves through God-knows-what. On top of that, one of your sleds this morning had wrapper leaves with cabbage looper worm holes – and at least two leaves still had loopers on 'em, eating an even bigger leaf hole on the way to the barn. Your daddy would never let this happen: OK, now nigger, let's get this thing right!"

All Goldwire could say was, "Yes sir, Mr. Red, we'll get it right."

Goldwire immediately pulled his field hands – primers and toters – together on one end of the shade. He thought he knew where at least part of the problem was – Joe Black, Jr. and his buddy Alonzo. Labor at La Camellia was in short supply this summer so Moses drove the old school bus to Quincy early each morning to get pickup laborers who gathered at the downtown King Edward packing house. Goldwire knew the two very well – they were on the JV basketball team at Carter Parramore High. Both had convinced Goldwire they were experienced primers, and therefore eligible for the $4 day rate, rather than the $2.50 rate for toters. Goldwire had a loud and profound speech for all the field hands, explaining the importance of quality workmanship. The toters – including two of Goldwire's younger sisters – were lectured on the need to look for worm damage on the wrapper leaves as they carried them to the end of the row. Any looper worms found were to be ground into the soil with a heel.

"Now, today is the day we gather the eighth leaf – and ONLY leaf number eight. If you have a question at all, count the leaf scars from the bottom of the plant stem. Call me if you have any question. WE ARE GOING TO GET THIS RIGHT," he bellowed.

Goldwire was in charge – no question.

~

Maybe he could show some leadership, thought Goldie.

AB noticed Goldie stretched out on his bunk.

AB did the same on his bunk. His upper body was crimson from the hour or so of shirtless PT and the relaxing hot shower. The J C Penney white jockey shorts provided a sharp contrast to his sunburned chest. It occurred to him that the mature body and chest hair revealed his age – particularly in contrast to most of the 18-19 year old fellow recruits. So far, somehow, no one had openly questioned his age or educational background , which he was determined to keep to himself. Goldie had been warned early on regarding this subject. There were a couple of fellows in the second and third squads he suspected of having more than a high school education, but he had not approached them on the subject.

Maybe it was time to relax and evaluate the events of the past few days…..

First, there was a need to review his fellow recruits in the first squad – men he would eat with, laugh with, do KP and Guard Duty with, drink beer with, and yes, grow up and live with for the next four months.

There was Zack Marley from Samoa. AB could easily see why he was squad leader, with his prior experience in military school, even though it was British military style. Zack had the body build of a football lineman. AB decided he needed to get to know Zack better. He noticed Zack also stretched out on his lower bunk reading some kind of long forms from a brown envelop.

AB knew Goldie well, but would he be aggressive and assert himself in a leadership capacity when called upon? AB decided it would be somewhat difficult, considering their previous relationship, but he could take an order from Goldie. He'd have to!

Barrigan – AB had him figured out from the first twenty minutes in his presence. A loud-mouthed Brooklyn kid who was completely out of his element when away from city streets. Barrigan really lacked confidence in himself, but used his mouth to cover himself. A big guy who was really not in good physical condition. He called all Orientals "Gook"—and all the Islanders knew it and disliked him.

AB's mind continued to search down the formation of the first squad by height. In platoon formation, and always to his left would be Alex Silva. Alex made his local heritage known early on – he liked to talk. He was of rural Portuguese descent and was from Maui. Alex had a maritime background with the family involved in inter-island freighter activity. He appeared to be a nice guy whom AB thought he would like to know better. He noticed Goldie seemed to like Silva, too.

Matthew Knight was a black kid from the streets of Detroit, who surprisingly never said very much. He mostly stayed close to two other black guys from the third platoon. AB thought Goldie was probably somewhat intimidated by Knight.

Next to Knight was Joshua Forsythe, and at the opposite end of the personality spectrum from Knight. He was a skinny blonde kid from North Carolina tobacco country who spoke in a deep country accent—and non-stop to anyone in hearing distance whether they were listening or not. AB was somewhat surprised how close Goldie and Josh had become, even with their apparent black/white Southern differences. Come to think of it, it was their similar tobacco-growing heritage and possibly their similar religious beliefs that provided the common background. It may be only their skin color that could have prevented them from being kinfolks. AB liked Josh.

In AB's view, Tad Sato was `class'—someone he really wanted to get to know better. Tad seemed to relate to most everyone in the squad regardless of color, heritage or lifestyle. AB thought Tad had leadership capability, and felt he probably should have been at least the assistant squad

Half Way There, Haole

leader. He recognized, however, that to have two Islanders in leadership position in the same squad probably would not happen; certainly not under Sergeant O'Conner's direction.

To the left of Tad was Vinnie del Fucci, the Italian kid with the Boston accent and sidekick to Barrigan. AB wasn't so sure about Vinnie. On his own, Vinnie was a comedian with a great sense of timing, but around Barrigan he became a lackey and parrot -- losing his own personality.

Then there was Wilfred Ching, a Chinese kid who was from inner city Honolulu, according to Silva. AB was yet to hear him say a word to anyone.

AB was uncertain about George Oxendine, who had been transferred mysteriously to the first squad several days ago when Aaron left. "Ox" was certain to have an impact with his presence in the first squad. He was an American Indian from Lumberton, North Carolina. Ox talked a lot – to anyone, it didn't matter. Ox had classic Indian features and coloring. And then there was the small tattoo of a tomahawk on his right buttock. Interestingly, Ox and Loa had immediately become close buddies.

Bernard Loa was the only known pure Hawaiian in the 55th Company. He had a stocky body build and blue-colored gums that somehow became a focal feature every time AB tried to speak with him. Loa carried dice in his right pocket at all times and brought them out at every cigarette break. He informed Ox of the action at the message parlors on Hotel Street in downtown Honolulu, and expressed immediate dislike for Barrigan and Vinnie. Loa could be trouble for Zack or anyone in authority. Loa didn't appear to accept any of the mixed breed Hawaiians in the squad and tended to defy authority in his own way.

Sam Allen was from Nebraska. He was short and chubby. No one knew anything about Sam except that he was from Nebraska and seemed to have an excess of folding dollars in his pocket at all times.

AB had trouble keeping the identity of the two Guamanians separate. Reyes and Rapolla were not related, but really were carbon copies of each other. Both carried dice – reportedly `loaded.' Their main objective was to learn to take larger strides to keep up with everyone in front of them in the first squad.

~

AB stretched his sweating body on the woolen GI blanket. His mind was scrambled eggs, thinking about the ethnic diversity of the first squad trainees. He and Goldie grew up understanding and accepting the `rules' of the two groups with different backgrounds and living in one community – but what are the `rules' of six or eight – or maybe more – ethnic groups living in community? Yes, it would be interesting these next few months.

Zack sat down on the footlocker near AB's bunk, surprising AB. Zack began to pull forms from a brown envelop. "I need some help," said Zack, "And I think you're just the one I need to talk to." AB swung his legs to the end of the bunk, deciding this was just the opportunity he was waiting for to get better acquainted with his squad leader.

"What's the problem?"

"Well, I'm planning to bring my wife and daughter from Samoa to Hawaii. They are New Zealand citizens and want to join me here, but they need to become US citizens. Here are the forms and are they ever confusing."

AB picked up the forms, "How much time do we have?"

"Oh, we have some time. They can't come here until after we finish basic training."

AB glanced down the first page of the long form. "I don't know anything about this, but we can figure it out together."

~

Lieutenant Soong addressed the entire 55th Company, "Men, we have an important decision to make. Even though this IS the Army, we are going to take a democratic vote."

"What the hell is he talking about, " said AB to anyone who might be standing nearby. "There is no democracy in the Army. You do what you are ordered to do – and that is it."

Lieutenant Soong continued, "We are going to take a vote on rice versus potatoes. Most of you know that those of us from the Islands grew up on rice. Many of you haoles grew up on potatoes. It will be a private vote – platoon sergeants have blank notebook paper for you to use."

An hour later, the vote was announced by Lieutenant Soong "It's rice by a fifty-eight percent vote. You guys from the States needn't be concerned though. I have ordered the Mess Sergeant to serve potatoes at every Sunday night meal.."

AB mentally accused Goldie and Forsythe of voting for rice. He remembered Tad playing with his plate of potatoes at their first meal together. Barrigan and Vinnie were outraged, but somehow speechless. Ox didn't seem to know or care what they were talking about.

Chapter 16

"Last week was a friggin' snap," said Sergeant O'Conner

"We did all the easy stuff like military history, map reading, use of the compass, distance estimation, military courtesy, and all that shit. Now, we get down to the really good stuff beginning with the third week. There's always a weekly training schedule posted on the bulletin board near the dayroom. Read it! Now we RUN at port arms with light field pack to every training site at Schofield. The first platoon WILL be in physical condition."

Kam smiled. This is what he has been waiting for.

The platoon, indeed the entire 55th Company, was beginning to show some progress – particularly with the marching formations and the addition of the drum beat. Maeva, the only other Samoan in the Company had been selected as the designated drummer. He had previous high school drummer experience and did the troops like the beat! Goldie particularly liked having the drum to beat the rhythm of ninety steps a minute.

AB had checked the weekly training schedule by the dayroom and was curious about the two hours blocked out and designated "Chaplain," for Monday afternoon. As the hour approached, it became obvious that only the haoles were scheduled to meet with the Chaplain. The locals were assigned to rifle cleaning in the squad room.

Haoles were marched to the Chapel area. The Chaplain met briefly with each recruit individually, reminding him of his responsibility to write home at least weekly and to attend religious services of his choice. Then he casually tossed this hand grenade! It was Army policy to send Schofield-trained infantrymen directly to FECOM – the Far East Command -- that is -- Korea. Each recruit would be given a seven-day leave to be spent `on the Islands.' FECOM was to become a much-used word in the vocabulary of all trainees.

Although he had heard rumblings about this policy, AB was left almost speechless. "But, Captain Goodman, what about all those guys taking training in the States? They get leave to GO HOME after completing basic training!"

Captain Goodman managed to display his most reverent smile, "I know, I know, but this is the policy of the Department of the Army at the Pentagon. There are no funds to provide transportation from Schofield to the West Coast. A number of men have reacted the same as you; here is a card with the address of a Congressman you can write."

AB's time was up. He was directed to go outside the chapel office where Goldie and three others waited under a palm tree. An Army photographer had the group grab shoulders in a football huddle and ordered smiles while he took a photo of the "buddies." AB rechecked – his " buddies", other than Goldie, were haoles from the second platoon whose names he did not even know.

AB pulled the card given to him by the Chaplain from his fatigue pants pocket. It read:

Senator Lyndon B. Johnson, Chairman
Senate Armed Services Committee
United States Senate
Washington, DC

AB and Goldie walked back to Quad K by themselves. This was their first opportunity for a private conversation in days. Without thought, they stepped off in unison with the first squad stride.

"AB, I was shocked when Sergeant O'Conner called my name as assistant squad leader. I'm not sure about what I'm into."

"Hey, you can be a leader," said AB. "Weren't you co-captain of the basketball team at Carter Parramore High? You had a crew at the shade tobacco farm. Hell, you can do it."

"Ya, I know but there are some dudes in the squad I'm not so sure of. What about Barrigan and Vinnie?"

I'll tell you what," said AB as they approached Quad K, "treat 'em like anybody else in the squad, and when either of 'em call you a nigger, you tell him that will be the last time. If there is another incident, you tell him you'll bust his ass. That's it. Get right at them nose-to-nose."

Goldie smiled, "OK, but what about some of the other guys."

"Well, first thing, don't ever call anybody a "gook." I think you know that. Tad, Silva, and Forsythe are OK, but I'm not so sure about Loa and his new-found buddy Ox. They could mean trouble, I'm not sure. Maybe you know how to figure out Knight. The Guamanians seem to be OK, but don't say very much. I think you know they both are gamblers and carry dice that I hear are loaded. It's going to be tough when the entire squad gets a police-up assignment and you have to post individual jobs to everyone. But you can do it."

There wasn't time to discuss the other members of the first squad.

Goldie and AB were stunned when they returned to the 55th Company area. A large group of trainees – all haoles – gathered on the lanai and were in a state of near-revolt. Barrigan and Vinnie were among the most vocal. They, too, had just returned from the meeting with Chaplain Goodman.

"What kind of shit is this?" yelled Barrigan. "They bring us to these fuckin' islands, half way around the world for infantry basic training. Then they have the CHAPLAIN tell you that you ain't never going back to the States; that you're just dogface red meat headed to the front in North Korea. Who the hell wants seven days leave in Oahu – we've already seen the place. Something's wrong! I'm writing that Senator guy from Texas."

"Ya," said Vinnie, "I just got a letter from a buddy I was drafted with in Boston. They sent him to Fort Jackson, South Carolina. He'll be finishing fourteen weeks of basic in February and is already planning a big fuckin' ten days in Boston. Rumor is they're headed to Fort Devens, Mass. for artillery training. How do you like that shit?"

Goldie nudged AB, "Wait until they hear the rumor that ninety-five percent of the 20th Battalion that graduates from here next Saturday is headed to FECOM."

Goldie pulled the card from his pocket. "Who is this guy Senator Johnson, anyway?"

I don't know much about him except he's from Texas," said AB, "but I'm going to get to know him better. I'm going to write to Quincy and tell my parents to write him and protest the situation. You ought to do the same. Everybody needs to. These guys from the Islands are lucky – some of them even can get a weekend pass and go home from this place."

Sergeant O'Conner was expecting this. He emerged from his room in underwear and ordered everyone to his bunk.

"Knock it off you shitheads. Report to your bunk and stand at attention for inspection."

AB knew he didn't really mean it. Sergeant O'Conner was not going to conduct an inspection in his underwear.

Barrigan, Vinnie, Ox, AB, and Goldie moved inside the squad room. The locals showed little interest – continuing to mess around with rifle cleaning.

~

Tad was excited and smiling.

"AB, PFC Kong tells me he heard Lieutenant Soong and Sergeant Rubinal talking about weekend passes for as many as twenty-five percent of the trainees at a time. You have to get by Saturday morning inspection without a gig. You can leave after the parade on Saturday and return by six PM on Sunday."

AB and Tad had become good friends over the past few weeks. AB's M-1 rifle had previously been poorly maintained and was hard to keep clean enough to pass an inspection. Among other things, it rusted on the base plate and the barrel. Tad had shown AB how to clean it in the mop sink in the latrine using soapy hot water, a toothbrush, and very hot water poured down the length of the barrel and into the chamber. After the soapy water was rinsed, the mechanism and barrel would actually shine – reflecting the light when held to the eye – the way Sergeant O'Conner liked to do when he was really looking to gig someone.

Inspection haircuts were always a problem. A Monday haircut would not pass a Saturday inspection. The barbershop was in the same building as the PX, but the six barbers were somehow there to serve the entire Battalion on a Friday night. The lines were long but service was quick – three minutes and thirty-five cents later you were out the door, and don't ask for anything other than a GI haircut.

AB decided to forego the Friday night chow line and hit the barbershop early. He would go to the PX for a double strawberry sundae afterwards. About seventy-five others had the same idea, but it really didn't take that long. The surprise came when he entered the PX. There was Lou Sample, an Allegheny College SAE fraternity brother. They had graduated together. Neither could believe the other was at Schofield, much less in the same battalion. Lou was in the 51st Company just across the Quadrangle. They renewed acquaintance and brought each other up to speed. Lou had belatedly decided to go to grad school at Pitt after job opportunities did not develop. He, too, had been caught in the October draft, gone to Fort Meade, Camp Stoneman and traveled on the USS Altman. Somehow their paths had not crossed. They ordered ice cream sundaes and decided to vacate the crowded PX for a quiet conversation behind the PX building.

Lou was usually considered a 'hustler' by other fraternity brothers – someone who was always checking out the situation to better himself personally – but not necessarily at the expense of other frat brothers. Lou somehow had advance copies of Econ tests, but passed them around to the brothers. Lou was an opportunist, but he often made his own opportunities -- maybe that was where AB first developed his *theory of positioning*.

"So, have you checked out the S&P Program at the Central Personnel Office," said Lou.

"What are you talking about? S and P? and what is Central Personnel?" asked AB as he finished the last of the double strawberry sundae.

"Scientific and Professional," replied Lou, "It's a program the Army has for trainees with a college education or maybe a career. The Army evaluates your application and your background and attempts to place you in a position where your talents can be utilized. It might be in the Pentagon, but more than likely it will be an assignment to a military/industrial complex in the States, Alaska, or maybe Europe. Some guys are assigned to Counter Intelligence School. You do not get commissioned, but you might land in a spot where you get a technical rating as a sergeant. You ought to check it out. Central Personnel is down by the Post movie theater." Lou glanced at his Timex, "Hey, I got to get back to 51st Company. Got to clean my rifle and polish brass for inspection tomorrow. I'm in second platoon. Stop by next weekend."

~

Sergeant O'Conner stood on the lanai near the stairs. "Company, Attention. Prepare for inspection."

"Trainees scampered to pre-assigned spots near bunks and footlockers. Goldie glanced at his shined boots and gave each boot a quick rub on the back of the lower leg of his khaki pants to remove last minute dust – an art he had learned from Loa who stood across from him at inspection.

Lieutenant Fujimoto and Lieutenant Soong, followed by two corporals with the ever-present clipboards approached the top of the stairs. Sergeant O'Conner clicked his heels and snapped to attention.

"The company is ready for inspection, sirs."

"Thank you, sergeant," replied Lieutenant Soong, "Lieutenant Fujimoto will take the first and second platoons. I will take the third and fourth platoons."

The attending corporals followed with pencil and clipboard in the ready position. Trainees strained to be at attention—eyes straight ahead as instructed. Within minutes, Lieutenant Fujimoto had nearly destroyed the first squad.

Loa's bunk had been ripped apart, blankets and sheets dumped on the floor. Knight, Ox, and one of the Guamanians were gigged for dirt on boot soles. Vinnie

Half Way There, Haole

caught it for unpolished brass. Tad, somehow had received a compliment.

Lieutenant Fujimoto, short in stature, approached AB. The officer's eye level was at AB's necktie knot. AB glanced down to establish eye contact.

"Burns, haven't you been told to look straight ahead during inspection?"

"Yes, sir."

"Well, then do it. I don't want anybody looking down at me!" The good Lieutenant kicked at AB's second pair of boots appropriately lined up beneath the bunk. He ripped the pillow from beneath the blanket, in disgust, but did not inform the corporal to make a note on his clipboard. The officer then ignored Goldie to get to Barrigan. He stood back to read Barrigan's name on the helmet liner, and then approached the recruit.

"When did you last shave, Barrigan, on Thursday? You look like shit."

He turned to the corporal, "Write up Barrigan on personal appearance. Needs a shave and a short haircut. Next time, Barrigan, stand closer to the razor."

The Lieutenant passed by Zack with a hint of a smile and proceeded to rip apart a bunk in the second squad. First squad members stood in amazement and relief as they observed the second squad be devastated and criticized. Nothing was acceptable. This was the first real inspection for 55th Company. It had not gone well.

It seemed strange to go on parade immediately after a destructive and demoralizing inspection -- to go out and compete with others in parade formation when nothing went right in the personal inspection. Yet there they were, strapping bayonets to field belts and getting ready to fall out in parade formation.

"The son-of-a-bitch said I hadn't shaved since Thursday, and now he wants me to march in the front row, five steps behind him and parade for the General," groaned Barrigan, as perspiration already had begun to appear around his collar and from his armpits.

"This army sucks," mumbled the kid from Boston.

Chapter 17

Tad returned from weekend pass with two packages. One was small and wrapped in a bright print bandanna. The other was a cardboard carton.

"This is for you," he told AB as he handed him the smaller of the two packages.

"If you learn to use the chopsticks, I'll bring you some more next time."

"What are you talking about?" asked AB.

"Well, we had tempura shrimp and vegetables for Sunday night dinner and my mother fixed an extra pan for you"

He smiled, "There's also some rice."

AB was completely taken aback – almost shaken. Tad must have told his family of his haole friend from Florida and this was the result. He untied the bandanna knot as he sat on his bunk – shared atop with his Japanese friend. Amazingly, the pan was still warm. AB looked at the black lacquered chopsticks.

"Here, let me show you how to use those things," said Tad. He picked up the utensils and placed them carefully between the thumb and third finger of AB's hand. AB instinctively shifted the chopsticks to his left hand.

Tad grinned, "This may be a little more difficult than I counted on." He showed his friend how to pick up a serving of the sticky rice; then the shrimp and vegetables. The full-length tempura fried string beans were the most difficult to handle.

"Eat 'em with your fingers," said Tad, "That's what I do at home when nobody is looking."

It took several adjustments, but AB was soon handling the chopsticks with some degree of skill. The food was delicious – the first home cooking in weeks!

"You're OK," smiled Tad. "I'll bring you some more the next time I get a pass to go home.

"You can go home every weekend, as far as I am concerned," said AB, licking his fingers as he wrapped the chopsticks in a clean handkerchief for future use.

"Hey, what's in the cardboard box?" asked Josh.

"You'll never guess – it's my radio from home."

Tad extracted the small red plastic Westinghouse radio from the box and pulled out a short extension cord. "Now we got tunes."

The policy of radios in the squadroom had never come up – no one had a radio except Sergeant O'Conner in his private quarters. It seldom was heard.

Tad cut the box with his bayonet to form a cardboard "sling" to hold the radio beneath the bed frame. He pulled cord from his pocket and proceeded to mount the radio in a remote area beneath AB's bunk – somewhere away from the prying eyes of an inspection officer.

"This is the 8 o'clock news from Station WNAQ in downtown Wahiawa. From Korea, there is again severe fighting in the T-Bone Hill area near the 38th Parallel. UN troops advanced against the North Koreans, but not without casualties. There is considerable North Korean troop movement in the Chorwan River area. There is no progress to report on the Panmunjon peace talks."

Tad looked at AB, "I don't like the way things are going over there." AB somehow wished he had not heard the news update. Goldie just sat there with eyes closed. It was the first Korean War news they had in days – maybe weeks.

The news continued, then after a pause: "Now for some stateside tunes. Here is Rosemary Clooney singing 'Half as Much.' We dedicate this song to all the haoles at Schofield Barracks."

Sergeant O"Conner emerged from his corner room with a hidden smile on his face. He looked at his watch. It was seven-thirty and the sun was resting on the mountains to the west. The first platoon was scattered – some writing letters; some preparing laundry lists; Zack, Goldie, and Silva in GI underwear were sitting on a bunk exchanging stories; the showers were nearly full; Ox lay naked beneath a towel reading a paperback novel.

Sergeant O'Conner eased out onto the lanai and down the well-worn steps. He swung open the double screen doors, put his whistle to his lips and let go . . . . .

"Fall out," he bellowed.

The men of the first platoon readily recognized the voice and the command. All hell broke loose as recruits grabbed for whatever clothing was handy. The showers emptied with a scramble for towels. Zack, Goldie, and Silva grabbed ponchos to cover their GI underwear. Ox, at a loss, grabbed the towel and flip flops, and streaked almost naked down the steps. Each searched for his particular spot in the platoon formation – arm's length from the next man. Vinnie, in fatigue pants and no shirt was the last to fall into position.

Sergeant O'Conner looked at his watch, "Forty-seven seconds, that's too frigin' long. You guys are going to do this in thirty seconds. We'll keep it up until we get it right."

He covered a grin at the display of humanity in various stages of dress and undress, then yelled, "Dismissed."

The men of the first platoon trooped back up the stairs to the second floor. After three more attempts, and an improved state of dress, yes, they did get it right.

Half Way There, Haole

On the last formation, Sergeant O'Conner congratulated the troops and said, " All right now, who's got a fuck book I ain't read yet."

There was total silence ......finally Ox pulled a paperback from the side pocket of his fatigues. Sergeant O'Conner approved the book from the cover picture and returned to his private quarters.

AB sighed to himself, "This guy is a first class idiot."

Chapter 18

At the end of a hard day of field training, mail call was always a great change of pace! Tonight was no exception – particularly when AB received a brown envelop from Quincy. He opened it and found several items of interest. The first was a 4 x 6 photo of five Army recruits in a football huddle in front of a palm tree. The chapel was in the background. There was AB, Goldie, and others from the first platoon. Included in the envelop was a letter addressed to Mrs. Lucinda Burns, Quincy, Florida. It read:

> Enclosed is a photograph of your son, Allendale, with a group of his friends training together here at Schofield Barracks, Hawaii. They really enjoy and appreciate the climate here. It is ideal for basic training.
>
> I have met with Allendale recently and he is doing well, and is responding positively to his training here. He advises that he attends chapel services at times and writes home frequently. Please be aware that training at Schofield Barracks is intensive and recruits are often extremely tired at the close of a day of training. If Allendale should not write to you as often as you desire, please be reminded of the intense training schedule. If there are any health related problems with your son, you will be advised immediately.

Enclosed is a memorandum from the Office of the Commanding General, United States Army, Pacific entitled "Assignment and Leave Information."

The letter was signed by George L. Goodman, Corps of Chaplains.

AB examined the picture again – he looked pretty good in his uniform. He re-read the letter from the Chaplain and then turned to the attached memorandum, It read as follows:

ASSIGNMENTS
1. In the Army, as in civilian life, the manner in which a young man recognizes and avails himself of opportunities governs to a marked degree his ultimate assignment.
2. During the period of basic training, tests are given to determine the qualifications of applicants for Officer Candidate School, Leadership School and technical schools. Qualification standards for these schools are high, competition is keen, and quotas are limited. In fact there are times when recommended applicants cannot be scheduled for attendance due to the quotas being filled. These quotas are filled by selection from a list of recommended personnel in accordance with their earned ratings; the soldier with the highest grades being selected first, and so on down the list.
3. The trainee is subject to world-wide assignment. An assignment to the Far East Command is most probable. The Philippines, Korea, Japan and other islands of the Pacific are included in that command

AB's eyes were wide open. What was that about assignment! He re-read: AN ASSIGNMENT TO THE FAR EAST COMMAND IS MOST PROBABLE.

So all the latrine talk about Hawaii being half way to Korea is really true, along with discussion of FECOM with the Chaplain. Barrigan is right – we are all dogmeat for front line duty in Korea. There it is in writing – an assignment to FECOM is most probable. That thing about FECOM including Philippines, Japan, and other Pacific Islands is crappola. We're all headed to Korea as infantry replacements for front line duty. That's what our cadre have been trying to tell us.

AB continued to read from the memorandum:
> For trainees assigned to FECOM, who spend their seven days Of post basic training are hereby granted four extra days of travel to and from mainland USA. The Army has not received funds for travel to mainland for leave, consequently the expense to the mainland must be borne by the trainee.

AB now had the official word that been rumored – you stay in the Islands for leave and don't return to the States. Who has six hundred dollars to fly to the West Coast, much less across the country to Florida? We are really getting screwed – all because you have a Class A Profile. No wonder the Chaplain gave me that card to write that Senator from Texas.

AB finally read the accompanying letter in the envelop from his parents. He was requested to return the photo and the letters, but more interesting was the letter-writing campaign to Senator Lyndon B. Johnson that had been initiated by his parents. His father had prepared cards on the company mimeograph machine with the Senator's address. These cards had been taken to the Tuesday Rotary meeting at the Quincy Women's Club and to a Chamber of Commerce meeting by his father, with a plea to write on behalf of

Half Way There, Haole

Allendale and Goldwire to return to the States for leave before Korean assignment. The high school principal – a Rotary member – had agreed to take the letter writing campaign to his senior Civics Class. Others agreed to respond, including the State Senator for the North Florida area.

Lucinda had taken the project to PTA Board meeting and to a church meeting and had received similar positive response.

Senator Lyndon B. Johnson of Texas was about to learn where Quincy, Florida was on the map. AB's father had even sent a message by Pocket to Moses Cohens to suggest a letter from Moses and his church members.

AB's reaction nearly brought tears, as he again re-read the letter. His thoughts were interrupted by Tad, who announced that he had just been downstairs where he read on the bulletin board that he and AB had KP duty next day. AB's first thought was a flashback to the KP scene at Fort Meade, the second day of his army career.

This lead to an in-depth conversation with Tad on the merits of various KP assignments.

"Without question," said Tad, "The best possible assignment is DRO – that's dining room orderly. The disadvantage is that you usually report directly to the mess sergeant and that can be a real pain in the ass. There are two DRO's and you are responsible for cleaning the dining room after each meal. This is OK except when the mess sergeant decides to do what he calls "in depth cleaning" where you have to wash windows – inside and out – dust everything including the overhead light fixtures. To be a DRO, you have to be one of the first ones to report for duty at five AM. The last guy to report gets the worst assignment."

Tad continued, "Some say the next best job is CRO – crud room operator, but I'm not so sure. You work in the little room where the empty trays are returned and operate the dishwasher. You dump the leftover food from the trays into the garbage and then run the trays and cups through the dishwasher in wooden trays. Don't ever get CRO when they have liver on the menu – it all comes back on the trays. It can really get hot and nasty in the crud room, but the real advantage is that the CRO's are the first to knock off at the end of the day – that is if you are with a guy who will really work with you and get it all done."

"The other jobs are garbage detail and cook's helper. Some like garbage detail since you sort of work on your own. The worst part is making the empty garbage cans SHINE from the inside to the outside. That is a lot of scrubbing with hand brushes and a hose. The mess sergeant NEVER approves garbage cans on the first inspection. You serve the food on line when you are not scrubbing the inside of garbage cans."

Tad finished, "Cook's helper can be OK – it depends on the cook. All our cooks are Chinese and they give us Japanese guys a fit. I try to stay away from them. You have to do whatever they don't feel like doing, including scrubbing pots and pans. Our haole mess sergeant can really get on the cooks when he feels like it – then the cook's helpers really catch it."

"So, even though you may have a choice of jobs – none of 'em are any fun. At the end of the day there isn't anything left of you."

~

Sergeant O'Conner spoke with authority. "Listen up, men. Next week we go on bivouac in the Waianae Mountains. It will be a three-day-two-night campout and you will be prepared! This is a warmup to a full week of bivouac in Week 16 of the training cycle here at Schofield."

"One of the first things you need to do is select a tent buddy. You already know of the shelter half – that piece of canvas you carry in your backpack – forms a pup tent to sleep two when properly assembled. You need to select a buddy from within your squad – and this means you too, Kam. Notify your respective squad leader by this time tomorrow of how you want to pair off. Squad leaders, give me a written report by noon tomorrow."

"Now, Kam, let's double time to the mortar range."

AB did some quick math – with Corporal Kam involved, there was an even sixteen men in the first squad. He noted, too, with the variety of ethnic backgrounds involved in the first squad of the first platoon of 55th Company, there would be some interesting thoughts going through these sixteen minds. Instinctively, he noticed some eye contact among several of them as the good sergeant was closing his little announcement speech. Ox and Loa gave it the thumbs up. Vinnie, standing beside Loa, observed the interaction and caught Barrigan's eye with a repeat of the thumbs up routine.

AB's mind was working overtime as the platoon double timed the step to the mortar range near Kolekole Pass. He had sensed covert lack of appreciation for haoles by the locals from the very first day of their arrival at Quad K. In his mind, he emphasized the 'covert'part of his thought processes because of his relationships with Tad, Silva, and Zack. He still had not become acquainted with Ching – mostly because Ching seldom reacted with him, or in fact, with anyone else in the squad. Loa and the Guamanians were not much for accepting or even acknowledging the haoles.

AB jogged on, in step with Barrigan in front of him. Then another thought passed through his mind – what about his *theory of positioning*? Who would he want to pair off with in the first squad if he had a complete choice? Let's see now, what are the facts? His mind was racing with various thoughts. First, AB, you haven't been on a campout of any kind since Boy Scout camp at age fourteen. Secondly, you have no idea what a tropical mountain jungle might be like. Answer: AB, you better position yourself with one of the Islanders if you want to survive this thing called bivouac in the Waianae Mountains of Oahu.

That thought process automatically eliminated his Stateside best friend– Goldie. Come to think of it, Goldie was a great friend, but he himself probably wouldn't want to ask to bunk with a white guy – and maybe the feeling was mutual. But who would Goldie share a pup tent with in the first squad? The only other Negro was Knight from Detroit and they had little in common.

Goldie didn't really mind the double time to the mortar range. He was in great physical shape – even before infantry training began. The mountainous outline of Kolekole Pass came into view – and somehow his mind turned to Sergeant O'Conner's announcement about bivouac and selection of pup tent partners.

Goldie jogged on, tracking easily the step of the man in front of him. His mind was searching for options for a pup tent buddy. AB would be a natural choice, but he would only wait for AB to make the first move. Knight was out – the black jive talk with other city blacks in the second platoon left him out. He would ask one of the Islanders, but that wouldn't be easy.

Kam held up his right hand as a signal to stop. It was time for a ten minute break. Forsythe sat beside Goldie along the roadside, offering him a Camel cigarette.

"What do you say we pitch a tent together, " said Forsythe.

"Sounds good to me, " replied Goldwire, trying not to show any degree of absolute surprise.

Forsythe continued, "Besides you may be the real squad leader some day and it might just pay off for me to know my squad leader better."

"Ah, get off that crap, Josh. We can figure out this pup tent thing together. OK?"

"Ya," said Josh, pulling on the last drag on the Camel. He field stripped the butt without even thinking, and took a quick swig of water from his canteen. Goldie did the same.

The 55th Company, including Sergeant O'Conner, heaved a sigh of relief as they passed a small sign on the roadway with an arrow "Danger, Mortar Range." With sweat streaming from all body parts of the 55th Company recruits, Field First Sergeant Rubinal. declared a twenty-minute break in the noonday Oahu sun. A small dark weather cloud hung half way up the mountainside at Kolekole Pass. Zack laid aside his M-1 rifle and field pack as he reached for his canteen. He sat beside AB on a mound of Johnson grass.

"I've been thinking, suppose we bunk together on bivouac? If we have any free time we could work on the immigration forms."

"Sounds good to me, Zack," AB reached to shake hands with his Samoan friend.

Captain Paaluhi introduced himself as being in charge of the Mortar Range and made it very clear to the men of the 55th Company that there were dangers involved in learning to handle live mortar ammunition. The Captain reminded the troops that they had had training with live ammo on the M-1 rifle range, but this was to be a heavy duty training session in learning to fire mortars. He ordered the platoon sergeants to form each squad into two-man teams. AB was paired with Tad – both were pleased to train together on something each had actually anticipated eagerly.

It was meal time. The mess trucks arrived with cooks and swarms of KPs who began setting up the noon day meal in a grove of trees remote to the mortar training area. This was the day the first squad of the first platoon was to proceed through the chow line first – something every recruit looked forward to, particularly since this occasion happened only about every three weeks. Corporal Kam ordered the men of the first squad to remove their mess gear from field packs and to separate their folding-handled cup from the canteen fastened to the ammo belt. Goldie hoped it wasn't liver day again.

AB was the fourth man in line. The first KP ladled hot coffee into each metal cup. The next serving station – a large dishpan of sugar – was manned by Lieutenant Fujimoto with a wooden-handled tablespoon at the ready to supply sugar to the coffee. The Lieutenant had decided, at the last minute, to serve on the line and greet each recruit by name—as printed on the helmet liners. He called out: "Marley, Cohens, Barrigan," and then, "Burns." AB didn't take sugar in his coffee. He declined and withdrew the steaming cup toward his ammo belt in an effort to prevent the Lieutenant from shoveling a mound of sugar into his cup. In the process of doing so, the cup somehow became entangled with the

Half Way There, Haole

ammo belt, disengaged the folding handle and dumped the steaming cup of coffee into the dishpan of sugar—turning the entire dishpan into an ugly shade of brown.

Lieutenant Fujimoto's eyes snapped as he stared at AB's name on the helmet liner.

"You dumb son-of-a-bitch, Burns. Look what you have done – and you are only the fourth man through the line." The Lieutenant thought a minute, "YOU come around here and YOU serve this stuff to the rest of the Company."

Lieutenant Fujimoto disappeared. AB was embarrassed at his stupidity, as he picked up the spoon and offered sugar to Silva and the rest of the first squad. As others approached the chow line, they stared at AB and asked, "What is this crap?"

AB finally recovered and responded that it was brown sugar and was all that was available with today's coffee. It sold pretty well under the circumstances.

The process of pairing off for bivouac continued as the men scattered to find a shady spot beneath a tree. There weren't too many pairing choices left for the first squad members. Allen and Knight paired off, somewhat by default, but to fend off any close association for either of them, with native Islanders – Korean or Chinese. This left Tad and Silva as bunk mates -- and even more interesting, Ching and Kam. Of course, the Guamanians became tent mates.

The primary advantage to be the first through the chow line was the opportunity to take an even longer after-meal break. On this occasion they stretched out for a brief snooze under the shade of the palm trees. All this while the last in line finished their meal. AB skipped chow and found a shady spot to rest his tired legs. His mind again shifted to the bivouac pairings.

Tad and Silva had not shown much interest in each other. These were no open hostility. Kam and Ching could be a very interesting pairing.
    Somehow, AB's mind wandered to his sophomore year at Allegheny where he struggled in Professor Cares' World History class. Going into the second grading period with a "D" average, AB was searching for a way to get through the class with a passing grade. Professor Cares had proposed a special research paper for those struggling with grades in his class. AB had become interested in the Treaty of Portsmouth that had ended the Far East war between Russian and Japan (in favor of Japan) – and how this Treaty had set up what was to be a continued and long-standing hatred and mistrust among the Koreans, Chinese, and Japanese. In 1905, as a result of the Treaty, the Japanese were given full control of the Korean peninsula – setting aside Chinese and Russian interests in Korea. Manchuria, of significant interest to both the Russians and the Japanese, was unquestionably to become Chinese territory.
    Here he was some forty or fifty years later, taking military training with Orientals in the Hawaiian Islands to engage in a war in Korea between the Russian/Chinese supported North Koreans and American/Japanese supported South Koreans. And now some of these Orientals were obligated to take training together and somehow accept and understand each other—even to the point of bunking together in a two-man tent in the mountains of Hawaii. Where would all this lead? Professor Cares might be interested!

~

"Men," said Captain Paluuhi, "This is an ideal area for mortar training. It is about five thousand yards to the base of the mountains on the far side of the valley – that's almost three miles. If you look carefully, you can see a stream of water winding through the jungle at about three thousand yards. Beyond that is a narrow roadway cut through the jungle. It winds through the area and generally follows the path of the creek bed. This is considered ideal for mortar training since you can actually see your target. In real battle conditions , you seldom see your target – you are usually getting telephone instructions from an advanced observer position. Anyway, in this case your target is an old orange school bus parked along the roadside. You may not be able to see the target with the naked eye right now, but when you are divided into two-man teams and have a pair of binoculars you will be able to identify it. Now will the first squad approach the mortar base training area for further instructions from team cadre trainers."

The eight field training positions were about three yards back from the steep precipice; each attended by a corporal mortar cadre trainer. AB and Tad were directed to the mortar position furthest to the right of the training area. Each cadreman explained the use of the bubble leveling device that was used to adjust the angle of the mouth of the mortar. He had each man make adjustments designating such as "six clicks to the right, or four clicks to the left" to perfect the aim of the mortar in terms of distance and angle by yards. He then demonstrated the proper technique to drop the shell into the tube and move the hands and body immediately away from the mortar tube for self protection. Both AB and Tad practiced with dummy runs on the procedures and felt comfortable with their instructions.

"Now," said the corporal, handing the binoculars to AB, "Find your target – it is a school bus parked near the roadside and beyond where the creek bed curves toward you – at about twenty-five hundred yards. Take your time and get it right."

AB adjusted the glasses and pointed in the direction of the target. He finally located the school bus in a tangle of weeds and vines. The bus had obviously been there for some time as heavy vines grew through the broken windows, and in and around the raised hood and over the motor area.

AB passed the glasses to Tad with instructions on how to locate the target. The broad grin below the binoculars told AB that Tad had zeroed in on the school bus.

The corporal then gave the team instructions on how to proceed. Each team would be given three live mortar rounds. Instructions were to try to fire the first round intentionally long on the target. Watch for the puff of smoke from the explosion, and estimate the yards toward the target in terms of clicks on the bubble leveling device. The second round was to be targeted short of the school bus, and following the same procedure to estimate the yardage short of the target by the location of the exploding shell. Having done this, the third round was to be "on target" as explained by the corporal –who had by all appearances of having given this same set of instructions many hundreds of times.

AB and Tad grinned at each other, "We can do this."

The other seven teams in the mortar training area received similar instructions and were confident of their mortar firing abilities.

The team of Barrigan and Vinnie was the first to fire. All rounds fell safely and well beyond the school bus. Other teams had similar experiences – spraying mortar shells throughout the jungle valley.

It came time for the team at Mortar Position #8 to perform. Tad had carefully observed Team #7 next to him – Silva and Zack. Their first round had landed well beyond the target. After bubble adjustments, the second round also fell beyond the target. From an apparent over adjustment, the third round fell at least two hundred yards short of the school bus.

AB was now trained as an 'ammo dropper;' Tad was the master of the bubble aiming device. -- and readily targeted the first round about five hundred yards beyond the orange school bus. AB located the exploding shell in the glasses. He suggested two clicks right and four clicks to raise the mortar barrel. Tad took the field glasses and found the small swirl of smoke of the first round. He agreed with AB on the bubble setting and made the adjustments while AB placed the round into position at the mouth of the mortar barrel. Within seconds the puff of smoke broke from the jungle – right on line and five hundred yards short, as planned.

They grinned at each other, as Tad adjusted the piece by two clicks. AB watched through the field glasses as shreds of orange metal bus parts blew violently through the tropical jungle. Tad grabbed the glasses. A small curl of smoke arose from what was left of the bus frame. He grinned, "I knew we could do it."

Captain Paluuhi, smoking a cigarette behind the training tower, arrived at Position #8 in a matter of seconds. He was livid.

"You dumb bastards! Look what you have done! You wiped out my target. I've had eleven companies of men come through here for training – several thousands of two man teams. No one ever came close to my school bus. Now because of you two guys, I got to find another goddam school bus and drag it through the jungle out there. Screw you two guys."

AB and Tad looked at each other in amazement. After the Captain stomped off, Tad winked at AB, "I thought that was what we were supposed to do."

Captain Paluuhi found Field First Sergeant Rubinal, " Tell the rest of 'em to fire at any friggin' thing out there they want to."

Chapter 19

Loa ambled up the stairs to the lanai. He paused to look out over the Quadrangle as Sergeant O'Conner brought the first platoon to parade rest. Loa had just returned from early morning sick call and had been instructed to rejoin his unit, as he had no fever – just a head cold. Loa had also just passed the main floor bulletin board where he noticed the company clerk post a fresh duty roster – and his name was on it! Battalion guard duty tonight! The other posted name was Private Allendale Burns.

Loa had missed the morning "Sweet and Sour Hour", which after all, was the primary objective of going on sick call. He looked for AB to inform him of their guard duty assignment.

"Hey, AB, did you check the bulletin board?"

"No.

"Well, we got tagged for Battalion guard duty tonight."

"Well, OK," hesitated AB.

This was a first for both of them. AB decided to check with Tad for the inside story on guard duty. He would need to *position himself* for this new assignment.

"Well," said Tad. "It's really not all that bad – except you have to report for regular duty the next day without much sleep. The key to guard duty is to get the right duty assignment. You know guard duty goes from 6 PM to 6 AM. You are on duty for two hours and off for four. The first relief is by far the best – 6 to 8 and 12 to 2AM. Then you are off for the rest of the night and get some sleep. Further, the Battalion Officer of the Day doesn't bug you during the first relief. He likes to show off to challenge the guards between ten and midnight. The worst duty is the third relief – 10 to 12 and 4 to 6AM. It stinks. Hardly any sleep at all."

"But, how do you get to be on first relief?" replied AB.

"You don't have much to say about it. The Sergeant of the Guard hands out the duty assignments and he KNOWS which are the best duty hours. He conducts the troop inspection before you go on duty. You better have your brass freshly polished, boots shined to a glow, and your best pressed Class A uniform. After that you are on your own."

Sergeant O'Conner later advised Loa and AB of the guard duty roster and sent them from field training back to the barracks by jeep at mid afternoon to prepare for inspection.

On the ride back from the pistol range, AB decided to share with Loa his knowledge of guard duty learned from Tad.

Loa seemed interested, but still somewhat indifferent to AB, who remembered Loa's haole comments on the first day at Schofield. AB decided he would use this guard duty assignment as an opportunity to get inside this guy's head. AB knew Loa was the only pure Hawaiian in the Company, and he wanted to get to know a little more about him.

A Field First Sergeant from the 51st Company was Sergeant of the Guard. He didn't appear to know anyone on guard duty that night. Inspection went well for Loa and AB, although four others were gigged for having red clay on the soles of their boots. AB and Loa somehow both got assignments to the second relief.

The Battalion guard room was equipped with five double bunk beds with mattress, no pillow, sheets, nor blankets – just a place to rest between guard assignments.

After their shift was completed, Loa and AB stretched out on nearby bunks.

AB searched his mind for some way to open the conversation. He well knew that Loa didn't much care for haoles. His only buddy in the Company was Ox who, in his mind, was not a REAL haole.

"Which one of the islands are you from?"

"Right here on Oahu."

"What did you do before you joined the Army?"

"I didn't join the Army. I was drafted just like you. I was a swimming pool attendant at the Moana Hotel on Waikiki. If I hadn't been drafted, they were going to make me a beach boy -- showing hotel guests how to surf."

AB decided to avoid the beach boy comment. "Tell me, Loa, you don't use pidgin English like some of the Islanders – how come?"

Loa hesitated, "I'll tell you why. I graduated from Jefferson High. We had haole English teachers – all of 'em sons-of-bitches – but you learned to talk right or you didn't graduate from Jefferson – no 'pau or mo betta' or any of that stuff."

Loa breathed heavily and continued, "You seem to want to talk about me. What about you? Why do they call you AB and how come you and Goldie are such big buddies?"

"OK," said AB, swinging his legs from the bunk and sitting up to face Loa. "First, Goldie and I are from the same small town in Florida. We didn't go to the same schools but we knew each other before we were drafted together back on October 15th. We both had Class A profiles – just what the Army was looking for at the time, to become Pineapples and take off for Schofield for infantry training."

Half Way There, Haole

"As to my name, you know it is Allendale Burns – AB is short for that. My mother had twin brothers, one named Allen and one named Dale. They both died in a car accident when they were in high school. I was supposed to be a twin also, but only one baby survived at birth. So I got named for both of my uncles that I never knew. And that's it. AB is easier to say than my full name."

"You want to know more about me?" said Loa. I'll tell you about me! First, let me say I really don't like haoles. You are a haole, but I'm going to tell you anyway. I've been waiting a long time to tell some haole this."

"You may not think so, but I know my history of this place – these Islands. I learned it at home and at Jefferson High. It wasn't only about one hundred years ago that we Hawaiians were the only ones here. We had a monarchy, a Queen, and our own government. We were doing OK, when those damned haole missionaries from Boston showed up with their ideas about teaching us their religion. Then some of 'em got to foolin' around with our women, married, and started to take our land."

"Then the haoles started to grow sugarcane – it was already here – as a field crop. They started to ship it out to the States and everywhere. The haoles tried to get the kanakas – that's us Hawaiians – to do the dirty field work, but we wouldn't. So what did they do? They went to China in the 1860's and brought the Chinks here as slave labor to do their field work. Paid them almost nothing and the haoles began to make millions on the crop. And these guys were missionaries! Then a guy name Whip – somebody—he was a real son-of-a-bitch, got smart and brought pineapples here to grow. Then they really needed a lot of slant-eyed Chinks to work the fields. The deal was that the Chinks were supposed to go back home after twenty or thirty years – but of course they never did. This place was still a lot better than working those rice paddies in China for some warlord."

"As they hung around here, many of the older ones started small businesses – mostly selling food and stuff to other Chinks. About 1900, the haoles went to Japan for more cheap labor. They made contracts with those Jap bastards to work for a specific period of time and then return to the homeland. Just like the Chinese, they stayed
around, some buying land, some intermarrying with the Hawaiians to get more land. You didn't see any Chinks marrying Japs – they couldn't stand each other. Later, some of the older Japs became involved in the labor union movement and became politicians. Both the Chinks and Japs sent some of their young people to the States for education. They came back as lawyers and other professionals and really all got involved in our government. Meantime the English, the Chinks, the Japs, the French, all have plans for these Islands becoming part of their Pacific empire. That's when, in 1898, the US government decided to take in the Islands as a Possession—mostly for military reasons to keep the Pacific for the Americans. Somewhere along in there, the Portuguese showed up as sailors with whalers and they settled in, mostly doing things related to shipping and boats. You didn't catch the Portuguese doing much of the dirty field work for the haoles."

"So what do we have now? Well, the haoles still own most of the land and they are looking to bring in Filipinos and a few Koreans to do the dirty field hand work, along with some Chinks and Japs. Because the Japs attacked Pearl Harbor, the US government decided to make them US citizens and keep 'em around to work the fields – they needed all of 'em. Some were drafted into the Army. Now with the Korean War everyone is a US citizen and subject to the draft and that's why I am here. I wanted to join the Navy – I'm a good swimmer – but the Navy won't let anyone from here in. You can be a house boy for a Navy officer, but who wants to do that?"

"Now do you see where I am coming from and why I don't like haoles? They keep talking about Hawaii becoming a state, but nothing is going to happen for a long time."

"And we haven't even talked about what the British did to Fiji. They brought in slave labor from India to work the sugar plantations. Took the land from the people and completely screwed up the place. The French did the same in Tahiti. We Polynesians have been worked over by the haoles – just like the native American Indians in the States – just ask Ox!"

AB paused. For the first time in a long time, he really didn't have a response.

The 2 to 4AM guard duty seemed to go on forever. No foot or vehicle traffic to challenge. There was plenty of time for AB to think about his conversation with Loa. No wonder he didn't much care for Tad, for Ching, for Kam, for Silva or anyone else from his Island homeland. As for Barrigan, Vinnie, and other haoles, it was a no brainer – particularly Barrigan with his big-city-know-it-all attitude. And Loa knew everyone from the Islands was a just another "Gook" to Barrigan.

No wonder Loa and Ox developed a relationship right off. AB recalled overhearing a latrine conversation between the two of them. They were discussing where the action was in Honolulu. Loa's suggestion was when they both got their first weekend pass, they would go to the Malacca Bar on Hotel Street where the favorite drink was the Singapore Sling. Loa explained that on the second floor of the Malacca was a combination tattoo and massage parlor. According to Loa, "After you get Singapore Slung – anything can happen upstairs."

AB continued to walk his assigned post – about fifty yards in each direction from the main entrance to the Battalion Headquarters building. Everything was quiet beneath an almost full moon. No sign of any of the usual tropical shower clouds hanging around the nearby mountain passes.

Chapter 20

Sergeant O'Conner spoke to the first platoon, "Men, tomorrow we leave for the three-day bivouac. You have the entire afternoon off to prepare for this. Your squad leaders have been given instructions. Be ready for the Buna Busses at 0900 tomorrow. I need to see Cohens right after this formation. Dismissed!"

Goldie approached Sergeant O'Conner. "You wanted to see me, sergeant?"

"That's right. Lieutenant Soong is leaving at 1300 hours with an advance party to the bivouac area. He asked me to volunteer a man to accompany Sergeant Rubinal and another man from the fourth platoon. You are to go with the team to help set up the Company command tent and equipment. Sergeant Rubinal will drive the jeep. There may be a couple of trucks. Have your full field pack ready to go by 1230 hours today."

Goldie said, "Yes sir," and turned to go toward the lanai.

"Oh, by the way, tell your squad leader about this assignment. And, who is your bivouac tent mate?"

"Forsythe and I are bunking together," replied Goldwire.

"That's fine, tell him you will meet him out there tomorrow. Your work with the advance party should be finished by the time the Buna Busses get there."

Goldie struggled with the full field pack, M-1 rifle and steel helmet. His ammo belt with poncho, bayonet, and filled canteen were all strapped to his waist. Maeva, from the fourth platoon arrived fully equipped in the day room, before Goldie.

"How'd you get picked for this duty?" asked Maeva.

"I can't even guess," said Goldie. "Maybe Sergeant O'Conner was pissed at me about something. I don't know. You never know about him."

"Why did Sergeant Mapa pick you?"

"I dunno," said Maeva. "I guess they won't need anybody to beat the drums on bivouac."

Sergeant Rubinal entered the day room in his usual rush. He carried his clipboard and flipped to the second page.

"Let's see," said the First Sergeant as he studied his notes. "You are Maeva and you are Cohens."

"Yes sir," they replied in unison.

"Lieutenant Soong wants this bivouac to go without a hitch. He wants it done right. That's why we are leaving today as the advance party to set up the command post. We'll have a jeep, a six-by-six truck to carry the equipment, and a tank truck to carry potable water for the troops. The water truck is down at the motor pool now being filled and should be back here by 1300 hours. The six-by is already out front with the tent and command post equipment."

"Lieutenant Soong got inside word from a buddy at Battalion Headquarters that Colonel Cottingham is planning to observe the 55th Company on this bivouac and the Lieutenant doesn't want anything to go wrong. Do you both understand?"

"Yes sir."

Lieutenant Soong entered the day room. All stood at attention and saluted.

"At ease, men."

Surprisingly, he shook hands with Maeva and Goldwire. He looked at the Samoan, smiled and said something about not needing drums on this trip.

"Let's go," said the Lieutenant.

The water truck was really a six-by-six with a tank temporarily mounted on the truck bed. The unit pulled to the curb as the team departed the building. Like the Buna Busses, the water tank truck and the six-by truck were driven by older drivers—US Army civilian employees.

All four advance party members placed their baggage and equipment in the back of the jeep. Goldie and Maeva were instructed to keep their rifles and to climb in the rear seat of the jeep, as Sergeant Rubinal spoke with the civilian drivers giving them final instructions and a map to the Bivouac Area C in the Waianae Mountains. The trucks pulled from the Quad K area, as the jeep was delayed while Lieutenant Soong gave last minute instructions to Lieutenant Fujimoto who was to bring the troop-filled Buna Busses the next morning.

Finally, all was in order and the jeep departed Quad K with Sergeant Rubinal behind the wheel. As they left the main entrance to Schofield, Goldie realized this was his first trip outside the compound since his arrival – which seemed like months ago. The jeep passed through the small town of Wahiawa and on through the countryside lined with fields of pineapple, then proceeded up the curving road toward the mountainous northern part of the island. The two advance trucks were not to be seen as the jeep turned from the paved road at a sign pointing to "Bivouac Area C." The rutted roadway, suitable for wide axle trucks proved to be a major challenge for the narrow wheel base of the jeep. Sergeant Rubinal held the steering wheel with white knuckles while the three passengers reached for the overhead support bars to steady the ride in the bounding jeep. The vehicle plunged into a deep cut in the roadway. The motor stopped – dead!

Half Way There, Haole

Sergeant Rubinal switched the key off and on; then the starter switch – nothing—totally dead!

"Oh shit," groaned the Sergeant. "Now what."

He crawled from behind the steering wheel and lifted the hood. Sergeant Rubinal had been with the 24th Infantry Division in Korea, and somehow escaped much of the terror of the Pusan Perimeter – and that was only about a year ago. This was a mere frustration.

The Sergeant glanced about the interior of the engine. Lieutenant Soong joined him in the mystery beneath the hood.

"I'm an infantryman, not a jeep mechanic. I don't know anything about what I am looking at," he murmured.

Lieutenant Soong was silent. He, too, was puzzled by the interior workings underneath the jeep hood.

"I can check the oil and water on a '48 Chevy. That's about it," commented the Lieutenant.

Goldie looked at Maeva, "What are WE supposed to do?"

Maeva hunched his shoulders as though to say, "Damned if I know."

Goldie eased from the back seat and exited the passenger side of the jeep.

"Sir, the way the motor stopped so sudden, it may be an electrical problem," said Goldie, approaching the open hood of the jeep.

Lieutenant Soong hesitated, then finally spoke, "Cohens, do you know anything about jeep engines?"

"No sir, this is the first one I've ever seen. I used to work some on a '38 Chevy school bus and a two-cylinder John Deere tractor. This don't look nothing like a John Deere."

"Well what do you think?" said Sergeant Rubinal.

"I think we should check the electrical system first, sir."

Lieutenant Soong could see things going terribly wrong on his first bivouac as Company Commander. There wasn't anything in the ROTC Training that offered instructions on repairing jeep motors. He had to get the bivouac command post set up and organized before dark. He trembled at the thought of the Colonel making an appearance to inspect the 55th Company in the field.

"Cohens," he said, "We got to figure this thing out. Get on with it."

Goldie checked the spark plug wires and the distributor system. Everything seemed OK. He crawled beneath the front wheels to see if there was any obvious damage from the rutted roadway. He lifted the hood to full upright position to check the battery and cables.

"Looks like this may be the problem, sir."

He showed the officer where the battery support frame had somehow cracked, allowing the battery to be partially dislodged from the frame. The negative battery cable was hanging loose from the battery post. Further, the post had somehow cracked and had a small split top to bottom.

"Got any ideas," said the Sergeant.

"Sir, I'll give it a try."

Goldie found a small wood chip along the forest roadside and wedged it in a place to bring the battery to a level position within the damaged frame. The battery cable could then be re-connected to the damaged post.

"Try the starter now, sir."

Sergeant Cabral returned to the drivers seat. It started – then, cut off immediately.

Goldie re-connected the cable to the battery post and held the cable in the appropriate position with his hand. The motor started. It continued to operate. Goldie tried removing his hand. The motor hesitated – then restored operation, but only after he held the cable in position.

Lieutenant Soong forced a smile, "It's obvious this thing is not going to run unless you hand hold that battery cable."

"We can do it, sir."

"How?"

"Well, I'll sit in the front passenger seat, wrap my arm with my poncho, put my arm around the windshield, and hold the cable in position while we get to where we are going. We'll have to go slow. Maeva, get a piece of wood to prop the hood open about six inches. Then get the tent rope from your shelter half and tie down the hood to the bumper so Sergeant Rubinal can see to drive. Sergeant, we got to take it real easy."

Within minutes the jeep was moving slowly up the mountain path toward the bivouac area. The Lieutenant joined Maeva in the rear seat – proud of their success. He made mental notes of Cohens' take-charge attitude, his problem-solving abilities, and his willingness to be awkwardly inconvenienced – holding his well-protected right arm around the front of the windshield and beneath the bouncing hood.

The advance party arrived at the site. Sergeant Rubinal parked the jeep beside the two trucks where the drivers napped. Lieutenant Soong leaped from the rear seat of the jeep. He and the Sergeant surveyed the area to determine their next move.

They ordered the supply truck to back up to a level area to unload the command post tent and equipment. The tent was easily raised and the wooden crates containing supplies and equipment placed inside. The officer supervised the two recruits in setting up the field tables and the standup operations desk, holding the rolls of detailed maps of the mountain area. Sergeant Rubinal removed the radio equipment, set up an antennae and established contact with the base radio operation at Schofield.

The first radio message was to the Schofield motor pool to advise of the damaged jeep and an immediate request for a replacement.

The tank truck backed to the nearby water tank – a large unit sitting atop a stack of timbers. There were pipes leading from the tank on each side with numerous outlets for troops to fill canteens.

The civilian employee hooked a fire hose to the truck tank pump and climbed the wooden timbers to place the hose in the overhead tank. He started the small engine and released the clutch to start the pump. Nothing happened! The motor operated, but the pump wouldn't move the water through the fire hose. He called the Sergeant to come from the radio equipment to explain the situation.

"Damn, what else can go wrong. We got to have water for these two hundred and fifty men arriving in the morning. Goddam the luck."

He called to Cohens. "You know anything about pumps?"

Goldie smiled, "I used to work on the irrigation pumps on the farm."

"Get on over here," ordered the Sergeant.

Goldie examined the situation. He stopped the gasoline engine and inspected the equipment. There were no valve handles to open or close. He re-started the motor, but the pump still would not deliver.

"I'll bet it needs to be primed. Maeva, take my helmet and go over to that little stream behind the tent and get me a bucket of water."

Maeva returned with a helmet of water. When Goldie poured the contents into the open pump valve, water started immediately to flow through the fire hose.

"Damn, Cohens, you really know what you are doing," said Lieutenant Soong. "Sergeant O'Conner knew what he was doing when he volunteered you to be with the advance party."

~

The four platoon sergeants of the 55th Company joined Field First Sergeant Rubinal at the standup table inside the steaming command post tent. On the table was a detailed map of Area C of the Waianae Mountains. The Sergeant brushed the red volcanic dust from the map surface with the back of his hand.

Outside, the recruits, organized by platoon, were on break – smoking and lounging in the tall grass. No one noticed the mid day cloud formations to the east. The first squad Guamanians had located the remains of a wooden ammunition box and were rolling dice against the inside of the box. It was several days to payday – no one was interested. Loa was telling Ox in vivid detail of the haole female from Atlanta he slept with in the most expensive suite in The Moana. Vinnie and Barrigan lay back in the tall grass, smoking and griping about the C Rations they had to eat for the mid day meal. They also complained about the lack of mashed potatoes. Zack reminded AB that he had brought some of the Immigration Forms and instructions – maybe there would be time to look them over. Forsythe and

Silva were listening to Goldie tell of his experiences the previous day with the jeep battery and the water pump. Everyone expected rice or noodles for dinner that night.

Sergeant O'Conner approached the lounging first platoon and called for the four squad leaders and Kam to join him at the jeep where he had unrolled a map on the hood.

"Kam, listen up." said Sergeant O'Conner. "You are going to help me with this. We are proceeding to different areas of this mountainside. We have to defend this entire area from the aggressors. You are going to have the first and second squads, and I'll be with the third and fourth. We'll set up platoon headquarters here (pointing to a spot on the map). The first squad will be the mortar squad and hike to this level area near the peak of the mountain. Fourth squad carries the backup radio equipment and stays with me along with the third squad....... You can pick up the mortar from the Supply Sergeant."

He hesitated, "Kam, have your men chow down on their C Rations and check their canteens for water. We leave here in forty-five minutes."

Kam instructed the second squad leader to move his men to the area behind the command post tent. Second squad was in reserve. The squad leaders checked their walkie-talkie radios.

"Zack" said Kam, "We got taksan work to do."

Zack was well aware of Kam's experiences in Korea – much like that of Sergeant Rubinal in the Pusan Perimeter area. Zack was more concerned about Kam's ability to communicate in the English language.

The first squad finished C Rations and began uploading back packs, ammo belts and rifles. The disassembled mortar lay on the ground nearby.

Half Way There, Haole

"All right," said Zack, "The first squad will take turns in carrying the mortar pieces. Kam has tied a loose tent rope to each end of the barrel. You throw this over your back pack and keep the loop of the rope in your hand. As far as the base plate is concerned, it's about fifty pounds of metal plate. When it comes your turn, you'll be on your own on how to tote it. I'll start off by carrying the base plate – then I'll pass it to Goldie and so on. Reyes, you're the tail end of this squad. You start off by carrying the barrel – then pass it on to Rapolla and so on to the front of the squad."

"There will be no bunching up on the trail. Keep ten to fifteen paces behind the man in front of you – just like you have been trained, as on patrol. But don't let the squad stretch out too far – no more than fifteen paces. We'll take a break in forty-five minutes. Does everyone understand?"

Kam studied the map, then proceeded with the squad up the narrow foot path carved along the side of a deep ravine. The path itself was relatively clear of jungle brush, but the mountainside was heavily wooded with short brushy trees. Everything seemed covered with vines and heavy undergrowth. The sagging humidity could be carved with a bayonet.

Zack carried the awkward mortar base plate for almost ten minutes. His forearms – even though heavily muscled – ached severely as he passed the plate to Cohens. Goldie, also thought he was in good condition, but he soon passed it to Barrigan.

Barrigan sagged. He nearly dropped it as he soon passed the monster to AB, who was convinced he would do his share regardless of how readily Barrigan handed it off. AB tried various means to handle the thing: first, he tried it in his left arm – carrying the metal plate like a fifty pound book. The backpack and the rifle obviously failed to balance the load. Secondly, he tried stuffing it in the front of his ammo belt, carrying it across his chest. That didn't work either. He finally settled on just carrying the plate with both hands in front of him like an overweight loaf of bread. That worked best but didn't last for long. He passed it on to Silva who had closed in behind him.

Within what seemed like twenty minutes, the barrel was passed up from the rear to AB. He threw the barrel over his back, held the rope and took off.

Zack held up his hand to signal the pre-planned break. In spite of instructions, the men grouped together and smoked in a secluded area along the trail. The base plate had already returned from the rear – to Silva.

Silva dropped the heavy metal piece at his feet and pulled a damp Lucky Strike from his soggy shirt pocket. For no particular reason, he turned the plate bottom side up. He read aloud from a metal tag attached, "This mortar base plate cost the U. S. Government $42.50."

Barrigan, resting on his back in the tall grass, overheard the Silva comment. He learned over and spoke quietly to Vinnie, "How much is $42.50 divided by fifteen?"

Vinnie thought carefully, "I dunno, almost three dollars, I guess."

Zack signaled for the squad to stand and proceed up the winding trail. AB reluctantly picked up the base plate and proceeded with the 'carry-it-in-front-of-you-like-the-loaf-bread' approach.

AB checked his watch and decided five minutes was his limit. He caught up with Barrigan and passed it off. AB slowed his pace to establish the required number of paces between squad members.

Within seconds there was a tremendous clatter. It sounded like a giant rock rolling down the side of the

Half Way There, Haole

mountain ravine. There was a splash of water. The first squad continued up the trail.

Kam finally signaled to the first squad. They were approaching the target bivouac area.

After what seemed like hours on the difficult ever-upward trail, the real surprise was the sight of Sergeant O'Conner standing near a chow truck – smiling and, of course, having a cigarette break.

"Kam, give the squad a ten-minute break. Then we'll set up the mortar and determine the perimeter for the squad defense of this position." A heavy mist began to roll from the atop the mountain.

Kam ordered Zack to set up the mortar. Forsythe stepped forward with the mortar barrel.

"Who has the base plate?" hollered Zack.

No one spoke.

"Who had it last?"

No response.

"I gave it to Loa," piped up Ox.

"I gave it to Tad," said Loa.

Tad was confused. "Just before the last trail break, I passed it to Josh."

And so it went. Barrigan claimed he gave the base plate to Goldie long after the break. Now Goldwire was confused. He recalled carrying the plate on at least four different occasions over the two and one half hour trail hike. All he knew it was returned to him by Zack after some reasonable period of time.

Sergeant O'Conner lost his cool. "All right, now somebody knows where the goddam base plate is. Who has it?"

Kam and Zack were confused and embarrassed.

Kam ordered the squad to fall into formation. He and Zack questioned each man individually, but to no avail.

AB had an opinion, but wasn't about to let it be known.

Sergeant O'Conner was furious, "You sonsabitches are going to pay for this. Payday is next week. You better be ready!"

It was late afternoon and the defensive perimeter of the first squad was yet to be determined. The sweating recruits assembled around Zack awaiting instructions. Four men were alerted to guard the designated squad post area while others were assigned to specific spot locations for erection of the two-man tents. Zack selected an elevated ledge on the mountainside for his site. He wanted to be able to observe each foxhole location.

The area was relatively clear of tropical underbrush. The soil was red volcanic ash. As instructed, the squad members retrieved entrenching tools from backpacks. The shovels appeared to just bounce off of the hard volcanic soil. Zack and AB traded efforts trying to dig in the hard soil formation. Finally, they moved the site about ten yards to an area where a streak of dark soil appeared. With much greater success, the foxhole was completed. Zack proceeded to make the rounds of the first squad to pass on information about how and where to dig foxholes. Each foxhole was to be at least six feet by six feet by eighteen inches deep.

Zack returned to AB and showed him how to pile and pack the loose soil in such a manner as to divert the flow of downhill water. He then took his bayonet and began cutting an armful of Johnson Grass. AB did the same. The grass was placed in profusion on the dirt floor of the foxhole, making the soil a dry 'mattress' on which to lay the poncho and blanket.

AB smiled, "Now I know why we are bunking together on this bivouac."

"Well," smiled Zack, "all you have to do is lay in a cold wet foxhole for one night and you know there must be a better way to survive this thing. That's one thing I learned in military school."

Zack and Kam relieved the men on guard duty, and ordered other squad members to assist them in preparing for the night exercise.

As Sergeant O'Conner arrived with the chow truck, it began to rain heavily. The troops were given trays as they formed a line near the rear of the truck. Rain pelted down as KP's served noodles with beef tips and soggy bread. The men sat as a group in ponchos. The rain continued to fall on the meal as rainwater filled the tray compartments while noodles and beef tips were spooned to hungry mouths. What could be more miserable?

Sergeant O'Conner instructed Kam and Zack to inform the squads that no two members of any tent team were to sleep at the same time. One was to stand guard while the other slept—alternating hours throughout the night.

Zack and Goldie visited each foxhole to relay orders. The downpour continued – both men doubted their sleeping instructions would be followed, as darkness closed in on the first squad.

Zack returned to his foxhole overlooking the perimeter. An occasional match, lighting a cigarette was the only real way to identify specific foxhole locations. The men had not been denied smoking privileges – after all, this was still their warmup bivouac for the 'big one' scheduled for Week 16 of training.

AB sat beside the tent, holding his M-1, and tried to keep dry beneath a floppy poncho.

"I'll take the first four hour guard shift while you catch some rest," said AB.

Zack didn't agree. He checked his watch. "I'll take two hours now. Wake me at 2300 hours and I'll change places with you."

"OK by me," replied AB.

Zack checked the interior of the covered foxhole. The tent had been well placed and was secure. Rainwater moving down the mountainside was diverted from the campsite, as engineered. He removed his damp poncho, stowed his M-1 and lay down on the pile of Johnson grass. It worked – a dry bed in a damp foxhole.

AB sat outside as the rain continued to pelt down. Maybe it was one of those kona tropical storms he had heard Tad talk about. There wasn't much to observe. He just sat there.

Maybe this would be a good time to sit back and review his situation, particularly in relation to his favorite pastime, *theory of positioning.* The fact is, unless something really changed, AB was "half way there" – on his way to Korea as an infantryman. If so, who in the first squad would he really want to go with? Who could he trust? First to come to mind was Tad. Tad seemed to be on top of any situation at all times – whether it was a mental or physical challenge. He could rely on Tad.

Close behind Tad were Goldie and Zack. Both were reliable and responsible. Josh Forsythe and Silva were good buddies, but lacked some level of self confidence and were followers rather than leaders. They would be ok, though. AB had discussed with Goldie, the experience with the jeep and water pump. AB was certain that Sergeant Rubinal and Lieutenant Soong saw something special in Goldie's practical hands-on approach to problem solving.

Half Way There, Haole

AB's mind wandered again – this mixing of haoles and Islanders for eighteen weeks of togetherness may well be a social experiment on the part of the Army. Sending Islanders direct to Korea from infantry basic training at Schofield with little or no exposure to haole leadership could quite possibly create major personnel problems with stateside-trained officers and noncoms who probably were running the war on the Korean Peninsula. Further, it was painfully obvious that the various Oriental groups in Hawaii were indeed still separated to some degree from each other by ethnic background. Over the years, there had been intermarriage with the native Polynesians by the Orientals – but little or no Oriental inter-relationship with each other. The Japanese clearly looked down upon all others – even Tad in his own way……..And what about home? No, he really wasn't homesick for Quincy. Certainly, he wanted to return to the family business. The Burns & Johnson business would be his some day and he could run the thing to his liking – without any parental direction. He knew he could do it! And, oh yes, he would want to find a challenging and rewarding place for Goldwire in his business. As planned previously with his father, Goldie would be sent to John Deere school for tractor mechanics   He would be a natural at that. He might eventually try to get Goldie involved in tractor and equipment sales. On second thought, that would probably be a real challenge – not so much for Goldie, but for the typical farmer-businessman in North Florida. Would they be ready for a black salesman? That might take some time to develop in rural Gadsden County. If anybody could be a black salesman, Goldwire could do it. With incentives, the Sales Department is where money could be made – both for the Company and for the salesman……have to think about that some more.

AB agreed with Barrigan and Vinnie on one thing – he has had enough rice – probably for the rest of his life! We are supposed to have potatoes once a week, at Sunday night supper. But what do the Chinese cooks do? They make what they call potato salad – it is really cold whipped potatoes and black olives with the pits still intact. Who ever heard of eating potato salad and spitting out the pits? Oh well, some day…

Some home cooking sure would go well one of these days…..

Speaking of home -- reckon I'll ever get there before going to Korea? Nobody is saying its not going to happen. And who has six hundred dollars to get to the West Coast and back? Last radio news out of Korea wasn't all that great. And what about that Senator Johnson from Texas who was supposed to be looking into this situation?

The wind began to pick up. The raindrops were now blowing sideways and running down the front of his shirt – soaking his T-shirt in spite of the poncho. He sneaked a peak at his watch – twenty minutes to go.

Goldie and Forsythe were both miserable. Goldie was supposed to be on guard as Josh slept. Their foxhole was a disaster – water at least four inches deep and still seeping in beneath the shelter halves. They had agreed to re-engineer the whole thing at day break.

Goldie sat outside, his poncho spread to protect from the downpour. He, too, thought about home and wearing his Class A khaki uniform. Come to think of it, he hoped it might be cool enough to wear his wools and Ike jacket. That would really look sharp on south Munroe Street!

Goldie felt good about the food situation. The rice was OK – he ate a lot of the stuff at home. That Sunday night potato salad crap had to go! And those black olive things with the pits –who ever heard of eating that stuff?

As for his position within the squad, he felt good about it. He'd seen a Japanese kid one time in Tallahassee – but beyond that he couldn't tell a Chinese from a Korean, from a Japanese, from a Guamanian. Where is Guam anyway? He would have to get a map somewhere. Samoans were OK – you could tell them apart. He liked Zack and Maeva.

Without much thought, Goldie had become more independent of AB. They still talked a lot, but not much of Quincy. He wanted to return to Burns & Johnson and get that promotion to tractor mechanic – he had toted enough bags of fertilizer.

"Josh, it's your turn to sit out here. I'm going to roll up in my poncho and try to sleep outside. We got to fix this hole in the morning."

Sometime, just before dawn, the rain suddenly ceased. A bright sun pushed over the mountain and into the damp and steamy tropics below. Water dripped from everything – pup tents and everything the first squad possessed.

Zack and Kam made the rounds of the living quarters of the squad. Barrigan and Vinnie seemed to be worst off – a foxhole with at least ten inches of water. The Guamanians, Reyes and Rapolla, were in great shape. Zack ordered most of the men to come to his own foxhole location and demonstrated the engineering technique of diverting water and use of Johnson Grass in the foxhole pit. He suggested to some – including Barrigan and Vinnie – to fill in the hole and start again. There would be time allotted after breakfast.

So it went on the first night of bivouac.

Chapter 21

Lieutenant Soong held a brief morning staff meeting in the steamy headquarters tent. He wanted a report from the four platoon leaders on how their men survived the heavy rains of the previous night.

Sergeant O'Conner was the first to report. He stood, holding a clip board with dampened lined paper.

"Sir, the first platoon survived the night with no major incident. Many of the recruits were soaked from spending the night in fox holes filled with rainwater. I did notice some of the locals survived much better than the haoles. Many of the local boys are familiar with heavy rains and some have camped out in the mountains before. They know how to pitch a tent by selecting a location protected from downhill streams of water, and to dig channels at the base of the tent to divert water away from the tent floor and the foxhole. I saw where a few of them had lined the foxhole with bunches of Johnson Grass as further protection from the dampness."

"Sir, I must report to you that the first squad, which had been designated as the mortar squad, failed to perform. When the squad was ordered to set up the mortar at the end of the trail climb, they could not do so. The base plate of the mortar could not be located. I know, sir, at the beginning of the day the base plate was in hand. The men of the first squad have been told they will pay for the missing base plate."

"Sir, Sergeant O'Conner continued, "I request that the first squad of my platoon be placed in reserve for today's planned exercises. It is my plan to drive the first squad to the base of the mountain in the mess truck. These men

Half Way There, Haole

should climb the trail a second time with full field pack as a reminder of their error."

Lieutenant Soong conferred with Lieutenant Fujimoto at the rear of the tent.

"Sergeant O'Conner, your request is granted. The first squad indeed should pay for their lack of responsibility. See Lieutenant Fujimoto at the close of this meeting for further instructions regarding a test of the squad by arranging for harassment as they climb the trail this morning."

"Yes, Sir."

Barrigan bitched. So did Vinnie. The first squad climbed into the mess truck.

"Why do we have to do this all over again? Nobody else in the 55th is climbing this friggin' trail again – and with full field packs, too."

Zack bristled, "Look, first squad was given a responsibility to carry the mortar. We fucked up. Somebody left that base plate somewhere on the trail. Maybe we will find it. I don't know. What I do know is that we're going to climb this trail again and I'm going to be doing the leading. Goldwire, you are going to bring up the rear. Barrigan is moved to the rear of the squad – behind Reyes and Rapolla and in front of Goldwire – and Goldie is going to put his boot up Barrigan's ass when he starts to lag behind."

AB looked at Tad. He had never seen Zack so pissed, and so in charge of the squad. Zack had obviously been criticized for lack of leadership and responsibility. Without Kam on this mission, he really was going to take charge.

Tad mumbled quietly to AB, "Zack got his ass in a crack."

"Ya, and we're all going to pay for it."

The mess truck pulled into the clearing at the base of the mountain trail. The troops slowly dismounted from the vehicle – rifles and field packs in place.

Sergeant O'Conner called Zack aside for last minute instructions. He approved of Zack's plan of special placement of men – especially having Cohens bring up the rear of the squad.

Zack looked at his Timex, "We take a trail break at ten-fifteen. Everyone keep ten paces from the man in front of you. DO NOT LAG BEHIND. Move it out."

The heavy rains had affected the footing on the trail. It wasn't going to be as easy as yesterday – even without the extra mortar pieces. With Barrigan in the rear, AB was now first man behind Zack. It was a pleasure, of sorts, to follow someone other than the clumsy, awkward, and stumbling Barrigan.

Zack held up his right hand – signal for the ten-minute trail break. The men kept the prescribed ten pace intervals, resting and smoking in place.

At exactly ten-twenty five Zack signaled the return to the trail hike. As the squad approached a gradual curve in the trail, Zack stopped briefly to observe the men in the rear of the squad. He signaled AB to keep moving up the muddy trail, but soon passed him – jogging as he returned to the squad point position.

That's when all hell broke loose.

A machine gun placement across the steep ravine on the opposite mountainside opened fire. All men instinctively hit the shallow and muddy ditch to the right of the trail and fumbled to position their rifles. The 30-calibre machine gun continued to rake the trail with blank ammunition. It then ceased as abruptly as it started.

A sergeant stepped from behind a vine-covered tree and pointed to Zack and AB.

"You and you are declared casualties. Do not move. Stay where you are."

He smeared a red chalk-like substance on Zack's right arm and on AB's lower legs. He disappeared behind the same vine-covered tree.

Silva, behind AB, at first nearly panicked. He couldn't speak. Then he sent a distress message to the rear, "Zack and AB have been hit – tell Goldwire to come up here --- now!"

Goldie proceeded cautiously up the trail, his M-1 rifle at the ready in a hip-firing position. He arrived at the scene with Silva and Tad close behind. Goldie ordered Josh to proceed fifteen paces up the trail and stand guard and look for any additional harassment. All others were ordered to maintain trail position with rifles at alert.

He approached Zack, then AB.

"You've been hit?"

"Ya."

He hesitated, further evaluating the situation, "Don't move."

"Tad, you tend to Zack. Make a sling for his arm out of your T-shirt. Sylva, take the bandage from your first aid kit and take care of one of AB's legs. I'll get the other one."

The first aid effort was completed in a matter of minutes.

"AB, can you walk?"

AB offered a weak smile, "Nobody said I couldn't."

Goldie turned to Loa, "Go find a walking stick for AB. Ox, cut a pole to carry the field packs of the wounded. String the pole with back packs. You and Loa carry the load between you."

"Tad, you're the assistant squad leader now. Go to the middle of the squad and keep everything together there. Watch for hand signals from me, and keep the rear of the squad up with the rest of us. Move Barrigan near you, but keep ten-paces between the men."

He paused, "Silva, you and Josh stay close to the wounded."

The squad moved out. The sergeant behind the vine-covered tree made mental notes of the activity.

~

The troops finally had a decent meal. It wasn't C-Rations and the rain had ceased. The ham and scalloped potatoes were devoured by everyone – includes the Islanders.

Lieutenant Soong spoke to the Company as the men stood at ease in platoon formation, "This afternoon we go on patrol by squad. First, though, you must have the experience of fording a stream of water. You will wade in water up to your belt, then pass through a low swampy area IN COMPLETE SILENCE while we seek out enemy positions. You will leave your field packs here with the trucks. Take your rifles, ammo belts and ponchos. After the patrol exercise you will pick up your field packs from the trucks and proceed to a level valley area where we will again dig foxholes – no more mountain exercises for this bivouac. Sergeant O'Conner, get the first platoon ready to leave in fifteen minutes. The other platoons will follow in about thirty-minute intervals."

Sergeant Rubinal and Lieutenant Soong preceded the first platoon down the road in a jeep. Kam lead the first platoon while Sergeant O'Conner brought up the rear – observing the movement and attitude of the men.

AB whispered to the man in the second squad marching beside him, "Do you hear that?"

"What!"

"The roar of the mountain stream up ahead."

"Is that what that is?" I'll bet that rain last night will make that stream look like a river."

Sergeant O'Conner jogged along side the platoon formation to catch up with Kam. "Hey, do you hear that mountain water up ahead? I'm not so sure about this whole thing."

Kam just kept on leading the troops and shrugged his shoulders in reaction to the Sergeant's comments.

The company commander's jeep pulled up near the roaring stream. Sergeant Rubinal and the Lieutenant were standing on the low bank looking at the white water scene. This was supposed to be a slow-moving three-foot deep mountain stream.

Kam approached with the first platoon in tow, "Hell, we can do this. Lemme' go first to checkie it out."

Sergeant Rubinal looked at the Lieutenant who was registering a look of great concern on his face. He hesitated.

Finally, Sergeant Rubinal spoke, "Let Kam go first, I'll follow to the far side. If I think it is ok, we'll do it."

Lieutenant Soong gave a nod of approval.

Kam searched his pockets and came up with two packs of Chesterfield cigarettes. He handed the packages to Sergeant O'Conner for safe and dry keeping, and waded into the white water. The 'over six-foot' Korean was soon in water over his ammo belt. He proceeded cautiously as the water raised to his arm pits. He edged slowly toward the high bank on the far side, turned and smiled, showing all of his teeth and gave it a big thumbs up.

Sergeant Rubinal selected a slightly different path about two yards downstream and proceeded. The water was chest high. AB carefully observed all this and decided when it came his turn he would target the Rubinal path.

Barrigan and Vinnie were sneaking an unauthorized smoke behind a cluster of palm trees.

The steep bank on the far side proved to be an additional challenge. Sergeant Rubinal sent Kam to the jeep to retrieve an entrenching tool. Kam forded the stream a second time and proceeded to dig toe holds in the steep muddy bank. He cut a hanging vine and secured it to the base of a tree, then threw it down the bank near the toe hold ladder. Sergeant Rubinal tested the makeshift ladder and pronounced it a go! He signaled the officers to send the first squad.

Sergeant O'Conner and Lieutenant Soong conferred. They decided the five-foot-three Guamanians would be exempt from this exercise, and directed Zack to lead the first squad into the water. The squad entered the water as ordered and in the established formation with Zack, Goldie, Barrigan, AB, Silva . . . . AB was convinced he would attempt the path established by Sergeant Rubinal, and moved several yards downstream where he followed Zack and others in front of him.

AB lifted his rifle above his head, as instructed, and soon was in white water above the waist. He looked up suddenly and was surprised to see a helmet liner bouncing in the water in front of him. What the hell was going on! He glanced upstream. Barrigan had disappeared! Zack was yelling, while Kam, standing on the bank, leaped into the racing water.

Barrigan's head suddenly popped up in front of AB – he was grabbing for AB's ammo belt and spitting muddy water in all directions. Kam appeared immediately and dragged Barrigan and his rifle to the stream bank near the toe hold ladder. Sergeant Rubinal retrieved the floating helmet liner from downstream. Barrigan struggled to regain his breath and hung to the nearby vine. Kam quickly climbed the bank and instructed the clumsy Barrigan to follow.

AB struggled to reach the muddy bank of the roaring stream, water nearly to his arm pits. Barrigan held the vine while Kam pulled him slowly up the side of the riverbank. The carefully dug toe holds disappeared as Barrigan used his KNEES in the toe holds to support the effort to get him to the top of the bank.

AB, and now with Silva close behind, took turns trying to climb the bank with the vine and the now-defunct toe hold ladder – so carefully prepared by Kam.

Sergeant Rubinal shouted, "You stupid shit, Barrigan, look what you have done – the toe holds are now just part of the muddy bank. That was for the entire company to use."

"Kam, take the entrenching tool and dig another track of toe holds. All you guys see what happened. Use your FEET to climb the ladder, not your knees."

The stream fording exercise was completed without further incident, and the silent 'swamp patrol' by squad finally got underway. Kam and Zack gave instructions – particularly about the need for complete quiet movement through the area. It was not easy terrain to cover, as the recent storm had downed a number of trees. Kam carefully selected the route through the downed tree limbs, but at one point there was no choice but to climb through the downed tree branches. He showed Zack by hand motions how to step on two branches with both feet at the same time and then proceed. The technique was passed on to Zack and Goldie, who carefully demonstrated the two-feet-on-a limb routine to Barrigan. The clumsy one immediately created the second scene within the hour, for the patrol. He misjudged the position of his left foot, causing the right foot to slip and jerking up the tree branch in such a manner that it caught Barrigan by the ammo belt and lifted him two feet in the air.

"Help, somebody come and get me loose from this sonofabitch."

The silence of the patrol was broken, as Kam cussed and returned to get the dangling Barrigan back to ground level.

Lieutenant Soong appeared from nowhere.

"Barrigan, you're a dumb bastard. You have completely screwed up the day's training exercise. Corporal Kam, have Barrigan report to me when we get back to the barracks tomorrow."

"Yes, sir," said Kam.

~

Sergeant O'Conner called the platoon to attention, as he made squad leaders aware of areas for digging foxholes for the last night of bivouac.

"Now look, you guys, there is a Dole pineapple field just beyond the tree line in back of me. There is a strand of barbed wire with "No Trespassing" signs. You now have a direct order from the Company Commander to STAY OUT OF THE PINEAPPLE FIELD."

The foxhole-digging routine was relatively simple in comparison with the dark red volcanic mountain soil. The level-land soil was easy for trainees to prepare shelter for the

Half Way There, Haole

last night. Most gathered Johnson Grass to make the two-man shelters more comfortable.

The next morning came almost instantly.

Reveille was held with a platoon formation and a formal headcount by squad.

There never was any question as to who had raided the pineapple field – each culprit had a telltale and painful red rash ringing his lips and cheeks. Unbeknownst to all, the pineapple field had been recently chemically sprayed! Breakfast for most of the first squad was a painful non-event. All Islanders, except Zack, but including Vinnie and Barrigan, and a most-embarrassed Kam, were hurting.

Sergeant O'Conner called for the platoon to meet with him informally. "Relax, smoke 'em if you got 'em. You guys had a direct order about the pineapple field. I hope all of you – and that includes you, Kam – enjoyed your little game last night. Nobody is going on sick call for a sore mouth. You can just have a good time with it all day, today. Good luck! Now, the Buna Busses are going to be here around 1100 hours. I suggest you spend some time getting your equipment in order. Scrape off the red mud from everything you can. We'll have an equipment inspection Monday – be ready."

"One other thing, Zack, have Private Burns report to Lieutenant Soong at the command post tent in ten minutes."

AB stiffened. What had he done? It was Barrigan who screwed up yesterday.

He straightened his fatigue uniform, scraped some of the red mud from his boots, felt his jaw and wished he had taken time to shave earlier.

"Private Allendale Burns reporting as ordered, sir."

"At ease, Private Burns," responded Lieutenant Soong. Lieutenant Fujimoto was at his side, as usual. Both were sitting behind the field table on folding chairs in the command tent. AB assumed the at-ease position – feet apart, hands behind back, looking straight ahead.

Lieutenant Soong spoke with authority. "Private Burns, we received a memo yesterday from Central Personnel that you had applied for a Scientific and Professional Army assignment. Is that true?"

Taken aback, with a puzzled look on his face, AB finally responded, "Yes sir, I did -- maybe about sixty days ago."

Lieutenant Fujimoto spoke up, "Private Burns do you really have a college degree?"

"Yes, sir."

"Then what are you doing taking infantry basic with all these people?"

"It is a rather complicated story. At one time I did have a Navy commission, but I don't think you want to spend the time now on the details of this, sir."

"OK," said Lieutenant Soong, "We'll get to that some time later. Right now this is to inform you that you are being considered for this assignment, but only after successfully completing the infantry training course here at Schofield. Where did you go to school?"

"I have a BS degree in Economics with a minor in Business Administration from Allegheny College – that's in Pennsylvania."

"Can't say as I have heard of Allegheny! Thank you Private Burns."

"Thank you, gentlemen," replied AB, snapping to attention with a sharp salute.

AB returned to the platoon area wondering if Lou Sample had heard anything from Central Personnel. He decided to continue to cover himself by further not revealing his background to other members of the squad. *So much for his theory of positioning – right out here in the Wainai Mountains of Oahu.*

Chapter 22

The barracks at Quad K never looked better. The mud-covered Buna Busses pulled up to the blue 55th Company sign. The Chinese cooks were leaning on the railing near the garbage cans – just like they were when the Pineapples arrived, many weeks earlier. The grungy troops unloaded slowly from the rear gates of the Buna Busses, rifles and mud-covered field packs somehow in order.

The hot shower line extended from the shower room, through the latrine and out onto the lanai.

Zack, AB and others decided to stretch out on their bunks until the shower line disappeared – evening chow wasn't available until after 1800 hours. The once highly buffed barracks floor was a mass of muddy clothing and equipment. All shelter halves, ponchos, field packs and ammo belts would have to be scrubbed with stiff brushes in the showers and in the two small mop sinks. And then – there was to be a cleanup detail assigned to scrub down the mud-encrusted latrine. The next few hours, and maybe days, were not going to be a fun time at Quad K barracks.

Tad plugged in his radio. He missed his tunes. Patti Page was singing, "Tennessee Waltz." The announcer continued, "There is a strong rumor making the rounds at Schofield that Miss Patti Page is bringing a live show to The Bowl at Schofield soon after the holidays. We'll keep you posted. And now for some news from Korea. Fighting continues near the 38th Parallel while at the same time Panmunjon Peace Talks continue with no progress to report."

Goldie asked what the 38th Parallel was.

"I'll show you on the world map in the dayroom sometime," replied Silva.

Half Way There, Haole

Tad lay on his upper bunk. He leaned over the side to ask AB, "What did Lieutenant Soong want? You got a problem?"

"Naw, they're checking on personnel records and had some questions."

"Right in the middle of bivouac?"

"Yes, who knows why the army does things when they do."

Tad wasn't exactly satisfied, but he let it lay for now.

Corporal Chang appeared in the door near Sergeant O'Conner's room and announced, "First platoon mail call."

The shower line and all others converged on the mail clerk. The three-day mail accumulation took much longer than usual to dispense the word from home – there seemed to be letters for all the haoles and a few of the locals – some getting three or four.

Zack eagerly opened his one letter. It was from his wife in Samoa. He read carefully line by line. Reference was made to a large brown envelop mailed the same day containing important papers – certified copies of New Zealand birth certificates for Melanie and little Moana. The brown envelop did not accompany the letter, and mail call was over. Zack was frustrated.

Corporal Chang was CQ that night. As he passed through the first squad sleeping area to remind all that lights go out in fifteen minutes, Zack approached the Corporal regarding the brown envelop.

"Oh, ya, I think I saw that. It was with the wrapped newspapers and other bulk mail. I didn't have time to sort all that shit. I'll get around to that in a couple of days."

"A couple of days!"

"Ya, and don't fuck with me, Private – especially when I have CQ duty."

Zack lost his cool, doubling up his fists. In an instant the Corporal was draped over the nearby rifle rack, his mouth bleeding and eyes blinking.

Vinnie, Goldie, and AB immediately were at the scene, trying to separate the two, and to assist the surprised Corporal Chang.

At reveille, Zack was ordered to report to Sergeant Rubinal. He was immediately relieved of his squad duties and informed that a general court martial hearing would be scheduled in about two weeks. It all happened so fast. Zack was dazed.

Lieutenant Soong was the first to speak, "Private Marley's actions are completely disappointing and out of order. Maybe that British military training in New Zealand is different from what I thought it was. We can't have him set an example for anyone in the 55th Company as a squad leader."

"Sergeant O'Conner, you are ordered to put Private Marley on restricted quarters and extra duty until the court martial hearing. Maybe he would like to clean the latrine of all the bivouac mud. You are further ordered to appoint Private Cohens squad leader of the first squad. Private Cohens exhibited outstanding leadership skills while on bivouac. The selection of the assistant squad leader is to be at your discretion."

"Yes sir," replied the Sergeant. "I propose to promote Private Sato as assistant squad leader."

"Your suggestion is accepted."

In the first platoon formation of the day, Sergeant O'Conner instructed Goldwire and Zack to change places in the squad formation. The platoon was advised of the change in leadership, but Tad was instructed to remain in his squad

Half Way There, Haole

position next to Josh Forsythe so as not to disrupt completely the squad formation of graduation by height.

AB decided he would talk to Zack and Goldie at the first cigarette break.

"I lost it, AB. It looks like I may have really screwed up everything with my plans to bring my family here. We never did get to work on the immigration forms while on bivouac. I guess I should have known there wouldn't be any time for that. I'm sick. I'm restricted to the barracks until my hearing. I have extra duty. I'm assigned to get all the red mud out of the latrine by myself on after-duty hours. I have really screwed it all up."

AB hardly knew how to respond. "Well, maybe you really have made a mess out of everything. If you don't have extra duty on Sunday afternoon, let's go to the dayroom, lay out all the papers, and get this immigration thing done."

"OK" was all Zack could reply. After a pause, he quietly added, "I wish Goldie well as squad leader. I know he can do it."

AB redirected his thinking. Why not let Goldie come to him? Goldie was the leader now. It wasn't but four months ago that AB was giving instructions to Goldwire: unload this truck of peanuts; fix the conveyer belt in the peanut warehouse; drive this semi trailer of peanuts to the Gold Kist warehouse in Marianna; we're working extra hours, there is a hurricane in the Gulf south of Panama City; get the John Deere and drive this wagon load to the peanut dryer; see all of you at seven AM sharp tomorrow; go help Albert and Raymond unload that 20-ton fertilizer truck . . . .

~

Sergeant Rubinal's order to resume the speed march brought AB's mind back to reality. The speed march with light field pack was just the beginning of an accelerated effort to bring the 55th Company into a second and final phase of conditioning. It was early in the day, but legs were tightening from the strain. The FULL field pack routine would come next week, when the Company would RUN to Kolekole Pass and back. The cadre were getting serious about having everyone ready for duty in the mountains of North Korea – no question.

Goldie approached AB as they finished another meal of the army version of spaghetti as prepared by the Chinese cooks, and eaten from mess pans toted to the field by all, just for that purpose.

"I don't mind eating out of this mess kit pan," said Goldie. "It's just like sitting on that old truck seat in the scale room at the warehouse – except Pocket, Raymond, and Albert ain't around. I sorta' miss those guys."

AB knew Goldie really wanted to talk about something else. The reference to the Quincy warehouse was just part of a cover.

AB, ignoring the comment, responded, "Congratulations on the promotion. You have earned it. You have a knack for leadership and you can handle every one of the guys in the squad. That includes working with Kam and the platoon sergeant."

AB continued, "Look, everyone knows you and I are kinda' close. We came into this thing together. I expect you to treat me like anyone else in the squad."

Goldwire gave a sigh, acting somewhat relieved.

"OK," and then with a typical Goldwire grin, "Mister AB."

"Smartass."

~

Vinnie and Barrigan griped about the lousy Chinese spaghetti, but ate it all and went back for seconds.

"Well, I don't look forward to taking no orders from a lousy nigger, but I guess we don't have no choice, Vinnie" said Barrigan. "You know it wasn't but two or three years ago that the Army kept all them niggers together in the same field unit. This is a new experience for the most of these guys and some of 'em can get big ideas if they get to order a bunch of white guys around."

Barrigan continued, "I figure we got a few more weeks of this training shit here in Hawaii. Taking an order from a nigger ain't much different that takin' an order from a Gook. They're all the same. Sergeant O'Conner is one of us, and look at what a bastard he can be. I want to see what the nigger does when it comes to handing out duties on shit details – you know he is going to look after his number one buddy, AB."

"You got that right."

Loa and Ox stood beside each other in the squad formation. They were seldom seen apart. They seemed to just ignore everyone else. They both accepted orders from anyone in authority without much reaction – just a job they had to do.

Loa commented, "Zack isn't from these Islands, but he is one of us. At first, I couldn't hack all the British military school crap he came out with. I told him so one day. He backed off and said to give him a break. Since then, he has been ok by me. He really screwed up by punching out that Chinee corporal, but that guy had it coming. He is a wise ass. I don't know about Cohens. I didn't grow up with no black guys – there just wasn't any 'round my neighborhood. He's still a haole, but if I were you I wouldn't call him no nigger."

Ox spoke up, "I don't intend to. There are plenty of black people in North Carolina. They know their place, just like us natives do. That doesn't mean we like it. Plenty of them black women like us native guys – we do all right. I'm not so sure about Cohens. I heard him tell Josh one day he worked a crew in the tobacco fields. He hadn't better treat us guys here like no field hands. I know how that goes and I don't want any part of it. I say give him a chance. Then there is that smart guy, AB. He and Cohens arrived here being big buddies – we'll see."

The speed march back from Kolekole Pass wasn't any easier, even though much of it was downhill. The exhausted troops stood in company formation outside Quad K barracks.

Sergeant Rubinol spoke, "Men, this is pay day. Go to your quarters upstairs, dump all your gear and come back down here in ten minutes. You all know by this time the payroll records are in alphabetical order. The Company clerk will get you in the right order, with the assistance of the squad leaders. Dismissed."

The dayroom had been rearranged for the payroll event. All furniture was moved to the area near the pool tables. There were two long folding tables with wool army blanket carefully arranged atop. Lieutenant Fujimoto sat behind a stack of currency – twenties, tens, and fives. To his left was Lieutenant Soong with a long list of names and money amounts. At the end of the table was Sergeant O'Conner with a small stack of one dollar bills. The number of men in the room was carefully controlled by Sergeant Rubinal -- standing just outside the dayroom entrance. There was total silence in the hallway of the alphabetically arranged recruits.

Half Way There, Haole

The line moved slowly but in military fashion, with most of the first squad of the first platoon appropriately in alphabetical order.

AB approached Lieutenant Wong and saluted, "Private Allendale Burns, US 52113169 reporting for pay, sir,"

"Seventy-five dollars," responded the Lieutenant.

AB stepped aside and in front of Lieutenant Fujimoto who quickly withdrew three twenties, a ten, and a five. He surprised AB with a small hint of a smile as he handed him his month's pay. Sergeant O'Conner beckoned AB to the end of the table.

"That will be three dollars for the mortar base plate." He offered to exchange two one dollar bills for a five. AB complied without comment and turned to leave the room. He climbed the steps to the second floor. *What more could happen in twenty-four hours?*

Chapter 23

The holidays came and went. It really didn't seem much like Christmas. There was a traditional holiday meal with turkey and dressing – no rice and no pineapples, this time. There was a printed menu, even though everything listed on the menu wasn't available. All this to impress the Schofield Commanding General with family, and his visiting Air Force General and family from Hickam Field. The first platoon had somehow escaped the long hours of holiday KP duty.

With time for weekend passes, Ox and Loa finally made it to the Malacca Bar on Hotel Street and got Singapore Slung. Ox returned to the barracks with a matching miniature tomahawk tattoo on the other butt cheek.

Zack was restricted to the barracks. AB decided to pass on previously made plans for a two-day stay at Fort DeRussy on Waikiki Beach. Early Christmas morning they did sneak out to play several sets of tennis at the officers' courts near the swimming pool complex. The locals disappeared for most of the holiday period – much to some haole resentment.

During the holidays, the long-awaited move by the third and fourth platoons to the third floor of the building was accomplished. Double deck bunks were eliminated – Tad no longer slept on the bunk above AB – just to his left. The extra space and with only half as many troops to use the latrine, made for some level of peace and quiet not seen before. Tad was given the bunk location near the electrical wall outlet in order to provide continued use of the radio which was now carefully mounted beneath his own bunk with duct tape and cord.

It was announced that the upcoming Saturday would be a big event. The 40th Battalion would graduate from eighteen weeks of infantry training and there would be a parade in celebration of the event. The Commanding General would have Admiral Radford as his guest and there would be artillery available for a seventeen-gun salute for the Admiral.

Rumors that ninety-five percent of the 40th Battalion was going to FECOM raced through all companies of the 50th Battalion at Quad K. Further, Tad's radio news reports were discouraging. Most of the first squad gathered around Tad's bunk to listen to a news report that major replacements were needed in Korea, as numerous National Guard and Reserve units called up early in the war were now returning to the States. Many newly-trained infantrymen would be needed for replacements. And some UN troops from Australia, New Zealand, Turkey, and Colombia had completed time assignments and were due for rotation.

"There is no question," said Josh, "Schofield is half way there to Korea. If those National Guard Units are leaving, we're dog meat for the front lines. Maybe we should start a rumor that the 50th Battalion is going as a unit – along with cadre and officers. That should get the attention of the cadre locals with the soft jobs."

"That will be the day," responded Barrigan. "Hey, it's a great idea. Let's start the rumor mill right now. I can see the headlines in the Honolulu newspaper – *50th Battalion at Schofield Goes to Front Lines in Korea.*"

The CQ flicked the lights and Tad turned off the radio. It would be dark, but not quiet as the bitching about FECOM continued endlessly into the night.

The latrine lights, however, remained on as Zack continued to struggle with cleaning the red mud from the shower floor tiles. The grout between the tiles was severely stained, requiring much effort on hands and knees with a scrub brush. The tedious work with toothbrushes was beginning to show progress as Zack worked on the final shower corner to be done. A work detail from the second platoon had scoured the latrine area and the mop sinks – the shower work had to be done when showers were not in use – which was seldom. Zack finished at 1130 hours and fell exhausted into his bunk. He was reminded of work details at military school. That seemed like years ago.

His court marital was scheduled for Wednesday morning. A Captain from another Battalion had been assigned as his counsel. A board of three officers from 50th Battalion Headquarters was to hear the case. AB was to be a character witness. Zack had visited Chaplain Goodman on two occasions. The Chaplain had advised him to "be honest, tell the truth, and very little would come from the incident."

The Chaplain was right. The case was essentially dismissed, with a thirty-five dollar fine. AB was available, but never was called to testify. Zack was denied any future leadership positions for the balance of the training cycle. His plans to attend Leadership School were dead as he would not be recommended by 55th Company officers. Zack, however, still planned to bring his family to Oahu, even though his Army career could be in jeopardy. All this had been discussed with AB in a Sunday afternoon in the dayroom as immigration forms were finally completed. Zack had temporarily put on hold any arrangements for a freighter voyage for his family to Pearl Harbor from Samoa.

Sergeant Rubinal spoke to the entire company formation. "Now, listen up, everyone. The parade this Saturday is an important event. The 40th Battalion is graduating. The Commanding General is making a special event out of this one. His guest is Admiral Radford and the General will be showing off how sharp Hawaiian Infantry Training can be. There will be a 17-gun salute from an artillery unit and the

HITC marching band will be at its best. The 50th Battalion will be recognized, and in a way this will be a practice session for our graduation in about six weeks. Colonel Cottingham has been observing all the companies within his command and his staff has selected the 55th Company to be the honor unit. We will lead the 50th Battalion in this week's parade. You guys are going to be good and you will get it right. Is that understood?"

The Sergeant repeated louder, "Let me try it again, IS THAT UNDERSTOOD?"

"Yes, Sir," yelled the 55th in unison.

Barrigan had to respond with some kind of comment, "Now ain't that a bitch. The 55th is going to be the honor company and the first to lead off this sonofabitch. I can remember when we looked like a bunch of stiffs."

Loa winked at Ox, "Some of us still look like stiffs – particularly that haole bastard that is sounding off."

Saturday morning inspection was scheduled a half hour early in order to have everyone in first class appearance and to allow time for needed corrections.

With Class A khakis and necktie, polished brass and shined boots, the first squad passed inspection with colors flying. The first platoon behind the Battalion and Company officers would actually lead the parade.

Sergeant O'Connell addressed the first platoon, "Now look, it is already a hot day out there and we haven't even started all the marching and the standing at attention. When we get to the parade ground for assembly with the other HITC units, you will see the medics there with stretchers and ambulances. If the guy next to you flakes out and falls on his face – you DO NOT DO ANYTHING. Let him fall on his face or his ass – just don't do anything but stand there eyes straight ahead as though nothing has happened. The medics are there to pick up the fallouts – that's what they do."

"Now, we will march with fixed bayonets. All you do is hope it isn't the guy behind you that falls on his face with his rifle in hand and rips your ass with a bayonet on the way to the grass. That is a chance you take when you joined the infantry."

As the 55th approached the parade field, they could hear the post band practicing behind the reviewing stand. Sergeant Rubinal stepped up the volume of his marching tempo in order to prevent the troops from picking up the step from the beat of the drum, rather than the tempo he had established. It worked!

The Battalion stopped abruptly at the prearranged spot at the end of the parade field. Other marching units approached and did the same. The medics were nearby – and on standby.

At the designated second, the band struck up a familiar Sousa March, and stepped sharply onto the field. The recruits followed with bayonets flashing in the bright morning sun. They were led to a designated spot ready for the review of the Commanding General and his Admiral guest.

AB had never seen an army olive drab painted jeep with white sidewall tires. But there it was, especially equipped with a stand-up bar for the two officers to grasp as the jeep driver with long white gloves aimed the vehicle past the "eyes straight ahead" troops. The band suddenly changed to a swing version of "Charmaine" in honor of the Admiral's wife. The Admiral had to be impressed!

Sweat poured from around every knotted necktie, from every armpit and down the inside of every leg, as the two officers approached the steps to the newly-painted reviewing stand. From nowhere, came the thunderous roar of the 17-gun salute --howitzer rounds belching clouds of white smoke.

Everyone reacted to the booming guns, knees knocking.

"Look straight ahead, you bastards," mumbled Sergeant O'Conner.

The speeches began, congratulating the 40th Battalion on their graduation. The fallouts also began – Vinnie was the first to go, then Silva. Somehow, Silva lay flattened to one side. AB had instinctively made a first move to catch his falling partner, but at the last split second he reacted and stood his position.

Sergeant O'Conner mumbled from the side of his mouth, " Don't any of you bastards move."

The alert medics gathered the weapons and limp bodies and moved the victims to the rear where they were joined by numerous others suffering the same fate. An ice pack on the back of the head had accomplished miracles.

The speeches continued and so did the trainee fallout. Finally, the band again trooped the field followed by the white-sidewalled jeep and its shining brass. Local families of the 40th Battalion crowded onto the field with flower leis to congratulate favorite sons. The remains of the 55th returned to Quad K with the thought with many of the men, that the next one of these parades would really be in their honor.

Sergeant Rubinal held the men in formation at the request of Lieutenant Soong.

"Gentlemen," said the officer, "you can be very proud of yourselves today. The 55th has come a long way in their military presence. The Commanding General has already sent a message of congratulations by special messenger. The weekend is yours! Overnight passes are available for everyone not assigned to KP or guard duty. See the First Sergeant for your pass. Company dismissed."

All the sweat and preparation had paid off. AB and Zack, now off restrictions, immediately began to make plans to spend the weekend in Honolulu.

"AB, I've got it all figured out. We catch a bus to downtown Honolulu and check into the YMCA – that only costs a couple of bucks. If we're lucky we might even get a room with a bath. If not we'll take whatever we can get. We need to get there as soon as possible. We'll get some real food at a restaurant and take off from there."

The line at the Y was long, even though AB and Zack had made every effort to get there ahead of the crowd.

"We may have to go to Fort DeRussy after all. I hope not. I have stayed there before. The location is great, but it is just like another wooden army barracks in a room with twenty-four other guys and a latrine down the hall. You have to be up at 7:30 and make up your bunk army style. It's not really much of a weekend off from the regular army routine even though it is right on Waikiki Beach."

The line at the Y moved on and a room for two was available – no bath. Zack and AB signed on, as an Hawaiian band struck up a Polynesian tune in the nearby outdoor atrium.

Zack wheeled around, "Hey it's a concert by the house band from the Royal Hawaiian Hotel. Let's check it out before we go to the room."

"Why not," replied AB. Zack was already coordinating some body moves with the familiar rhythm. AB sat on the steps, enjoying the scene – sensing that this was some of the real Hawaii he had not yet really experienced.

"Let's go down to a restaurant on Waikiki and get some real Polynesian food."

Zack ordered for both. There was raw salmon wrapped in a steaming roll of seaweed, some deep friend shrimp with a cabbage-like vegetable and poi.

AB devoured everything but the poi – it reminded him of the art class construction paste from a quart jar, doled out by his kindergarten teacher and sampled by all.

AB initiated the dinner conversation; something he had wanted to do for a long time. "Tell me about growing up in Samoa."

OK…..I was born in what is now British Samoa, but we moved to American Samoa several years later. That's why my birth certificate and passport are so screwed up. My father is a land owner in American Samoa and owns a dairy farm. He has several hundred acres of land by the seashore that is pretty much tropical jungle. My father made good money during the war with your government. He conducted a sort of tropical island orientation for US Marines and Army officers. He went to military school in New Zealand, like I did. He showed the Marine officers how to train their men in survival techniques in the Pacific Island jungle terrain. I used to help him some, as a fourteen and fifteen-year-old. I showed the officers what jungle foods were edible and what to stay away from; how to fish in the surf and how to crack coconuts with a rock – drink the milk and scoop out the meat. We also identified poisonous lizards and snakes to stay away from."

"Out of all of this I learned to hate my father. He ordered me around just like one of the Marines. After that he sent me to New Zealand military school just to get me out of the way. Some day that land will probably be mine. I wanted him to send me to an agricultural school in Trinidad to learn how to grow tropical fruits and coconuts for export, but he wouldn't let me do it. He just wanted me as a farm hand at the dairy."

"And…..how about you?"

"Well," hesitated AB, "I have some trouble getting along with my father too, but nothing like you. My dad runs his own farm supply business and works hard at it. He just didn't have much time to spend with me as a kid – always something to do with work at the office, the warehouse, or in the tractor shop. I was working for him in the business when I was drafted into the Army."

Zack heard a ship's horn. "Hey, let's go down to the passenger pier. That sounds like the signal from the 'Matsonia' – a ship I used to work on."

On the way to the pier, Zack explained how he used to be an entertainer as part of the ship's crew – a knife dancer in the Polynesian nightclub act. The sister ship, "The Lurline" was in dock making preparation for a Sunday departure. Zack and AB climbed the gangway in their Aloha shirts where they were met by a friendly crew member. They were invited to come aboard.

Zack was familiar with "The Lurline" and offered AB a complete eye-revealing tour of every deck. They climaxed the tour in the nightclub where the Polynesian band and dancers were practicing a new routine. Zack was invited to join in.

Dressed in a borrowed lavalava, lowered to reveal the railroad track scars below the belt and carrying a machete, Zack leaped from the stage to the dance floor and gyrated violently to the beat of the Samoan drummer. AB sat on a nearby barstool in complete awe of the scene. Was this really his squad leader—make that former squad leader?

Chapter 24

The 30-mile hike scheduled for Week 16 in the Wainaie Mountains had been discussed – and discussed – by the squad since first revealed to the troops back in December. The planned five-day expedition couldn't be any more challenging than the first three-day adventure in the mountains, according to many in the first squad. Maybe it wouldn't rain for five days in a row!

The CQ had already turned off the barracks lights, but Josh and Goldie continued their conversation while sitting on footlockers in GI underwear. It was unusually warm in the squad bay this February evening. They had both just listened to the Korean War news on Tad's radio. It wasn't good news. A Peggy Lee tune was playing, 'Just One of Those Things.'

I just don't look forward to more days in the red mud and the mountains," groaned Josh.

"It's all just part of getting us ready for the Korean mountains – except there it will be cold as hell in the winter," replied Goldie.

Josh continued, "Do you remember that session we had at Camp Stoneman about how to escape from behind enemy lines? I still think about I sometimes. Ya' reckon we'll ever have to face up to that?"

"I sure do remember that thing. Like the part where your best chance to escape is within the first few hours after capture, and how you stretch out the line of march so you can make a dive for the underbrush in a curve in the trail. And when you jump off the train – make sure it is on the right hand side as the train moves, so the North Koreans have to shoot at you left handed."

"Ya', I remember," said Josh. "Wish there was some way to have a small light here in the barracks. I'd like to read my Bible at night. Don't you read the Bible?"

"Ya' sometimes," replied Goldie. "The Salvation Army gave me a New Testament when we got on the bus in Quincy. I don't much like the chapel service here. I been a couple of times but it's not like I'm used to on Sunday. At home we're in church for a couple of hours with a lot of good singin' – then if the weather is good we have 'dinner on the ground.'"

"You are kidding," said Josh. "We have 'dinner on the ground' with lots of fried chicken, fried okra, macaroni and cheese, potato salad and biscuits."

"That's the same thing we have in Quincy –'dinner on the ground' with lots of fried chicken. If you're lucky you might get a piece of coconut cake."

"I'd settle for a 'dinner on the ground' anytime. Guess it won't be for awhile . . . ."

"Hey, why don't you guys shut up and hit the sack," hollered Barrigan. "I'm tired of hearing about 'dinner on the ground', whatever the hell that is. You better be thinking about the 30-mile hike coming up one of these days."

~

AB and Tad walked out onto the lanai where AB untied the bandanna-wrapped package. He spread the contents on the window sill. AB turned and was surprised to see Sergeant O'Conner walking from the latrine area zipping up his fly. The Sergeant was dressed in a Class A uniform. He motioned to AB.

AB walked with the Sergeant to the end of the lanai and near to the door to the squad room.

"Burns, I need to borrow twenty-five bucks from you. I'm good till payday – week from Tuesday."

AB struggled with a response. First, he was surprised as he thought it was a bit unusual for a platoon sergeant to ask to borrow money from one of his trainees. Secondly, AB didn't have the twenty-five dollars.

"Sergeant O'Conner, I don't have twenty-five. I got fifteen to last me to payday. . . . . I guess I could let you have ten. I have to get a haircut and I'm out of toothpaste. Ya, I guess I can let you have ten."

"OK, I'll take the ten spot. You'll get it back on payday."

AB pulled out his wallet and handed over the ten dollar bill. He counted out the five singles left. Sergeant O'Conner disappeared down the stairway. The screen door slammed twenty seconds later.

"What was all that about?" asked Tad.

"The Sergeant wanted to borrow twenty-five bucks. I didn't have it, but I let him have a ten. What's going on?"

"I think I know" said Tad. "I hear there are some heavy duty poker games going on among some of the cadre here at Schofield. When my brother brings me back on the weekends, we drive by the Base motor pool. There are always quite a few non-coms hanging around there. I am sure that is where the action is."

"I've been going to tell you about what I heard Kam and Sergeant O'Conner talking about on a cigarette break one day last week. O'Conner was telling Kam about the big money he used to bring in from poker games when he had duty in China. This must have been in '39 or '40 – before Pearl Harbor. He was telling Kam about the big poker games going on among the Marines, Army guys, and I guess some big time Chinese gambling guys. Sergeant O'Conner bragged about having twelve-hundred dollars in a British bank in Shanghai."

"Then he went on to tell Kam about being a prisoner of the Japanese in China – apparently for several years. He was treated pretty rough as a prisoner. At some point he was sent to Korea by the Japanese and was used as forced labor to dig a tunnel with a bunch of prisoners – some of them Chinese – through a mountain in a place called Chinhae. He said all they had was picks and shovels, and their hands to dig the tunnel. Some years later, during the Pusan Perimeter, he drove a jeep through that same tunnel and said you could still see the pick marks on the tunnel walls. Kam said he knew where the tunnel was – it must be somewhere around Pusan."

Tad paused, "I can't say as I am very proud of that part of Japanese history."

AB ignored the comment, but stopped eating the shrimp when Tad was talking about the tunnel. "Man, that is bad stuff. I had no idea Sergeant O'Connell had been through all that. The only thing I ever hear him mention was about the 24th Division. I guess I was right when I estimated he was close to thirty-eight or forty years old – and he is still a buck sergeant."

"But, you see all those yellow hash marks on his sleeve for years of service. He must have fifteen or twenty years," said Tad.

"If he's still a big time poker player, I'll bet that is why he's only a buck sergeant. You can get busted for gambling. I don't know, maybe he didn't pay off his gambling debts."

AB turned to finish the shrimp. He wrapped the chopsticks in a white wash cloth. "Sergeant O'Conner is a tough nut. He knows his way around this Army, and he is tough on us at times. I've about decided he is pretty much a loner. He doesn't seem to hang around the other cadre here in the 55th. I don't know whether I'll ever see that ten bucks I just gave him. I'm just glad I didn't have twenty-five on me at the time. Just chalk it up to experience, I guess. Do you know if Allen ever got any money back from him?"

"I have no idea. Allen doesn't talk much to anybody, you know."

There was an obvious disturbance in the grassy Quadrangle near the 55th Company sign.

"Hey, Vinnie, fuck you. Knock it off."

Tad looked at AB. "It looks like they have closed the Fireman's Hat early again."

"Who cares?" said AB. "I can't stand that place. They have that 3.2 beer that is all watered down. I like a beer once in awhile, but not that stuff. For 30 cents you can get a whole pitcher of the stuff. It's awful."

The Fireman's Hat was a club for enlisted men that had been reconstructed, sort of, from what had been a temporary fire station. It was for the HITC trainees, but you had to be in your sixth week of training before being admitted to the place. It was only open on weekends. AB and Zack had visited the Fireman's Hat several times and decided it wasn't worth the effort. Barrigan, Vinnie, Loa and Ox were weekend regulars.

"I can get an Asahi beer at home on weekends" said Tad. "Some time I might bring you a cool one along with the shrimp."

"I like Asahi, but don't take a chance on bringing anything on Base. It's not worth it. Here comes Vinnie and Barrigan. It will be loud in here for awhile."

Chapter 25

Zack and AB sat on the curb in front of the 55th Company sign. It was mid afternoon. They were dressed in fatigues with light field pack containing mess gear and other essentials. Each had a full canteen of water. M-1 rifles were nearby. They were waiting for the Buna Busses to take them to the Wainaie Mountains for the scheduled night exercise. Vinnie, Ox, Loa, and Barrigan watched as the Guamanians practiced dice shots against the cement curbing – no money exchanging, just a few practice shots. AB surveyed the cloud formations near Kolekole Pass for evidence of rain showers. The possibility of showers had something to do with seat selection on the Buna Bus. Long benches were built along the open-top semi-trailers. Another row of benches was positioned toward the center of the truck bed – also long way of the truck bed. If you were seated along the preferred side seating – for more cooling and fresh air – you were subject to getting soaked by the driving rain. AB hadn't consulted his *theory of positioning* recently, but decided he would opt for a center seat. The clouds were hanging heavy and low near Kolekole Pass.

It hadn't been a good day so far. So why should things improve by mid afternoon? To begin with, the PT this morning was held with ALL the Company participating as a unit, rather than on the basis of individual platoon exercises. The Company exercise program was led by Sergeant Los Banos. He delighted in standing on the raised wooden platform on the athletic field and removing his shirt. He had a chiseled body and was damn proud of it. He even lowered his belt line to show off the deep horizontal lines of his stomach muscles. The exercises, as led by the Sergeant were all downhill from there – many more repetitions than usual of each individual exercise. He wanted everyone to know that his platoon was by far the toughest in the 55th Company. He even kept them fifteen minutes longer than scheduled. AB and Zack agreed that Sergeant Los Banos was a real GI asshole when it came to physical exercise. Lieutenants Soong and Fujimoto just stood by, smiled, and observed quietly.

After all that, the morning training experience deteriorated further. The schedule called for something identified as 'SA Inspection,' to begin at ten thirty hours. The 55th had marched (actually run) to the temporary buildings identified as "Medics" where somehow the 53rd Company was already lined up – two-hundred and fifty strong. It didn't take too much imagination to determine that "SA" meant short arm inspection. In other words, a pecker check where some five-hundred men stood in a long line within the temporary buildings to have their private parts inspected by a medic for evidence of a social disease. Short arm inspections were seldom announced ahead of schedule. Due to the confusion of two companies showing up at the same hour, it had taken nearly twice as long as scheduled, making noon chow at 55th Company mess hall run much later than planned.

AB and Zack agreed it had not been a good day so far. The announced night time exercise couldn't possibly improve the situation in any way.

AB spoke to Zack, as Zack was re-reading a letter from his wife. "I suggest we take the middle seat when the Buna Bus finally arrives. I don't like the look of those cloud formations hanging over Kolekole Pass."

"Sounds good to me. We got soaked that last time on those outside seats even though we had ponchos," said Zack

Howard Boylan

Zack lay back on the grass. "Wonder how long before those Bunas arrive? It's several hours to the mountains from here, and we have to have some kind of a meal in the field, as well as orientation on the night problem before it turns dark." Zack was still thinking as a squad leader, even though he had been relieved of his responsibilities weeks ago.

~

There was never any question when Sergeant O'Conner was in charge. He stood on the back of a jeep explaining to the entire Company exactly how this night exercise was to be accomplished. His shoulders were back, head erect, and he waved his arms to accentuate a point he was making. He was clearly in charge and loved every minute of it. Sergeant Rubinal had conferred with Lieutenant Soong and had suggested that the Sergeant provide leadership on the night problem because of his experience with night patrols in the Pusan Perimeter – less than twenty-four months ago. Darkness was moving in rapidly, as the sun had set behind the mountains some twenty minutes ago.

"Gentleman, listen up! We are going to talk about the fine points of conducting a night patrol into enemy territory. The purpose of the patrol is to seek information regarding the placement of defensive positions on the part of the enemy. The patrol is conducted by squad – fifteen men working as a team to accomplish a mission. Much of our training so far has been on developing individual skills. *This exercise is to determine how well your squad can work as a team.* Of course, the squad leader is in charge. He will be informed by Sergeant Rubinal of the specific intelligence that we have concerning the territory assigned by platoon. I can tell you that the site is relatively open – a few low trees and brush along with knee-high swamp grass. You can see from the low hanging clouds that there will be no moonlight tonight. It will be dark – and then some. I can tell you that the 53rd Company is defending the territory that you are seeking to patrol."

"Now," he continued, "there are four different sites to be patrolled – one for each platoon. Sergeant Rubinal will meet with the squad leaders of the first platoon in two minutes at that palm tree over there to my right. Other platoons will be oriented in just a few minutes."

Goldwire and the other three squad leaders followed Sergeant Rubinal to the designated palm tree.

"I am not too sure about this whole thing," said AB. He and Zack were sitting in the high grass sharing a Baby Ruth candy bar. Chow that evening had been a disaster. Another effort at the Chinese cooks' version of spaghetti was the main course – dumped into mess kits brought along for that purpose. The canteen cup of warm milk hadn't added anything to the experience. It had not rained in the 90-minute trip on the Buna Bus, so the selection of the steamy interior seating by AB and Zack had not added to any expected excitement of the experience of the night exercise. Their fatigue jackets were soaked with perspiration. The cool breezes normally available as darkness moved in were somehow missing.

Goldwire walked slowly back from the platoon squad leader meeting. He had listened carefully to Sergeant Rubinal and he had a tough decision to make. The 53rd Company had an outpost in the first squad area of patrol. The position was equipped with a 30-calibre machine gun to defend their area of fire. The objective of the patrol was to locate the machine gun position, and in a surprise move, to overrun the position by charging full squad to capture the position. This was to be accomplished by sending out a field scout as point man, ahead of the patrol. As a scout, he was to locate the machine gun position and report back to the squad leader, who was then to plan an attack on the position – all to be done in a time span of twenty minutes.

Goldie's problem was this: Sergeant Rubinal had told him to select his best man to be the scout. His first choice was Tad, but the assistant squad leader was to have another specific assignment. That left AB or Zack.

The first squad gathered around their squad leader. Goldie explained the plan in detail. He put Tad in charge of the seven men whose assignment was to be the second wave in the attack on the machine gun position. Goldie would lead the first group. All were issued blank M-1 ammunition and were to charge the enemy position, firing from the hip position.

"AB, you are the scout. You are to go ahead of the squad while we stay back under cover of the ditch here at the roadside. You are to advance about 100 to 125 yards and locate the position and then return here where we plan the attack. All this is to be done in twenty minutes.

AB accepted the assignment. His major concern was how, in this absolute darkness, to know when he had traveled the 100 or 125 yards. After some consideration, he decided to count his steps. Each stride would not be one yard, but it would be close. No sideway movement allowed.

Goldwire wished him well. AB, rifle at port arms, proceeded into the dark of the night – up a slight incline, counting each step as he proceeded into the knee-high swamp grass. At seventy-five paces he stopped to observe what appeared to be the outline of a palm tree with heavy underbrush nearby. He paused, then proceeded carefully,

Half Way There, Haole

continuing the pace count. At about a hundred paces he stopped short. He thought he saw a light – maybe the low flame of a cigarette. He crouched low. The cigarette glowed brighter – someone was taking a drag on a cigarette butt.

AB paused. What to do now? He looked to his left about fifteen paces. There was what looked like an overturned tree stump. He crawled in that direction. It WAS an overturned tree stump – a perfect place to seek cover and concentrate while he confirmed what he believed to the object of his scouting assignment. He crouched low and reorganized his thoughts. How far had he traveled? Where was he in relation to the squad crouched along the roadside? He made mental notes to describe the gun placement when he returned.

AB thought he heard voices. He raised up to get a better position. It was someone talking. He was telling his buddy of a recent visit to a massage parlor on Hotel Street in Honolulu. AB became fascinated by the detail described of two females massaging the naked butt and shoulders of the willing participant. In his mind, he imagined himself on that massage table . . . .

That's when all hell broke loose!

Rifles were firing at all angles from what seemed like behind him and to his side. The machine gun returned the fire after some pause. The first wave of M-1 firing began as bodies crouched low and moved forward. The second wave of M-1 firing began and moved forward. AB was confused. Was this another squad from another platoon? It couldn't be the FIRST SQUAD! He hadn't had time to return to Goldie and report his findings of the machine gun position. The M-1 firing continued, but at a reduced pace. Finally, it ceased completely. All was quiet.

What to do now? He tried to look at his Timex. It was 2125. He had no idea what time he had left the squad. Could that have been the first squad and Goldie had just passed him by? He now realized how confusing actual combat could really be.

He again heard voices. He stood in a crouched position behind the tree stump. There were now three lighted cigarettes at the machine gun position and some conversation about getting more ammunition for the next expected attack.

What to do? AB decided he had two options – return to the roadside or approach the machine gun crew. He decided on the latter.

Hesitatingly he approached the three lighted cigarettes.

"Who are YOU?"

"I'm with the first squad of the first platoon of the 55th.

"What are you doing here? Those guys sailed through here a few minutes ago. The second squad should be here in ten or fifteen minutes."

"What should I do?"

"Hell, man, catch up with your unit." A corporal pointed to his left with his lighted cigarette.

AB was really confused. Why had his squad advanced on the position without hearing of his advance report on the site location? Where did everyone go? He stumbled off to his left as directed by the corporal from the 53rd Company. It seemed to be getting even darker as he slowly moved forward among the high grass and passed by more palm trees.

He stopped. Were those more voices ahead of him? It sounded as though there were voices coming ahead of him and somehow BELOW him. Again he halted! He could hear running water, the sound of a jeep motor, and then more voices.

Half Way There, Haole

He stepped forward and quickly found himself sliding on his butt down a steep incline – or was it a cliff? He held his rifle overhead and continued to slide down the endless bank. His legs were spread eagle and he was collecting vines and grass in his crotch. AB hollered out as he finally slid to a stop. He could now hear the sound of a mountain stream. Someone was shining a light on the side of the cliff. The light finally focused on his body – hands high in the air holding his rifle.

"What the hell are you doing?"

AB replied, "Give me some help. I'm hung up on these vines and can't get loose.'

"Hold on. We'll come get you."

AB struggled to maintain his composure. It seemed like forever before he finally spotted someone climbing the embankment. AB could see he carried a machete.

"What the hell are you doing – walking off a thirty foot cliff in the middle of the night?"

"Just get me outa' here, won't you? Cut the goddamn vines hanging between my legs."

AB saw the stripes of a sergeant he did not know.

The vines were cut and both men slid down the bank and splashed into the shallow stream below.

AB stood at attention with his rifle in front of a Lieutenant he had never seen before – jeep lights shining in his eyes.

"Private Burns, you are a prisoner of the 53rd Company."

The sergeant relieved AB of his rifle to check for live ammo. The rifle was returned while his body was searched for other means of destruction. AB was ordered to sit in the rear seat of the jeep.

Later, in the exchange of prisoners, AB was returned to the 55th Company. Lieutenant Soong was relieved to have all his men accounted for as the Buna Busses pulled up to the 55th Company sign.

AB sighed, yes it has not been a good day, or night, at Schofield.

Chapter 26

The duty rosters for guard duty and KP continued, regardless of the advanced status and importance of the training cycle. The troops all had to be fed and military security of Quad K was obviously essential. Posted on the training bulletin board was an item designated as "Live Ammo Exercise –Site 34A" The KP duty roster was also posted: Wednesday 3 February 1952 – Private Francis Barringan, Private Allendale Burns, and four others.

AB read the posted notice and wasn't too surprised at the KP duty. He would have preferred to work KP with almost anyone other than Barrigan, but what difference did it really make? There had been other KP duty in recent weeks and it had become somewhat routine. AB decided he would report early to the mess sergeant in order to get a chance at a preferred assignment.

AB was still struggling with the oversized set of fatigues given to him at Fort Meade, Maryland. That seemed like years ago! He had carefully arranged to have his best fitting fatigues available for Saturday inspections, leaving the baggy set for most weekly work activities. This caused some concern with weekly laundry send-out, but he had worked out a suitable schedule. He had long ago given up trying to convince the Supply Sergeant for an exchange.

The Mess Sergeant arrived late that Wednesday morning. All six KP's lined up at parade rest. The Mess Sergeant briefly studied the group and immediately assigned Barrigan and Lee as dining room orderlies. AB was assigned to Corporal Dong Soo as cook's helper. He decided the grungy and outsized fatigues may have brought the least desirable KP assignment. He resigned himself for a day of hell with

Corporal Dong Soo, who had a reputation for being impossible to work with. He would just have to make the best of it.

"My name is Dong Soo – not just *Dong* as most of you haoles say it."

"Yes, Corporal Dong Soo," replied AB obediently, as he tried to start the day with some degree of optimism.

Dong Soo disappeared into the walk-in refrigerator storage area. AB checked the kitchen bulletin board for the menu of the day. This often determined how the day might go for the KP staff. The menu seemed simple enough: scrambled eggs, bacon, and toast for breakfast; noon meal (served in the field) was baked ham, rice – of course—and broccoli casserole; dinner was beef tips with noodles, steamed carrots, and apple cobbler. AB knew most of the broccoli and carrots would end up in the garbage cans, but the meal preparation itself should be relatively easy.

Corporal Dong Soo returned from the cooler with a stack of eggs separated by flats of cardboard. He motioned for AB to begin breaking the eggs into a large pot. The other cook began frying bacon by throwing large flanks of cut bacon on the grill.

The second kitchen KP kept busy by pulling individual bacon slices from the hot, snapping grill. The meat separated into slices and turned a dark reddish color. This was hot work with grease snapping and popping in all directions. The white gloves did help. some.

AB was directed to start the commercial-sized toaster – stacking individual slices of bread on a revolving metal belt and returning brown toast in a matter of seconds.

In no time, the serving line was set and the troops were in line. Scrambled eggs and bacon were a favorite of the 55th. Seconds were available and all food disappeared!

A ten-minute smoke break was declared. AB sat on the loading dock while the entire kitchen staff puffed on cigarettes. He still had no desire to smoke. He sat upwind from the trail of blue smoke on the loading dock.

After cleanup from the breakfast meal, the noon meal preparation began immediately. AB addressed Corporal Dong Soo appropriately and all went well. The ham slices were cut, but later the loading of the bulky pots and pans containing the rice and broccoli casserole into the six-by-six trucks proved to be a heavy challenge. He wondered what the dining room orderlies, that is – Barringan and Lee – would do to help with the noon meal in the field.

Sergeant O'Conner approached the Mess Sergeant as the last of the troops were served the noon meal. "Sergeant, you have two men on KP from the first platoon. I need to have these two for about an hour while they qualify on the machine gun range here at this site."

Barrigan and AB were relieved of KP duties and reported to Sergeant Los Banos to qualify with the 3rd platoon. Steel helmets and rifles were borrowed from others in the first squad.

As they were ordered to the machine gun site, the nature of the training exercise soon became evident. Two thirty-caliber machine guns were set up at one end of a field overlooking what appeared to be a tangle of barbed wire. Upon closer look, the barbed wire was strung in the form of a flat bed about fifteen to eighteen inches above the ground level. The field was at least fifty yards long. The objective of the exercise was to crawl the full length of the site, beneath the layer of barbed wire while live ammunition from the 30-caliber machine guns raked the area just above the wire. The height of the wire and the live ammo prevented crawling on hands and knees. It appeared to be a real

Half Way There, Haole

physical challenge – in addition to the major mental concern of real live ammo flying overhead.

"It must be this way in Korea," mused AB to no one in particular. He guessed he could do it if the others had succeeded, but it wouldn't be easy.

AB, Barrigan, and four others approached the barbed wire enclosure, fell to their bellies and proceeded to follow those in front of them. As he proceeded to crawl, he felt a ripping noise on one pant leg. Somehow a loose barbed wire strand hung low and snagged his fatigues. He hesitated, rifle in hand, then proceeded. The rip soon expanded upward to the knee area. As he crawled ahead, the other pant leg developed a small tear near the crotch.

Totally exhausted, AB plopped into the deep trench at the end of the field. Barrigan was nowhere in sight. As the bullets were fired into the mound above him, AB looked at his fatigue pants and jacket. The right leg was ripped from the knee to the bottom hem. The left leg was torn on the upper thigh. He smiled to himself and gently extended the rip from the crotch to the knee with both hands. After fifteen weeks, he could finally get a second set of fatigues – a set that would fit!

Sergeant O'Conner exclaimed, "Burns, what in the fuck happened to you? Are you bleeding?"

No, Sergeant, just tangled with a loose piece of wire."

"Well, that is going to cost you money," replied the Sergeant.

"Yes, sir," said AB with an inner smile.

"Report to the Mess Sergeant. See the Supply Sergeant when we get back to Quad K."

"Yes, sir."

Corporal Dong Soo exclaimed, "What the fuck happened to you?"

AB didn't respond, just kept loading the empty food containers into the truck.

Barrigan finally showed up. "What the fuck happened to you?"

"Nothing," replied AB.

The supply truck headed back toward Quad K.

After the dirty pans and kettles were stacked at the loading dock, the Mess Sergeant approached AB with four large safety pins and ordered him to look presentable.

Preparation began for the evening meal. AB and others attacked the food-encrusted pots and pans in two large sinks designed specifically for that purpose. Just more grunt work to make each utensil shine.

Dong Soo approached the KP's with the menu for the evening meal.

"Burns, you go to the food supply room and get six cartons of noodles. I put them out on the floor this morning. Fill this kettle with water from a hose while it is on the stove. Drop in the noodles when the water comes to a boil."

AB placed the kettle on the stove as instructed and used the hose from the nearby faucet to fill the kettle. The water soon came up to temperature and AB dumped in the six cartons of long, brittle spaghetti noodles. Dong Soo observed from a distance and without comment. He glanced at his watch as if to determine a time length for the noodle boiling process. AB returned to help finish scrubbing the crusty pots and pans still remaining from the noon meal. The other cook and helper chopped the beef into bite-sized pieces. The carrots had been scraped and were boiling in another huge kettle.

Dong Soo went to the loading dock for yet another Chesterfield cigarette. He looked at his watch again and yelled to AB to drain the water from the noodles. AB

Half Way There, Haole

surveyed the situation. He cut off the fire from beneath the kettle. The water continued to bubble slowly. He found two damp dish towels and placed each beneath the handles of the opposite sides of the sizzling container. The towels provided protection to prevent burning his arms. He cautiously lifted the heavy container from the stove. His knees nearly buckled as he struggled to tote the heavy vessel, keeping it away from his upper body. He struggled to raise the container to the edge of the mop sink. As he did so, one of the towels fell to the floor, immediately burning a red streak on his forearm. The hot kettle slipped, dumping ALL the contents into the sink.

AB panicked. First, running cold water on his arm and then jerking a dirty mop from the sink. He noticed a mass of black coffee grounds in one corner of the sink. He glanced around for Dong Soo. The cook was talking to the Mess Sergeant at the dining room doorway. AB immediately began to retrieve the hot wet noodles from the sink – but not before Dong Soo seized upon the situation.

"You dum sum-bitch, Look what you have did!"

AB continued to retrieve the slippery mass by the handful. It was impossible to separate the noodles from the black coffee grounds – giving the resulting mess in the container a very strange appearance.

Dong Soo looked at his watch. "You dum sum-bitch, we don't have time to cook those noodles again. He hesitated. You stand right there and separate them coffee grounds from them noodles. We start the serving line in about ten minutes. Burns, you are a dum sum-bitch."

AB poured the noodles with the black coffee grounds much in evidence into a large flat serving pan. His right arm was now blistered. He struggled to carry the pan from the rear of the kitchen to the serving line.

"You dum sum-bitch, YOU stand right there and serve this shit to the troops," yelled Dong Soo.

"What's the black shit in the noodles," exclaimed Sergeant Los Banos – the first man through the serving line.

AB didn't look up. He wondered if the wet mop had left a strange taste to the dish.

Zack, and others of the first squad were in line with their aluminum trays – ready to be served. Zack stared at the pan of noodles.

AB spoke quietly to Zack, "Better pass on the noodles, just eat the beef tips. Let the other guys know."

AB trudged upstairs to the second floor barracks area. His right arm throbbing, he mused to himself, "Looks like Barrigan won this one". Then his thoughts brightened. He would see the Supply Sergeant in the morning.

Chapter 27

Josh bounded up the stairway to the second floor lanai. He rushed into the first squad bunk area.

"Patti Page is going to be at the Post Bowl next Thursday night. She is super! I'm gonna' skip chow and be there on the first row."

"Sure you're going to be on the first row," said Silva, "but it won't be at the Post Bowl."

"Whaddya mean."

Silva responded in his usual nonchalant manner. "Don't you ever read the bulletin board downstairs? We leave on Monday for a thirty-mile hike to Kahuku. On Thursday night you'll probably be lucky you don't have guard duty somewhere up in those mountains."

"Ah shit, this will probably be our only chance to see Patti Page – live."

"You better start checking all your clothes and equipment for inspection tomorrow. You're going to carry with you everything you got and it better be ready," said Tad.

Sergeant O'Conner had mentioned the thirty-mile hike several times recently. Week Sixteen was intended to demonstrate the knowledge of military training that had been expended on the 55th Company for the past fifteen weeks. Some referred to it as a 'final exam'. Sergeant O'Conner said it wouldn't be a fun time.

The Friday equipment inspection is held with surprisingly constructive criticism on the part of Lieutenant Soong and his inspection team. Everyone is serious about this thing. It must go off without a hitch. There is no parade schedule on Saturday morning. A delayed breakfast at seven-thirty is a real luxury for the troops.

Half Way There, Haole

Barrigan surveyed the mass of clothing and equipment spread out on his bunk, footlocker, and the floor in between bunks. For once, he had followed instructions by Corporal Kam to a tee. It had paid off – no comment, no nothing—from Lieutenant Fujimoto, Barrigan's weekly inspection antagonist.

"This is going to be one son-of-a-bitch," mumbled Barrigan in his Brooklyn accent. "All this shit is supposed to fit in your backpack or hang from you ammo belt, somehow."

AB, who seldom responded to Barrigan's ramblings, looked up and said, "You better pack that stuff in the right order, like the Sergeant explained, or you're going to have fun getting the right thing out of there at the right time. Keep you shelter half and mess gear on the top of the pile in your backpack."

"Ya, sure, the Army can always tell you exactly how to do something—always by the numbers."

AB continued his packing – by the numbers, just as he had been told. Maybe it wouldn't be raining when he and Zack put their shelter halves together for a dry pup tent on the first night.

Sergeant O'Conner and Corporal Kam wandered through the first platoon barracks sleeping area.

"Everyone ready for the big hike?" inquired the Sergeant with a wry smile on his face. "We shove off at 1300 hours right after noon chow. We won't do all the thirty miles in one day. We'll make it part way to Kahuku and have some chow, and camp out for the first night. With a full field pack, you guys will be ready for a break."

The Sergeant returned to his room. He needed to check HIS pack for last minute details. Yes, he had packed the thing by the numbers and the vodka pint was near the top of the pile.

Silva spoke to Josh, "You know, this wouldn't be a bad time to have KP. For sure, the chow truck will go ahead of the Company to set up for late chow. You know those KP's will RIDE with their packs on the truck for at least half the thirty miles."

"Ya," said Josh, "but I think the fourth platoon has KP this week. Maybe they'll get to ride all the way. Oh, well."

At 1300 hours the 55th Company stood at attention with rifles and full field packs. Lieutenant Soong was giving last minute instructions to the cadre. He, too, had a full field pack, but with no M-1 rifle. He and Lieutenant Fujimoto opted to carry the lighter-weight carbines.

Tad assumed they would march through the Schofield compound, out the main gate and through the village of Wahiawa. Wrong! There was a seldom-used and remote entrance to Schofield that was unfamiliar to the troops.

The Company did take the now-very-familiar route to and through Kokekole Pass. The pace was accelerated, but not too difficult. Even the Guamanians at the end of each squad could keep the step. They had long since learned the awkward art of taking long strides to maintain the pace.

A ten-minute smoke break was scheduled after the first hour. Sergeant O'Conner was observed going behind a clump of palms – presumably for a pee break. Instead, he sampled the pint of vodka on top of his pack. He returned with a half smile on his face.

AB and Zack doffed field packs and lay stretched out in a grassy ditch nearby. As instructed, each only took a brief swallow of water from his canteen. That canteen of water had to last for all the thirty miles – including overnight. The familiar cloud formations in Kolekole Pass promised a shady early afternoon under those hot steel helmets.

"Field strip those weeds and fall in," shouted Field First Sergeant Rubinal.

AB took his usual squad position next to Barrigan. A quick 'right face' put him behind the kid from Brooklyn – for quite possibly the one-thousandth' time. AB noted to himself that Barrigan had finally stopped 'the goddam bouncing' and marched in formation and in step with others in the first squad. After sixteen weeks he had finally learned to stride properly. The same was not true for Barrigan's mouth – he still made unwanted comments and wisecracks at inappropriate times. This, in spite of many extra pushups and laps around Quad K as administered by Sergeant O'Conner, Corporal Kam, or anyone else in charge at the time.

AB's mind wandered as he plodded along. He speculated on what would really happen to Barrigan at the close of basic training. AB, for one, did not want to ship out to Korea with the likes of Barrigan. Almost anyone else in the first squad was acceptable—even Loa, Ox, or Allen, or any of the Guamanians. Come to think of it, that thought had wandered through his mind some time earlier at Schofield.

As the Company approached a steep incline in the road ahead, AB's mind turned to his possible special assignment. The Sergeant at Central Personnel insisted AB and Lou were assured of the commitment. But, AB had learned early on in his training at Schofield that nothing was a sure thing in the Army. There had already been some disappointments, so who could be certain of anything? AB plodded on – up the incline in the roadway and barely puffing. His leg muscles functioned without fail. After fifteen weeks of PT and training, he should be in shape for this thing.

On the other hand, AB rationalized, he had not really shown any leadership qualities in these weeks of training. Goldwire, had been made squad leader when Zack was in trouble. Yes, Goldie was assistant squad leader at the time, but had AB been even considered as a squad leader? Or even as an assistant squad leader? No, probably not. Goldie had stepped forward – in several ways on that last bivouac. Yes, AB had leadership responsibilities at Burns & Johnson – but he had inherited that situation; he hadn't really earned it. Yes, Goldie had really earned his position, and Tad probably deserved his promotion to assistant squad leader. So what!

He reminded himself of the extremely high percentage of trainees assigned to FECOM from the just-graduated 40th HITC training battalion. With just seven days in the Islands as leave time, they were probably at Pearl Harbor right now waiting to board a troop ship to Korea. AB heard a rumor there was a stop at a place called Camp Drake in Japan, where you had another clothing check, a review of shot records, and whatever else. The scuttlebutt somehow seemed real, and was probably accurate.

The hike continued though Kolekole Pass. The mid-afternoon sun danced among the low-hanging clouds. Again, AB felt in great shape. He could go on like this for some time. He just needed to keep his mind occupied. He could hear Ox and Loa behind him exchanging gripes about the length of the hike and the futility of just being there. AB was reminded again of his one-on-one conversation with Loa when on guard duty. How Loa felt about haoles and how those people from the mainland had taken their land and their freedom as native islanders. Rightfully so, he should be proud of his Hawaiian heritage. Ox had fortified this attitude with his story about how the white man had treated HIS ancestors. The two didn't talk much about this. It was just a feeling that had developed between them. AB looked at his Timex. It was about time for another break. Barrigan plodded on ahead of him, but still maintained his pace with the platoon.

"Company, halt! Take a break."

AB, Zack and Goldie all headed for the shade of the same palm trees. Zack fished a Hershey bar from his field pack. AB was reminded of that kid on the bus in Tallahassee eating a Hershey bar and throwing the almonds beneath the bus seat.

Suddenly, from nowhere, came two six-by-six trucks. Each slowed and passed the resting troops. From the rear of the second truck, Maeva and three other KP's from the fourth platoon waved frantically to the resting troops.

"See there," shouted Silva. "I told you there was a way to beat this thing. Be on KP and ride all the way. Not only that, you've had your turn at KP – maybe for the rest of your time here at Schofield."

"Ya could have volunteered, ya know," said Josh with tongue in check.

For AB, at least, the speed march was going OK. He decided that he would allow his mind to continue to wander as he plodded along. He casually mentioned this thought to Zack and to Goldie who was stretched out in the Johnson Grass nearby.

"OK, on your feet," said Sergeant O'Conner. "Now's the time to take on a little water if you need to – not much though. Our next stop will be for chow. Then we dig a foxhole and spend the night. Third and fourth squads will alternate on guard duty." He waited for the moans and groans from the affected troops.

"I can handle that," said Barrigan. "I can see me eatin' chow, diggin' a hole to sleep in, and then standin' guard duty for half the night."

"Ya," agreed Loa. "And then get up and speed hike for another fifteen miles."

Sergeant O'Conner stood aside with a wry grin. "Barrigan, you and Vinnie dig the latrine ditch for the first platoon. And fill it in just before we leave tomorrow."

"Ah shit," grumbled Barrigan.

"You get the idea," responded the Sergeant with a grin. "You're beginning to catch on pretty fast on the way the Army does things."

Barrigan decided a further response wasn't going to be in his favor.

"Why me?" moaned Vinnie.

The Company re-formed and stepped off at the accelerated pace.

Goldie, leading his squad in platoon formation, soon allowed his mind to wander. He didn't get much mail. His father wrote an occasional letter, but his mother didn't really write at all – she couldn't. AB had kept him informed on anything of interest from the Quincy community, but that was it. He wondered if his name was ever mentioned on the back page of the *Gadsden County Times*. Then, he considered how could the newspaper people know WHERE to put a military announcement about a serviceman – on the back page with the 'colored news' or on the other pages with the white folks news. Somehow, it didn't really disturb him – or ... did it?

Goldie decided that Mister AB had handled this thing of Goldie being in charge of the squad fairly well. AB certainly had encouraged him to take charge. And he had helped with advice in how to handle some of the rough guys in the squad.

Even Knight didn't seem to be bothered by Goldie ordering another colored guy around. At least, he didn't seem to say anything to others in the squad about it. Come to think of it, Knight probably mouthed off to his buddy in the third squad, but who knows?

Goldie plodded along, checking to see that the squad was maintaining the pace. Loa was griping to Ox but that didn't seem to prevent him from staying in step with the platoon.

Loa, he thought, didn't know quite how to take Goldie. With Zack in charge he bitched about how Zack handled the troops and assigned work details. He noted that Loa seemed to object to most of the Orientals and didn't much talk to any of them. Loa made fun of Ching sometimes even though Ching hadn't said a word to him – or anyone else for that matter. He noticed that Tad didn't take any of Loa's crap and Loa knew it. And the Guamanians – they were great. They just did what you told them to do and smiled back at you. Goldie figured that Tad would probably get a chance go to Leadership School. Goldie hoped he would get a chance at that, too.

His mind then returned to the occasion on the last bivouac when he helped Lieutenant Soong and Sergeant Rubinal with the jeep battery, the water pump, and then when he took over the squad as AB and Zack were 'injured' on the mountain trail. Maybe that would help him get into Leadership School – and as a CORPORAL you made a lot more money. How much? He wasn't really sure. You probably went directly to FECOM after Leadership School, but that would just have to be.

Sergeant Rubinal's voice commands brought Goldie back to the real world of the speed march.

"Company, halt! Prepare to eat chow and bed down for the night."

He hesitated, "Who goes through the chow line first tonight?"

The second squad of the fourth platoon held up their hands in unison. The troops might not keep up with a lot of training matters, but there was never any question as to which squad in the Company was the first to go through the chow line – either at the Quad K mess hall or in the field.

"That makes us close to the front of the line," said Silva. "I'm ready for something – anything."

The 'anything' turned out to be sliced ham with a covering of a sticky pineapple sauce, rice, sliced pineapple salad with lettuce, cold green beans, and banana pudding. It didn't look all that great when piled in the mess kit, but who really cared? AB thought again, he would never forget this place and all the damnable pineapple. He speculated that Dole must have a major tonnage contract with HITC.

Sergeant Rubinal got the attention of the troops as the meal was finished. "All right now. Be sure you dunk your mess kit and silverware through the hot water in the garbage cans. Do it twice, for good measure. No sick call out here. Now, you will be consigned to areas for squad sleeping tonight. You dig a double-sized foxhole – that is, a six by six, but only make it about a foot deep. Line 'em with Johnson Grass if you want. Each platoon digs their own latrine trench. All trenches are to be covered over before we leave in the morning."

"If all goes as planned, we arrive at Kahuku area about 1230 hours tomorrow. I will discuss our game plan for the next two days when we get there."

Tad's ears picked up. He had not heard the term 'game plan' since his high school football days. Maybe Sergeant Rubinal played some ball. With his physique and height he would make a great end on the team. Those long arms could snag a pass! But, then again, this would be a different kind of 'army game plan.'

It didn't rain. The night passed without incident.

Barrigan and Vinnie filled in the latrine trench and the troops were on their way to the second half of the thirty-mile trek. To most of the men it was even better than the day before.

"All right men," spoke Sergeant Rubinal, "we came through that OK. Now, let's talk about the next two days. This is your base camp right here. Wednesday, we become familiar with the tank – not the kind you get your water from – real Army tanks with tracks and heavy caliber weapons. We'll have five operating tanks and as infantrymen you will be familiarized with the technique of advancing on the enemy in unison with a tank company. The idea is that the tank with the heavy fire power clears away any enemy defenses, like machine gun emplacements, and you as infantrymen advance under the cover and protection of the tank. But, now listen to this. YOU are also protecting your brothers in the tank by advancing and being on the lookout for any stray enemy who might be harboring an anti-tank weapon of any type. That could be a bazooka, or any heavy caliber weapon capable of damaging the TANK TRACKS. A tank with a damaged track isn't going anywhere. A squad of infantrymen advances with each tank – keeping your eyes in all directions for the enemy while you advance at the same time."

Sergeant Rubinal paused. "Does everyone understand what I am saying?"

He paused again, allowing time for his thoughts to penetrate the skulls of the men in the 55th Company.

"I know what I am talking about. I advanced with many a tank through the rice paddies near the 38th Parallel. I saw some of my buddies ignore their responsibilities to protect the advancing tank and those North Koreans took 'em out with a well-placed shot from a heavy caliber machine gun emplacement. A tank with a damaged track can turn the tide of your advance in a matter of minutes. So, do I make my point – you are there to protect the tank. And the tanker is there to protect you, under cover of the advance."

The wide-eyed troops were silent.

"Take a ten minute break."

Goldie, AB, Zack and Tad looked for the usual shady spot. There wasn't any. Zack reached for his Lucky Strike pack and sat down on a rotting log. Others joined him.

"I believe Sergeant Rubinal knows what he is talking about," said Silva. "It would be easy to think you have plenty of protection from the tank and all its firepower when you advance under its cover, but you have to work with those tanker guys to protect them from some wise guy with a sharp eye."

Silva continued, "I heard the other day that Sergeant Rubinal was being considered for some sort of medal."

No one responded – hardly knowing what to say.

Chapter 28

The morning routine in the field passed without incident. Sergeant Rubinal had the Company stand at ease while he conferred with Lieutenant Soong concerning planned details of the morning activity.

He then spoke with the platoon sergeants.

The Company was regrouped into platoon formation. The exercises this day were to be by platoon – and at times by spread formation.

Sergeant O'Conner called the squad leaders aside. He looked for a shady spot, but there was none.

"Gentlemen," he said, "our first exercise has to do with familiarization of artillery fire. An offense is typically initiated by a pre-arranged cover of 105 howitzer artillery, firing from some distance behind your line of attack. In other words, it softens up the enemy defense and allows you to attack an enemy that is confused and probably suffering some losses. At the same time, however, the artillery attack forewarns the North Koreans and the Chinese that you are preparing to attack. The enemy can also track the location of the artillery and can quite possibly return fire with its own artillery in an attempt to destroy OUR artillery support."

He hesitated, then continued," The whole idea of this exercise is to familiarize the members of this platoon with the SOUND of our outgoing 105 artillery fire. They call it 'outgoing mail.' You need to be able to recognize this sound so that you are aware of the safety of the sound. It is being fired for your cover and protection as you advance"

The Sergeant hesitated again, "We won't have the advantage of recognizing 'incoming mail' – that is, the enemy return fire. But, at least you will be familiar with the 'outgoing mail' sound. We will also do this with the accompaniment of tanks. We discussed this yesterday."

"Now," Sergeant O'Conner continued, "I want each of you to return to your respective squad and explain this to your squad members. We will advance up that low hill over there to my left along with the tanks. It will be done by squad, with the first squad leading off when I give the signal. Remember, you are to advance up the hill firing from the hip position. You will be using live ammunition, so keep you squad in assigned positions and advance up the hill in an even formation – that is, in a solid front line of attack."

Goldie distributed the M-1 ammo – three clips per squad member.

Sergeant O'Conner signaled for the first squad to move to the base of the hill and to spread out in the squad attack mode, as practiced many times earlier.

From the rear came the explosions of the artillery pieces. The sound tracked overhead with a swoosh and loud echo – one after another – about every twenty seconds.

Goldie gave the signal to 'move out.' The sixteen men moved slowly up the hill, firing from the hip as instructed. Slowly, but surely, they advanced to about the halfway point of the hill – using the cover and concealment techniques they had learned earlier – moving from one clump of bushes or rock formation to another – eyes searching for enemy attack on the accompanying tanks. The artillery pace slowed, but the advance became ever-more realistic as the troops could now see the exploding shells land near the top of the hill.

AB felt confident of his situation as he advanced in the formation – the crack of rifle shells to his right and to his left. Suddenly, he looked up to see Loa bending over the base of a bush. His rifle was aimed at AB's groin.

"What the hell are you doing," shouted AB.

Loa smiled and reached again into the bush. "Picking guavas," announced Loa as he munched on his find.

"Look, you dumb bastard, you're aiming that M-1 right at my balls."

Loa reacted by moving his rifle with his left hand and aimed it in the direction of the line of fire up the hill. At the same time he moved to another guava bush to reach for more fresh fruit.

The advancing squad continued up the hill, firing for effect. AB kept one eye to his right – being assured that Loa was keeping his mind on the assigned task of taking the hill.

AB reconsidered his thoughts about going into combat in Korea with members of the first squad. No way was he going to FECOM with Loa. He was re-classified into the same group as Barrigan – and maybe a few others.

As the first squad approached the half way of the advance, the artillery fire suddenly ceased. As instructed, Goldie ordered a cease fire for the squad. All remaining cartridges were ordered removed from the rifles. The first squad returned to the assigned areas near the base of the hill. They prepared to observe the second squad in action.

AB was still disturbed over Loa's irresponsibility. He considered what action he should take – then on second thought – to hell with it.

Breakfast the next morning was a major flop – partially cooked pancakes with some sort of gooey pineapple syrup.

The Buna Busses arrived ahead of schedule for the return to Quad K. AB decided the buildup to the big hike and the Kahuku bivouac was somewhat of a disappointment. Everything just about went off without a hitch. This certainly went better than the earlier bivouac – the one right after the holidays. Come to think of it, maybe that was the

Half Way There, Haole

way it was supposed to be. The 55th Company was now trained and ready for Korea.

Chapter 29

The dayroom was crowded – some stood around the walls, but most of the trainees and cadre simply sat cross-legged on the floor. The Japanese-Hawaiians and some of the Chinese-Hawaiians assumed a natural position – sitting on their heels with knees beneath the chin – something no haole could do, or even tried to do.

The men of the 55th Company had been ordered to the day room for the reading of duty orders. Everyone had passed weeks of infantry basic training. All would be promoted officially from Trainee E-1 to Private E-2 and receive confirmation of this in the form of a multicolored certificate from the Hawaiian Infantry Training Center, United States Army Pacific, at Schofield Barracks, Oahu, Hawaii – and signed by the Commanding Officer.

Tad, Goldie, AB, and Silva, and most of the first squad had anticipated the crowd and arrived early to find space on the floor near the double door entrance to the dayroom. Tad crouched on his heels.

Lieutenant Soong stood on a chair in the back of the room with numerous typewritten sheets just received from Battalion Headquarters. Lieutenant Fujimoto stood quietly aside holding more papers and files, carefully organized by the company clerk alphabetically by platoon and squad. Field First Sergeant Rubinal and some cadre members leaned uncomfortably and silently along the same back wall. There was a sense of concern registered on the faces of most cadre members. They had heard a rumor!

Lieutenant Soong assumed the defined position of being in charge, as instructed in the ROTC manual at University of

Half Way There, Haole

Hawaii. His chin was firm, eyes wide and staring straight ahead.

"Gentlemen, we are assembled here for the reading of orders for the members of the 55th Company. I am proud of each and every one of you for completing your infantry basic training at the Hawaiian Infantry Training Center. Before I read individual assignments by squad, there are several announcements"

He read carefully from the top sheet, "With the graduation of the 80th Battalion, the Hawaiian Infantry Training Center will close operations. All training staff members NOT associated with the remaining training battalions will receive new assignments within the next thirty days. This does NOT mean that Schofield Barracks will close – only the HITC units are involved in this order."

The reaction among the cadre was one of no real surprise, just disappointment. The rumor mill was right this time – HITC really was going to close operations.

Barrigan poked Vinnie, "Some of these cadre bastards are going to FECOM along with us dog meat."

Vinnie didn't much respond.

"And now for the second announcement. By order of the Department of the Army and at the direction of the Senate Armed Services Committee Chairman, Lyndon B. Johnson, all stateside residents of the 50th Battalion of the Hawaiian Infantry Training Center are hereby granted two weeks leave time in mainland USA. Each enlisted man must provide his own transportation from the West Coast to his home and return. Travel time of up to three days is allowed in each direction. All trainees are to return to their West Coast base unless other specific mainland USA assignment is made."

The roar of applause within the dayroom was deafening. All haoles jumped to their feet instantaneously – whistling and yelling. Most islanders remained quiet – individual assignments were yet to be announced. Lieutenant Soong allowed the celebration to continue for several minutes. He finally signaled Sergeant Rubinal to bring the men under control. AB thought to himself – so much for the letter-writing effort.

Lieutenant Soong continued on the subject of the two-week leave. "The US Navy is cooperating with the movement of troops from Pearl Harbor to San Francisco. The aircraft carrier "Cape Esperance" will ship from Pearl eight days from today – that's Monday week. So be ready."

The celebration began anew. Sergeant Rubinal again brought order to the dayroom scene, with a firm hand but with dignity.

"And now for the last announcement before I read your orders. The Company party begins at 1830 hours in this same room. The beer is on the house."

This brought a major surprise response from all – haoles and locals.

For possibly the last time, Sergeant Rubinal stepped up and, in time, whistled the Company to silence. He continued, "Lieutenant Soong will now read the orders for the men of the 55th Company."

The officer was handed the filed for the first squad of the first platoon:

"Private Samuel Allen – FECOM

Private Francis Barrigan – trainee IBM machine operator, Wheeler Air Force Base, Oahu,, Hawaii."

Now, AB nor anyone else could understand the US Army. Here was a guy who was a real jerk; a guy who hated Hawaii with a passion, and, as he says, 'all the gooks on it' – assigned to the Air Force at Wheeler, right next door to Schofield. Most Islanders looked at each other – why?

Half Way There, Haole

Barrigan, for the first time had little or no reaction – no wise ass remarks to anyone.

"Private Allendale Burns – Scientific and Professional, assigned to 804th Signal Base Depot, Fort Holabird, Baltimore, Maryland, management trainee."

AB smiled internally, and mentally thanked his friend Lou Sample. Tad grinned broadly and offered a jab to the shoulder. Goldie gave him a big 'thumbs up. – with both hands. Barrigan mumbled something about ' that lucky sonofabitch.'

Others waited for their names to be called.

"Private Goldwire Cohens – Schofield Leadership School, FECOM

Private Vinnie del Fucci –FECOM

Private Joshua Forsythe –FECOM

Private James Knight – FECOM

Private Bernard Loa – FECOM

Private Zachary Marley – Ski Troops, Camp Drum, New York"

The Lieutenant paused and flashed an eye roll. AB dropped his head. What is really wrong with this Army? Here's a guy from Samoa who probably has never even seen snow, and now he is heading for the ski troops! Zack's world was about to collapse. The fight, and later the court martial, had screwed up his personal plans – and further, HITC was closing. There wouldn't be any future for him in Hawaii anyway. Zack cleared this throat. He had a stone-faced stare – looking at no one in particular.

Lieutenant Soong continued:

"Private George Oxendine – FECOM

Private Tadao Sato – FECOM"

Tad shed a tear – AB sensed his reaction and reached to return the shoulder nudge.

"Private Alex Silva – FECOM
Private Jesus Reyes – FECOM
Private Jesus Rapolla – FECOM"

Barrigan mumbled, "Jesus, I didn't know they were both Jesus."

Lieutenant Soong turned to retrieve the folder for the second squad. The damage was done. Somehow, the first squad of the first platoon had been exposed to being first in many training experiences. Reading these orders was no different.

All remained silent as the word FECOM was to be heard many more times during the next forty-five minutes. Personal reactions were mostly suppressed after the FECOM pattern became obvious.

Well, it was over – weeks of training and a primary MOS 4745 as an infantryman to show the effort. The men returned to the main second and third floor barracks – silently and slowly.

Finally, Josh spoke up, "Well, what did we expect? For weeks they've been showing us how to fight on the front lines. We've said all along that we are half way there. But, hey, we do go home for two weeks. I wonder how much the airfare is from California to North Carolina. Hope I don't have to take a Greyhound."

Tad and AB waited until most of the men had departed the dayroom. AB looked outside. There was a soft rain falling, along with a distant and somewhat unusual rumble of thunder. It was hot! Returning to the second floor, AB somehow noticed the metal step plates on the concrete stairway. Just last week, the first squad was given the duty of cleaning the lanai and the stairway. AB had been assigned, along with the Guamanians, the task of cleaning the red clay from between the ridges of the tow plates.

Tooth brushes were used. AB was reminded of the worn concrete steps in some of the older barracks at Schofield. No metal plates had been used in these building – the many footsteps of the earlier recruits had left a well-worn reminder on the unprotected steps. Oh well, there wouldn't be too many more trips to the second floor on these steps – graduation is Saturday.

Tad walked aimlessly down the aisle between the rows of bunks of the first platoon. He thought of his brother and his injuries from the war in Europe. He sat quietly on his foot locker. AB joined him.

"Slide over, pal, let's talk."

Tad made room for AB on the foot locker. "Tad, I've known and trained with you for about four months now. I made up my mind early on that if I went to the front lines in Korea, I wanted to be along side you. You are somebody I can depend on to do the right thing at the right time."

Tad's eyes brightened. He smiled, "I felt the same way – but even earlier. Like the time I carried your barracks bag to the second floor of this building. That was your first day at Schofield."

Tad continued, "You deserve the assignment you got in the States. Goldie told me a couple of weeks ago that you had a college education and that you missed out on a Navy commission. Goldie told me, too, that he worked for you in the family business in Florida; and that you helped him to find out what else was in this world beyond that little town you both live in, in Florida."

"That's interesting, "replied AB. "I made him promise to tell no one about my background. I got here to Hawaii and infantry basic just like anyone else. Goldwire Cohens is a very capable guy. He learned and developed leadership qualities in the tobacco fields when he was fourteen. He has good mechanical know how – been working on tractors, motors, and pumps since he was a kid. He deserves to be squad leader and headed for Leadership School. He'll make an excellent non-commissioned officer. I just hate to see him, or anybody else go to FECOM. All I can do now is wish you the very best of luck."

They shook hands.

"Hey, my family is going to be here for graduation on Saturday. I want them to meet you. My mom is packing a basket lunch – tempura fried shrimp – your favorite. I already got a place picked out for us to eat. It's under the palm trees across the street near the golf course." Tad grinned, "You're going to have to learn to sit on your heels, Japanese-style, to eat with us."

~

Silva spoke up, "Hey there's free beer in the dayroom. Let's go check it out."

For the second time the same day, the men of the 55th Company lined up to enter the company dayroom. The mess sergeant stood at the door – much the same as he had done for many dozens of days, feeding the troops in the company mess hall. But this one was different.

There were colored paper streamers hanging from the dayroom corners to the center of the room. The two pool tables had been pushed together and covered with white sheets as a tablecloth. In the center was a whole, well-stuffed pig with a red apple in its mouth and surrounded by huge trays of fancy foods – comparable to any spread presented by the hotels of Waikiki. Flowers and leis were in profusion. The record player gave forth with traditional

Hawaiian music with the highest volume possible. Maeva, draped in a red and white flowered lavalava, kept time with his own set of drums. There were four kegs of 3.2 beer – two at each end of the room to prevent beer line chaos.

This was truly the army version of an Hawaiian luau, and it had to compare favorably with any offered on the Island. With the watered down 3.2 beer, it was doubtful anyone could possibly drink enough to get inebriated. And it was all done without the help of squads of KP's. The cooks, with cadre assistance, had done all the decorations and food preparation.

The men rushed into the room in a state of excitement – even the Islanders were impressed. A line formed immediately to circle the pool tables piled high with food. The mess sergeant moved to the food table to offer massive servings of roast pig.

The beer flowed with ease. Suddenly, the music stopped and Maeva began a frantic and loud drum roll. Zack appeared at the door in his lavalava – lowered, as usual, to display the railroad track scars from the motorcycle accident. He leaped across the room as the men scattered to allow space for the flailing arms and machete knives. The room took on an extended festive air as Zack performed endlessly to the solid Maeva drumbeat. The beer lines overlapped and extended around the room.

The festivities continued but the beer supply began to fail. Ox came forward to demonstrate another of his many talents – the art of tipping a beer keg in just the proper manner to get just one more paper cup of beer.

A few men, including Silva, Loa, Tad, and Ox left the area with full cups of beer – headed for the second floor. Ox explained to Loa that in North Carolina, you always left a party with a 'toter' – one for the road.

The party continued on the second floor, as Barrigan and Vinnie carefully negotiated the twenty-two steps – empty handed. Observing a group of Islanders and Ox on the lanai with full cups of beer, Barrigan blurted out:

"Look at the fuckin' gooks. Wouldn't you know, they got all the beer!"

After seventeen weeks of gook comments, the fight was on. Brushing Vinnie aside, Loa and Silva jumped Barrigan and proceeded to dump him to the floor and flail away with all four fists. By this time, Tad joined in with a couple of football running back forearms to the head and nose.

Ox stood by, "I'm a haole, let these guys settle this."

Barrigan finally recovered sufficiently to flop in his bunk – nose bleeding on sheets and blankets.

Loa approached the foot of the bunk and proceeded to dump Barrigan's foot locker into a pile of shoes, clothing, and shaving supplies. Ox was standing at the head of the bunk – Loa at the foot. In one giant move the bunk was overturned, dumping a much confused Barrigan to the floor beneath the pile of bloody sheets, blankets, and mattress.

Tad's radio blared. Hank Williams was singing 'Jambalaya."

Loa, Tad and Silva returned to the lanai to finish their beers.

Silva spoke up. "That sonofabitch Barrigan has called us Islanders 'gook' for the last time. He deserved everything he got – and then some. I'll bet he won't even think of calling anybody a gook over there at Wheeler. They will have his ass in North Korea in a heartbeat."

The beer finally gave out. Ox and Loa returned to the bunk area to find Barrigan sleeping in a stupor – bloody nose in tact. Quietly, they picked up opposite ends of the cot and carried him through the lanai, into the latrine and deposited

Half Way There, Haole

the sleeping Barrigan, bunk and all, in the shower room. At a pre-arranged signal, six showerheads poured cold water on the sleeping Francis Barrigan. Vinnie was no where to be found.

Chapter 30

There was a certain feeling of finality as the men of the 55th Company prepared for their graduation parade. It would be their day. There had been numerous other parades, some for graduation ceremonies of earlier HITC training battalions. Other parades were held just because it was a Saturday at Schofield Barracks.

The usual pre-parade inspection went off without a hitch – no gigs for personal appearance, no gigs for dirty of faulty equipment. It was a surprise when Maeva arrived with his native training drum. The men departed Quad K in precision step. Colonel Cottingham observed quietly from his office on the third floor of Battalion Headquarters.

The 55th Company left the Quad area, while other companies of the Battalion were still conducting personal inspections in front of respective company areas.

AB was suspicious. Why the early departure? Why Maeva and the drum? The 55th approached the parade area while preparations were still underway. The marching band could be heard practicing from a remote end of the field.

Lieutenant Soong signaled for Field First Sergeant Rubinal to bring the company to a halt.

"Parade rest," ordered the Sergeant.

The company clerk drove up in a jeep. Lieutenant Soong leaped to the rear of the jeep, positioning himself so all could hear.

"Men, I have an announcement for you. The parade today also is in honor of our own Master Sergeant Orlando Rubinal. He is being awarded the Silver Star Medal for distinguished combat service in Korea,"

Half Way There, Haole

Corporal Kam led the company in a huge response of clapping and hollering. All joined in, in the informal and unplanned reaction. Somewhat chagrined, Lieutenant Soong joined in the response.

Sergeant Rubinal was pleased – embarrassed, but pleased – offering a broad smile to all. Sergeant Rubinal seldom smiled during these past eighteen weeks. This was a genuine response.

As other HITC training units converged on the parade grounds, the 55th Company was ordered to move to the position as honor unit for the ceremonies. Civilian family members gathered along the edge of the parade area – flowered leis in hand.

The graduation ceremonies began. General Almond complimented the 50th Battalion on successful completion of the training schedule. He then requested Master Sergeant Orlando Rubinal to approach the reviewing stand.

Maeva also stepped forward. He began a steady and isolated drum beat as Sergeant Rubinal approached the reviewing stand. It was a poignant and dramatic display of military custom. The drum beat ended with a flourish.

The General approached the rigid Silver Star recipient.

He spoke, "As Pacific Army Commander, I hereby award the Silver Star to Master Sergeant Orlando Rubinal of the 55th Company for distinguishing himself by courageous action in the vicinity of Chinju, Korea on September 18, 1950. Sergeant Rubinal displayed outstanding leadership with infantrymen in a tank-supported counterattack on the enemy. Congratulations, Sergeant Rubinal."

Sergeant Rubinal took one step foreward and offered a stiff and proper salute. General Almond returned the salute.

The Maeva drum beat escorted the honoree to his original position with the 55th Company.

The Schofield marching band trooped the parade field as parents and friends rushed to the 50th Battalion graduating class. Leis were formally presented to loved ones. Military discipline was ignored as dozens of civilians surround favorite sons. All first squad Islanders were duly honored with flowers. AB was shocked as Tad's teenage sister approached him with a lei – matching that given to Tad by the other twin sister. AB bowed at the waist to allow the formality of placing the lei around his neck. He offered a brief embrace to the surprised teenager.

The flower-bedecked 55th Company returned to Quad K, only to be met by more friends and relatives honoring the special day.

AB joined Tad and his family for a colorful meal of tempura fried shrimp, fried string beans, and seaweed-wrapped rice balls. The rice balls were now an AB favorite.

Later he reflected on his haole experience at Schofield – Tad's aloha greeting that first day, His early sharing of KP and guard duty knowledge. The radio. The Sunday night meals and the chopstick experience. The successful mortar wipe-out of the school bus target. This latest experience with the family meal.

He thought, too, of Goldie – he will do all right for himself in this army.

Schofield Barracks might be 'half way there, for many. For one haole, maybe it was 'all the way there!"